A Shade of Blood

Blood

A Shade of Vampire, Book 2

Bella Forrest

Also by Bella Forrest:

A SHADE OF VAMPIRE SERIES:

Derek & Sofia's story:

A Shade of Vampire (Book 1)
A Shade of Blood (Book 2)
A Castle of Sand (Book 3)
A Shadow of Light (Book 4)
A Blaze of Sun (Book 5)
A Gate of Night (Book 6)
A Break of Day (Book 7)

Note: Derek and Sofia's story completes in Book 7 of the series: *A Break of Day*, and the characters embark on entirely new adventures from Book 8: *A Shade of Novak*.

Rose & Caleb's story:

A Shade of Novak (Book 8)
A Bond of Blood (Book 9)
A Spell of Time (Book 10)
A Chase of Prey (Book 11)
A Shade of Doubt (Book 12)
A Turn of Tides (Book 13)
A Dawn of Strength (Book 14)
A Fall of Secrets (Book 15)
An End of Night (Book 16)

For an updated list of Bella's books,
please visit www.bellaforrest.net

Dedication

To each of my wonderful Shaddicts.
Thank you so much for your kind words, support and
endless encouragement as I continue writing this series.

Contents

CHAPTER 1: DEREK

A cold wind howled as it whipped through the giant redwoods surrounding us. The port was in sight. The crash of the ocean waves against the island's ragged cliffs was audible—even to human ears.

It wouldn't be long until I'd have to watch her go. I knew the risks that came with letting her and her friend leave The Shade. Still, I had no choice. She'd chosen to go and I had to respect that decision. It hurt that she didn't trust me enough to protect her, that she'd chosen the human lad, Ben, over me, but I knew she would be safer if I let her go.

Yet holding her in my arms, with my lips still tingling from the kiss I'd claimed—perhaps even demanded—from her, I was aware of every curve of her slim, fragile body flush against mine. My fingers were entangled with her long, soft auburn locks and her sweet scent invaded my senses. No other woman had ever made me feel the way Sofia Claremont did, and at that moment, I couldn't bear the thought of her leaving me.

Her beautiful, freckled face was buried against my shoulder as she broke down into tears for reasons I couldn't fully understand. Each sob cut me to the core.

Ben tentatively approached us. He had been watching us from the moment I pulled Sofia into my arms and pressed my lips against hers. I didn't need to look at him to know that his eyes were screaming murder.

I ignored him. The only reason he mattered to me was because he mattered to *her*. I didn't even trust him, but she did and that was supposed to be enough.

Sofia's arms tightened around my waist, clinging to me in much the same way I was clinging to her. The motion gave me hope that she might choose to stay.

"Sofia..." My voice came out in a husky, breathless whisper.

My heart sank when she slowly pulled away from me. I was surprised when she laid both hands on my shoulders, stood on her tiptoes and leaned into me, her lips brushing my own. It propelled all my senses into overdrive and it took all of my willpower to not let my passion take over. I didn't want to scare her, so I shut my eyes and let her take the lead. My fists clenched when our lips parted. I opened my eyes and found her emerald-green gaze fixed on me. She was studying my face so closely—as if she were trying to memorize me.

I did the same. I committed every part of her adorable face—every long eyelash, every freckle, and every other detail—to my memory.

Sensing how much she had begun to mean to me, I was unable to keep myself from voicing out what was going through my mind. I knew it was selfish, but the words flooded out.

"Sofia, stay."

I, Prince of The Shade, was begging her—supposedly my slave—not to leave me. Because I knew without a doubt that her departure would plunge me deeper into the darkness that had taken over my life five hundred years ago, when my own father had turned me into the monster that I was.

Chapter 2: Sofia

Sofia, stay.

The words took me aback. It sounded like a command and for a moment, it felt like I had no choice but to comply. It wasn't until I looked into those electric-blue eyes of his that I saw the statement for what it was. I bit my lip. *Is it possible that I really mean* that *much to him?*

"I promise you, Derek, I'll never do anything to compromise you, to bring harm to The Shade…"

His face tensed—offended—as he shook his head. "It's not about that, and you know it."

"Then what is it about?" I needed him to give me a reason to stay. I wanted to hear it from his lips.

He gritted his teeth and ran a hand through his dark hair. Derek Novak never was good at expressing himself in words—that much I knew about him. He spoke louder through his actions, and I admired him for this.

He opened his mouth, but someone grabbed my arm from behind.

"Let's go, Sofia."

Ben.

My eyes were still fixed on Derek's handsome face, the contrast of his blue eyes and pale skin never failing to make me catch my breath. His eyes darkened the moment Ben's fingers coiled around my arm. His muscles flexed when his hands balled into fists.

I tried to break away from Ben's grasp, but he held fast.

"We don't have time," Ben hissed. "Say your goodbyes and let's go."

The expression on Derek's face wasn't giving me much confidence about my best friend's safety. After all, it wasn't long ago that much—too much, in my opinion—had been said about whom I belonged to.

Derek's. Lucas'. Ben's. It's beyond me what I must do to make them realize that I'm neither object nor possession. I don't belong to any of them.

I had to intervene before a testosterone-charged battle could spark. I turned to look Ben straight in the eye.

"Let go of me, Ben. Now."

Ben's jaw tightened. Before our captivity at The Shade, I would've done anything he asked of me, but The Shade had changed us both.

When his grip on me didn't slacken one bit, Derek took a step forward. "You heard the lady." His deep, baritone voice took on a threatening tone.

I stared pleadingly at Ben, hoping that he wouldn't try Derek's patience. *Do you not realize that you don't stand a chance against him?*

Over the past few days since Derek had forced Claudia— Ben's mistress at The Shade—to turn Ben over to his custody, Derek had taken great lengths to at least be polite to him. Ben, on the other hand, had done nothing but shoot glares at Derek. I'd been on edge trying to keep them apart, fearing a confrontation.

I spoke more gently this time. "Let go, Ben."

He let go, but the glare he sent my way showed he was not giving in. "Don't even think about staying." The words came through clenched teeth and with a slight shake of his head.

"Sofia..." Derek spoke up as if to remind me that his opinion mattered too.

"I need time to think." I said.

"Now?" Ben protested.

"There's no time for that," Derek seconded.

Finally! You two agree on something. "Well, then make time."

They exchanged glances. It was almost endearing how helpless both of them looked. A smile threatened to creep over my face. *Who owns whom now?*

It was Derek who first relented. I was still mystified by what continuously made him give in to me. After all, of the three of us, he was the one holding real power. He could simply decide that neither Ben nor I could leave and that would be that.

Still, his eyes softened the moment they landed on me. He nodded and said, "Fine, but not here."

He scowled at Ben before laying his hand on the small of my back, pushing me forward.

"Unbelievable," Ben grumbled, throwing his hands into the air as he followed after us.

The moon was the only light to guide us as we made our way through the rest of the woods, weaving our way past rocks and bushes. My brain took note of the hidden paths that led us from Derek's penthouse to the port. The trees got smaller and smaller as we neared a clearing. The rustle of the twigs beneath us, the waves nearby and our soft, even breathing were the only sounds filling the air. The scent of the trees surrounding us and the sea nearby mixed with

Derek's intoxicating musk. It made me sense his proximity, along with the gentle heaving of his chest and the feel of his arm gripping my waist.

My heart ached at the idea of never again being as close as I was to him at that moment.

"We're close."

I snapped to attention. The port had been in sight even before we stopped to talk back in the woods. However, now that we had climbed down into a clearing, there was nothing in sight but high, rocky cliffs.

"What the hell is going on?" Ben said.

"I don't understand." I eyed Derek as I looked around. "Where's the port?"

I tried to slow down, but Derek tugged on me to keep me walking.

"Hey, your highness. Where are you taking us?" Ben used both hands to push Derek and me apart.

I stumbled aside, but Derek didn't even budge. When the prince of vampires turned to face him, I was half-expecting Ben to keel over and die from sheer fright. Derek looked nothing short of menacing.

Ben stood his ground. I guessed he didn't care that Derek was capable of breaking every bone in his body. Ben was never one to back down from a fight, and it seemed he wasn't about to start now.

I couldn't remember ever being around so much testosterone. The blood drained from my face the moment Ben stepped forward—a blatant challenge—and said, "We're headed nowhere, *vampire*."

I was torn between admiring him and slapping some sense back into him. *What on earth are you doing, Ben? Are you trying to get yourself killed?*

Derek stared him down. The presence and power he exuded reminded me of what he'd looked like just before he ripped the heart out of the vampire guard who'd tried to feed on me.

"Derek," I managed to choke, "where are we going? Those are boulders straight ahead."

Derek kept his eyes on Ben. I wasn't even sure if he'd heard me. A dozen prayers were going through my head. The last thing we needed was a fight—if we could even call it that.

Relief washed over me when Derek's eyes fell on me. Ignoring Ben, Derek took hold of my hand, pulled me closer to him and replaced his hand over my waist. Apparently, he didn't feel obliged to offer either of us an explanation.

"Stop resisting, Sofia. Just follow my lead. And make this idiot friend of yours shut up, or I swear…" He paused to reel in his anger. "You have no idea how close I am to maiming him." His grip tightened around me.

Derek. Ever the authoritarian. I didn't bother to look at Ben's reaction. I knew he would be seething after being brushed aside like that.

We were headed toward a solid rock wall. Derek didn't look like he was going to slow down. I looked at him several times to check if he had gone insane, but he kept his focus ahead, not slowing down as we got closer and closer to walking right into a rock wall.

All I could do was gasp when we finally hit the wall… only to find myself shocked when it enveloped us, feeling a lot like Jell-O. We emerged on the other side and found a staircase winding downward. We'd just moved down a few feet when Ben stepped out of the wall. He seemed fine, save for the scowl on his face. He wasn't used to being ignored.

At the bottom of the staircase we stepped into a cavernous hall enclosed by huge glass windows revealing that we were underwater. Had it not been dark outside, I'm sure I would have marveled at the sight of sea creatures. In the center of the room was some sort of control panel where Sam and Kyle, two of Derek's most trusted guards, stood.

Since I'd developed a bond with them over the time I'd stayed at The Shade, the glances—both fond and curious— they sent my way didn't come as much of a surprise.

Derek didn't even bother to look at Ben. He fixed his eyes on the vampire guards. "Kyle, take the boy to the submarine.

Make sure all the preparations for his departure are in order. Sam, take Sofia to one of the holding cells. She apparently needs to rethink her stay here."

I frowned. "Holding cells?"

"Wait. What submarine?" Ben asked. "I'm not gonna go anywhere without Sofia."

Derek set his eyes on me. "You said you need time to think. A cell is the safest place to do just that. Meanwhile, he will wait for you in one of the submarines. He will be sedated, just like you will be should you decide to leave. We can't afford for you to remember anything about your journey out of the island."

The thought of never seeing Derek again made me ache inside and I was fighting the urge to cry as I looked into his eyes. *How dare you kiss me, Derek. Tonight of all nights. As if this decision isn't already hard enough, you had to claim my first kiss from me.*

"I won't send him off until you've made your decision," Derek promised. The look he gave me was so intense, I was sure I would melt. I just nodded.

"What?" Ben began to protest. "Sofia…"

Before he could say any more, Sam stabbed him in the neck with a needle and he fell unconscious. Sam met my glare with a shrug. "What? He was going to get sedated anyway."

He picked up Ben and carried him over one shoulder. Kyle tugged on me to follow him. "Looks like you've got some thinking to do."

I heaved a sigh. *Understatement of the year.*

Chapter 3: Derek

We kept her in one of the rooms normally used for holding human captives before transporting them to the Black Heights, where humans were then either placed in the Cells—the island's prison system—or assigned their own quarters at the Catacombs, home to all humans who were not assigned to a harem.

Sofia, being a part of my harem, stayed at my penthouse at the Pavilion, which was comprised of lush tree houses atop a network of giant redwoods. Ever since my brother Lucas had attacked Sofia and killed Gwen, Sofia had been sleeping with me in my bedroom. The idea of her not being in my arms later that night made my gut clench.

It felt like an eternity before Sofia emerged from the room. When she did, the greater part of me wished that I could just shove her back in and force her to rethink her decision. One look at the apologetic expression on her face was all it took to know that I had lost her.

She walked toward me and placed her arms around my neck, pulling me close, pressing her lips against mine—returning the passion, the urgency, the hunger that I'd poured out on her when I'd first claimed her lips back at the woods. I both loved and hated that kiss. It hinted so much about what she felt for me, yet it was clearly a goodbye.

When our lips parted, her delicate fingers brushed over my hair, her green eyes fixed on me. She wordlessly walked away to find the guards.

Her choice was clear. She was leaving me. I knew I could stop her. I could've used my power and influence to keep her with me, but I didn't. I chose to respect her choice.

Kyle carried her unconscious form toward the submarine. Both guards would take them to the mainland where their bodies would be left on the same shore where they were first found.

The submarine faded into the distance. Just like that, she was gone. My one ray of light amidst the eternal darkness of The Shade was gone forever, leaving me to retreat back into the black night I'd spent my immortality failing to escape.

Chapter 4: Sofia

I was surrounded by darkness and the drumming of a heart. It got increasingly loud, so loud that I was certain my head would explode. I couldn't understand what was going on. I couldn't see, feel, taste or smell anything. My one sense was my hearing and it was overwhelmed by that mysterious heartbeat.

It was driving me to the brink of insanity when a sudden burst of light threatened to blind me. It took a couple of seconds to adjust to the light. That was when I saw him. Derek. He was staring at me, face pale and eyes listless. He fell to the ground, eyes open and blank. There was a gaping hole where his heart used to be.

The echoing heartbeat was coming from behind me... coming

closer and closer. Then came a chuckle and a cold, menacing breath down my neck. It was followed by a whisper—no, a hiss—barely audible. Yet fear began to envelop me and panic ran through my veins, because I heard the snake's words loud and clear.

"You're next."

Then came the crash of waves.

It was the high tide that woke me from the deafening sound of Derek's heartbeat and the foul sound of the snake's words. My pulse was double its normal rate and I could barely breathe. At first, I thought my face was wet only due to the warm wave of salt water that had just washed over me.

One name echoed through my mind: *Derek.*

I'd been so used to waking up in his bed that I blinked several times before I realized that the sun was just about to rise over the horizon.

The sun.

It jolted me into the reality that I was no longer at The Shade, because back at the island, the sun never rose. It was an endless night. Had it not been for my nightmare, I would've adored that sunrise. However, my anxiety about Derek stole all the joy away from my reunion with the sun.

Although the sun failed to ease my nerves, it did succeed in bringing me back to my senses. It returned to my usual state: being excruciatingly *aware.*

Back at The Shade, Corrine, the witch maintaining the island's protective spell, had begun to take a special interest in me after Lucas had first attacked me and killed Gwen. Having been a psychology major before the vampires whisked her to The Shade, she'd diagnosed me with low latent inhibition, or LLI. I was unable to filter out most external stimuli. It meant that I could sense everything, feel everything. I wondered if that was the reason my mother had gone insane and been taken away from me—apparently, only people with a certain IQ could handle LLI without going mad. I was used to my condition now. It wasn't as overwhelming as it used to be when I was younger.

The sun's oranges and yellows slowly rising over the ocean's blues and greens; the cawing of seagulls and the waves crashing against the shore; the salty aftertaste of sea water mixed with tears; the soft sand beneath my feet and the cool breeze blowing against my skin; the scent of the ocean mixing with the fresh morning air—I was aware of it all.

Someone was approaching me from behind.

Ben, I'm sure.

Sensation after sensation assaulted me, and yet my mind was still fixed on the way Derek had looked in my dream— pale, distant... heartless. Trembling, I pulled my knees against my chest, gathering the beach sand beneath my heels.

"Derek, please be all right. *Stay* all right," I whispered, hoping the morning breeze would carry the message back to The Shade.

"Why all the whispering?"

Ben looked at ease and relaxed for the first time since we'd discovered each other back at The Shade. Still, even with the lighter tone, every word he spoke came with a heaviness I couldn't completely shake. He plopped himself down next to me.

"Where do you think we are?" he asked.

"We're in Cancun." I had no doubt about it. "It makes sense for them to return us where they found us."

Le Meridien. That was the resort we'd been staying at when we got abducted by the vampires. Ben's family, the Hudsons, had been able to afford the long-awaited vacation because of the substantial sum of money my father sent to support me. The last time I'd seen him was when he had left me under the care of his best friend—Ben's father, Lyle Hudson. That was eight years ago. The only clue I had that he was still alive somewhere was the quarterly check he sent the Hudsons to continue caring for me. The check wasn't even sent in my name.

Memories of our vacation spent on the sugary beaches of Mexico felt like they'd happened a lifetime ago—to a different version of myself. The jealousy I'd felt over Ben dating a gorgeous blonde, Tanya Wilson, seemed frivolous and shallow. Even my bitterness toward my parents seemed to matter less in light of what I'd been through.

I remembered a time when I'd worshipped the ground Ben walked on. My hot and popular quarterback best friend, with his charming smile and sun-kissed skin... The young man sitting next to me was nothing like that.

"What do we do now?" I asked.

We'd been so bent on escaping The Shade, we'd never actually thought about what we would do once we got out. It took at least half a minute before Ben shrugged.

"For now, I don't think there's anything left to do other than go home."

"Right." I nodded, wondering where home was. The idea of going back to suburban California, back to the Hudsons' family home, made me sick to my stomach. That place had never felt like home to me. "But I don't think I'm ready to go back just yet, Ben."

I was relieved when he nodded. "I feel the same."

A comfortable silence followed, both of us focusing on the sun and its slow, steady rise. The view was magnificent, but it wasn't enough of a distraction to ease the thoughts roaming around in my head.

"Perhaps we should stay here for a day or two, gather our wits about us," Ben suggested. "Then we can go home."

"Sounds okay to me."

I paid more attention to what I was wearing. The bikini and the cover-up was the exact same outfit I had been wearing when Lucas had taken me from the beach and brought me to The Shade. Ben was wearing a black vest and red board shorts. I wondered if that was what he'd had on when he was taken from the beach. *Did they return us here with nothing but the clothes on our backs?*

"Relax. They didn't leave us empty-handed." He nodded toward a spot further down the beach.

I followed his gaze to a black backpack on the sand. I breathed a sigh of relief. I was bewildered by the scowl on Ben's face. *Why do you seem so ticked off?*

"Have you seen what's in it?"

He shook his head. "I'm not exactly excited to find out what I now owe them."

You and your ego. It was just like Ben to be too proud to accept help from anybody. Although, of course, the fact that this help was coming from the vampires who'd put him through hell made the whole thing much worse. The horrors he'd been through at The Shade constantly loomed over him... over us.

"Let's see what we have to work with." I walked over to the backpack, more concerned about our current predicament than pride.

I'd already reached the pack when I realized that Ben

hadn't even bothered to follow me. I knelt on the ground and checked the bag's contents. There were only a few items: two sets of clothes—one for Ben, one for me—a wad of cash and a sealed envelope with my name on it. Satisfied that we had enough to get by, I closed the bag and slung it over my shoulder before heading back to Ben.

"So?" he asked.

"We have clothes and enough cash to get us on a first-class flight from Mexico to India. Round trip. Twice."

I was expecting him to at least be somewhat relieved, but no. All he did was scoff.

"They throw us their scraps and expect us to be grateful for them. That's nowhere near enough considering what they put us through."

I knew he was right and I wanted to be on his side, but no matter how much I tried, I couldn't bring myself to hate The Shade as much as he did. At that point, I didn't dare ask myself why.

"So that's all there is?" Ben asked, glaring at the backpack.

I thought about the envelope addressed to me. Then I nodded.

"Yeah. That's it."

A tense moment ensued before he kicked the sand. "Fine. Let's go and indulge ourselves, using the oh-so-generous fortune they sent us."

As he headed off toward the luxurious resorts that lined the white sandy beaches, I lingered behind long enough to look back at the ocean and whisper, "Thank you, Derek."

Chapter 5: Derek

Focus, Derek. Ignore everything.

I stood still, my feet shoulder-width apart. My left hand kept a relaxed grip on my silver bow's handle. I retrieved an arrow from the quiver slung across my bare back.

Drown everything out. All that matters now is that you hit the target.

Beads of sweat trickled down my temples. I'd been at this all night. I'd started with boxing before moving on to sword practice, then firearms practice, and eventually every other training the Crimson Fortress' grounds had to offer until I reached the archery range.

The thick walls of the Crimson Fortress towered at least a

hundred feet above me. They surrounded the island, protecting us from everyone who'd sought to invade us throughout the centuries. The mere thought threatened to bring back a slew of dark memories that I'd long wanted to forget. I cleared my throat and refocused.

Shut it out. Don't let the past haunt you. Not now.

I shut my eyes as I nocked the arrow and positioned its shaft onto the arrow rest. I took a deep breath.

Let your instincts take over.

I positioned the weapon to hit the target that I couldn't even see. Using my back muscles, I pulled my right elbow backwards until my right hand was placed firmly against my jaw. I held my stance for a few seconds, trusting my instincts to aim right.

Then came the release. The arrow pierced through the cold night air and I heard a loud thud. Before I could even open my eyes, from behind me came applause.

I opened my eyes. The arrow had indeed hit the bull's eye, cutting right through the first two arrows. I longed for the sense of satisfaction that came with a shot like that. Nothing. It only served as a cruel reminder that most of what I knew about combat, I had learned from hunters—back when I was one of them, before I became the Lord of vampires and Prince of The Shade.

"Well done, your highness," the familiar voice of

Cameron Hendry, with his thick Scottish accent, boomed through the training grounds. "It seems four hundred years of being the Sleeping Beauty has not dulled your fighting skills one bit."

I tensed. The last thing I wanted now was company and it seemed I had an entire flank of soldiers surrounding me. I tried to relax as I faced my good friend. Cameron and his wife, Liana, were two of The Shade's fiercest warriors and had fought and bled with me many times on the battlefield. The Hendry clan represented one of the few clans among the Elite that I trusted with my life.

"Hendry." I nodded his way. "Up and about so early?"

"Early?" he scoffed, his red hair tousled as if he had just tumbled out of bed. "If The Shade had sun, it'd be midday. Yuri says you've been using every single weapon we have available to murder some unknown force for the past eighteen hours. What or whom are you planning to kill, Derek?"

"Midday, huh?" I asked, quick to change the subject. "Since when do we start training troops at midday?"

"Truth be told, we haven't trained much since the war ended and you went off to sleep." The large man, only twenty-eight years old when he was turned, threw his arms up in the air with a shrug. "There hasn't been a major attack on The Shade since your witch friend, Cora, first hid it with her curse."

My jaw tightened. "That has to change. We won't be safe for long. We can't afford to have untrained troops. Our adversaries are innovating their weapons, developing their skills, while we lounge around like there won't ever be a tomorrow."

Concern sparked in Cameron's brown eyes. He stepped forward and spoke in a low tone—just loud enough for only me to hear.

"What's going on, Derek?"

"I remain commander-in-chief of The Shade's military force. Am I correct?"

"Of course."

"Well, as of this day, the initiative starts. Within the next couple of weeks, I expect every single vampire living on this Godforsaken island to be drafted for duty." If I weren't in such a sour mood, I would've guffawed at the way Cameron's face contorted with shock. But I was dead serious. I stood to my full height, summoning all the power I had. "That's what's going on, Cameron." I looked at all the men listening in on our conversation. They were a sorry bunch to look at, weak and withered by time. "Does anyone dare object?"

I was met with downcast stares and a tense silence.

I smirked. "Of course not."

CHAPTER 6: DEREK

Steady footsteps echoed through the torchlit corridors of the Crimson Fortress' west tower. I was discussing with Cameron what had to be done over the next few weeks as we made our way to the Great Dome, where most of our military strategic planning was done. The west tower, standing as high as one hundred and fifty feet and roofed with pointed cross-arches, had been one of the first buildings erected in the fortress and had already witnessed many battles in defense of the island.

"We'll need to gather the Elite Council and the Knights."

The Elite Council was composed of twenty individuals who represented each of the Elite's clans. Liana, Cameron's wife, was one of them and so was my twin sister, Vivienne. The Knights, on the other hand, were members of the Elite's clans who had enlisted as part of The Shade's military force. They composed mostly of the high-ranking officers in our garrisons. As far as I knew, we had twenty-one Knights.

"Not many of them will understand, Derek. The Shade has become a small version of Ancient Rome. We've grown complacent and drunk with power. Some of the Elite call our citizens the untouchables."

"And you agree?"

"No." Cameron shook his head. "We've had it good for too long. The tides always turn eventually."

"Exactly. So you understand why we must prepare our people?"

"Of course. We fought side by side a long time ago. You know I recognize it when the winds speak of battle. I'm just telling you the situation as it is. Not many will understand."

"We'll make them understand," I said through gritted teeth. "There is no choice."

Before Cameron could respond, a familiar, shrill voice echoed through cavernous corridors.

"Derek! What do you think you're doing?"

I turned to find my twin sister, Vivienne, marching at full speed toward me. Vivienne was both feared and respected as the Seer of The Shade. Many of her visions and prophecies had saved The Shade throughout history. However, some of her prophecies had only placed me in trouble—especially with my father and brother. One in particular burdened me whenever I recalled it: *The younger will rule above father and brother and his reign alone can provide his kind true sanctuary.*

As my sister stormed toward me, the words echoed through my mind. Sometimes I wished that she could stop seeing into my future and just let me live without being pressured by what she saw.

"Hello, Vivienne."

"What's going on, Derek?"

Cameron shifted his weight from one foot to the other, always uncomfortable in the midst of a confrontation involving a woman. I couldn't help but grin. *Some things never change.*

"Hendry. You can go ahead of me. You don't have to be present to watch this bloodbath."

Relief washed over his face. He bowed his head. "Princess," he acknowledged, before speeding toward the Great Dome.

"So? What are you blazing mad about, my dear sister?"

"Come on, Derek. A draft? A census? Why?"

"You've been too lax with our citizens during my sleep. They've become weak, complacent. Father, Lucas, you... how did you let it get this way? What happens when the other covens decide we have it too good and attack us?"

"Father is doing everything necessary to take the road of diplomacy as we speak."

"Diplomacy, Vivienne?" I scoffed. "Tell me, does this road of diplomacy lead toward Borys Maslen?"

Her face paled. The Maslens were some of our fiercest adversaries and Borys Maslen in particular had an especially dark history with my sister. Her inability to come up with a response was enough indication of the threat the Maslens posed to us.

I smirked. "I thought so. I have serious trouble thinking that Borys Maslen will welcome an ambassador from us with open arms. Not unless *you* are part of the deal."

Vivienne's face hardened. My gut clenched at how insensitive my words were. I still couldn't wrap my mind around what kind of hell that monster Borys had once put her through. "Vivienne... I..." My apology froze on my tongue.

"He has a new girl, you know. Maybe he wouldn't want me as much now."

"A new girl?"

"Ingrid Maslen. No one's ever laid eyes on her yet. Borys keeps her under lock and key, his biggest secret. Some say she possesses some kind of power and that's the reason Borys turned her into a vampire. According to rumors, she's stunningly beautiful."

"Don't be a fool, Vivienne. Borys has it in his mind that he owns you. Only two things will make him forget about coming after you: your death or you back in his hands."

"We're still protected by Cora's spell." She composed herself after all the talk about her former betrothed.

"For how long, Vivienne? Corrine isn't Cora. Her loyalties don't lie with us as strongly. Do you really believe that a witch's spell can protect The Shade forever? Once we're no longer protected, what happens then? How do we protect ourselves from hunters? Bloody hell, Vivienne, how do we protect ourselves from *the world* once they find out how many human slaves we've been exploiting and murdering within our walls?"

Her silence encouraged me to go on.

"You never should've allowed The Shade to grow *this* weak."

Her beautiful face tightened as she took a step forward to challenge me. "We refused to just survive. We thrived. What's so wrong with that?"

"It was at too great a price. How many have died on this island, Vivienne? How many?"

"If I remember correctly, a good few of them died under your iron fist, Derek. Remember how your hands were tainted with blood while you were building this fortress?"

She'd stepped out of line and she knew it. She faltered and backed up a step at the murderous glare I sent her way. She knew how to hurt me, I had to give her that.

But to my surprise, she continued pushing my boundaries. "You let her go, didn't you? Sofia and that friend of hers, the one you forced Claudia to give to you... Ben, is it? You let them go."

How did she find out? I'd given Sam and Kyle strict orders not to breathe a word to anyone. Even the girls living in my house still had no idea that I'd let Sofia and Ben escape. Only Corrine had been informed, but only because—for reasons I didn't fully understand—Sofia had insisted.

I reminded myself whom I was talking to. Vivienne had a gift of prophecy and discernment. *Of course she knows.* She didn't even need me to answer her question.

"Is this why you're doing all of this? To keep yourself from thinking of Sofia?"

I grabbed my sister's jaw, every single muscle tensing as I stared at her. From the look in her eyes, she saw in me the Derek who had existed more than four hundred years ago— the one whose ruthlessness had built The Shade and all its fortifications over the spilt blood of thousands of humans. For the first time in a long time, my sister cowered.

I leaned closer to her, so that my mouth was directly in front of her ear. "The name Sofia Claremont is never to escape your lips again. Not in my presence. Not unless I give you permission. Do you understand?"

She nodded.

I let go of her, red marks forming on her porcelain jaw.

"This is what you're going to turn into without her in your life. You can only get worse from here. This is why you need her."

Gaining back her composure, she stood to her full height and gently caressed my face with her long fingers.

"You never should've let her go."

Chapter 7: Sofia

Ben and I checked in to the same resort we'd stayed at with his family. The moment we arrived at the hotel room, neither one of us could wait to get out. It mattered little to us how beautiful the suite was—in fact, it paled in comparison to the lavish penthouses of The Shade. What mattered more to us was the sun. We were in Cancun and we'd missed the sun for too long to spend that bright day indoors.

It became an unspoken rule between the two of us that for that morning, there would be no mention of The Shade, nothing dark or heavy. For a few hours, we tried to be what we had every right to be—teenagers having fun on one of the most beautiful beaches in the world.

Without even noticing at first, we avoided any kind of shade. We wanted to feel the sunlight against our skin, so we stayed clear of umbrellas and roofs and anything that would block the sun. I was sure that by the end of the day I'd be burnt to a crisp, but I didn't care. I couldn't even remember what sunburn felt like.

Breakfast consisted of fresh fruits and virgin piña coladas at an outdoor seaside restaurant. After that, we headed off to the ocean. At some point, I ended up building a sandcastle on my own while Ben remained in the ocean, enjoying a good, long swim. To my right was a pouch filled with seashells we'd collected for a half hour. Neither of us had any idea what we were going to do with the shells, but it had seemed like a great idea at the time. Lying on a bright red towel we'd bought from the hotel store were a bunch of snapshots Ben and I took after squeezing into a photo booth and goofing off.

It brought a smile to my face. We were making every effort to lighten up, to make a connection to our former selves. We wanted to forget even though we knew how impossible that was. Still, it was worth the effort to try—if only to hear my best friend laugh and see that dashing smile on his face again.

He emerged from the water and headed my way. Several

ladies nearby openly gawked at his handsome face and lean, well-built physique. With the sun shining down on him, the beads of water clinging to his body glistening, he looked like he'd just walked right out of a swimsuit catalogue.

Of course, I knew better. Beneath the shirt he had on, his upper torso was still covered with layer upon layer of scars, evidence of what he'd gone through at The Shade. My gut clenched.

I tried to go back to those days when I would lose myself in daydreams about being with him. Strangely enough, he didn't take my breath away like he used to. He looked incredible, but he no longer had the same effect on me.

It didn't take long for him to reach me and plunk himself right on top of my beautiful sandcastle.

"Ben!" I screeched.

He laughed. "Sandcastles always fall, Sofia. I thought you might as well bid it farewell sooner rather than later."

The smile on his face transfixed me. I realized how much I'd missed him—the old him.

"What?"

I shook my head. "You seem happy."

The smile on his face remained, but his eyes betrayed emotions—none of them happiness. I reached for his hand, but he withdrew from my touch. It was a harsh reminder that I could never fully understand what he'd gone through at The Shade.

I wanted to ask him, but Ben wasn't the kind of person who talked about feelings. If things were the other way around, Ben would've already found a way to make me laugh. I wondered if I should do just that—throw a shell at him or something—but the brokenness in his appearance made it seem insensitive. So I just sat there, hoping that my presence would somehow bring him consolation.

"I feel numb," he confessed a few minutes later. "Just numb."

What did she do to him? Ben had already told me about how the gorgeous blonde Claudia had tortured him, healed him by forcing him to drink her blood and then tortured him all over again. It was punishment for trying to escape. Something told me that it was just a glimpse of what Claudia had put my best friend through.

"What happened to you, Ben? Back at The Shade?"

I could never forget the look on his face the moment I mentioned the island. All traces of the charmer my best friend used to be disappeared. In his place existed a dark and broken character whose features were screaming murder.

"Do you really want to know?"

I hesitated. *Do I?* I tentatively nodded. "Tell me everything."

"You asked for it." He stood up and held out his hand to

me. "Let's take a walk then."

I grabbed his hand and he pulled me up. As his story unfolded, I found myself wishing—for his sake—that I had never asked.

Chapter 8: Ben

As we strolled over the white sands perfectly complementing the clear blue ocean water, I told Sofia my story, not mentioning that she was forcing me to live out the horrors of The Shade all over again.

I was distraught. I'd once again let Sofia down. Ditching her on her birthday for Tanya—total babe that Tanya was—was on top of my growing list of screwups when it came to the best friend I always took for granted. It felt awful to see the hurt look in Sofia's eyes, but I figured she'd take a walk and get over it. After all, she always did.

I sneaked into her hotel room just before dawn the next day, fully expecting her to still be in bed, with my five-year-old sister,

Abby, snuggled against her. I was disappointed to find my mom lying beside Abby. Even asleep, my mom had a scowl on her face.

I shook her awake. "Mom, where's Sofia?"

My mother blinked several times and frowned at me. "I have no idea where she is. What time is it? She was supposed to be here. Abby was terrified about having to sleep here alone."

"Perhaps she just went out for a walk or something…"

"At this hour? What's gotten into her?"

"I'll find her." I started to feel worse about what I'd done—or not done—to Sofia the night before. It was unlike her to just run off. She'd always been the responsible one.

Worried sick and knowing that I'd been a jerk to her, I set out to the beach to look for her. I walked half a mile down the shore before realizing that I was wasting my time. I kept trying to call her phone, but just kept getting her voicemail. I was ready to turn back when I bumped into a gorgeous blonde girl, wearing—of all things—a black leather jumpsuit.

She approached me with a sultry look in her eyes.

"I'm Claudia. You are?"

Distracted by how beautiful she was, I forgot about my quest to find Sofia. I forgot about Tanya. I flashed my best smile.

"I'm Ben."

To my surprise, she grabbed my neck and pulled my head down for a kiss. It was arguably the best kiss I'd ever had. When our lips parted, she smiled. Fangs protruded from her upper lip.

"You're perfect," she hissed before stabbing me in the neck

with a syringe.

It took mere seconds for me to fall to the ground, unconscious. The last sound that registered was the laughter in her voice when she said, "I'm going to have so much fun playing with you, Ben."

When I came to, I found myself in a large bed, my wrists cuffed to the bedposts. She was on top of me, kissing my neck, my shoulders. I was so much larger than her, and yet I felt helpless.

"What are you doing? Who are you? Where am I?"

She chuckled.

"Oh, so many questions, my pet."

I grimaced at the word, turning my mouth away from her when she tried to kiss me. She grabbed my head with both her hands before forcing a kiss on me. When our lips parted, she cocked her head to the side and pouted.

"I'm in such a nice mood, I've decided to answer your questions. What am I doing? I'm kissing you. Who am I? I'm Claudia, your mistress. Where are you? You're in my bedroom."

Her lips and her hands were all over me and all I could think about was the way she'd smiled at me back at the beach. "You're a vampire." Saying the words out loud made me feel insane.

"Smart boy." She straddled my waist and propped herself up over my chest as she looked down at me, the same manic smile on her face. "Now, I want you to shut up." She gagged me, and then she sank her teeth into my neck, drinking my blood for the first time.

Once satiated, she lifted her head, my blood dripping from the corners of her lips. *"You're as sweet as he was. The Duke..."* Claws protruded from her fingers and she began to trace one of them over my torso. *"Do you have any idea what he put me through?"*

Of course not, you insane bitch. *I fought the urge to scream when her claws sank into my skin, drawing blood. The way her eyes lit up with delight was sickening.*

"My mother was a whore, you know. We were so poor and she was so sick, so she decided to sell me to The Duke. I was only six years old." She began running her hand through my hair before gripping a clump of it with a fist. *"You remind me so much of him."*

My heart sank.

I felt myself inside her, every fiber of my being struggling against the restraints she kept me in, struggling against the degradation she was putting me through. All of it for nothing.

She backhanded me as she chuckled. "I struggled too, you know. I screamed and clawed and fought back, but he had his way with me still. He always got his way. I'm going to have my way with you too."

And she did. Everything about her made my stomach turn. Her moans, the things she was saying... When she collapsed over my body, panting, I wanted to murder her.

"When I turned into a vampire, I made him pay dearly for what he did to me." Her eyes lit up. *"You should've heard him cry and scream. He was weak. Just like you. I hold the power*

now and no one will ever be able to harm me again."

By the time she was done with me that first night at The Shade, I was battered, bruised, bleeding and exhausted. She left me still cuffed to the bed, gag in my mouth.

It took hours before someone entered the room. I flinched at the creak of the door. I was relieved when a pretty girl with raven hair motioned for me to be quiet. She took the gag out of my mouth before beginning to pick the lock of the cuffs holding me to the bed.

"You have to be deathly quiet," she whispered so softly, I barely understood what she said.

"Who are you?" ·

"I'm Eliza." She looked at my worn-down form. "Can you get up?"

I nodded. "I'm mostly just sore."

"Okay then. We're going to get out of here."

I was shocked at how quickly she was able to get the cuffs off me. I sat up on the bed, rubbing my wrists as she began rummaging through the closet for clothes she could throw on me.

"What's your name?" She threw me a pair of boxers and a navy blue hoodie.

"Ben." I put the boxers on. "How did you get here?"

"I was following Claudia. I saw her approach you at the beach and sedate you. I would've saved you, but she was too quick." Eliza threw me a pair of jeans.

I put them on, surprised by how well the trousers fit. "Saved *me? How could you possibly…"*

"There's no time for that now. If you make it out of here without me, find Reuben. He's a hunter like me. He'll help you."

She made me memorize a number as I pulled the hoodie over my head. We snuck out of the room, checking that no one was following us.

I was stunned when I realized that Claudia's penthouse was nestled on top of giant trees. It was an amazing sight.

Eliza pointed to a lift nearby. We crept past some guy wearing a white woolen tunic. I was certain that we'd be found, because of what folklore said about vampires having heightened senses. I was relieved to get past the guy, wondering if vampires weren't that attuned to their senses or whether he was human.

We managed to get inside the lift and punched a button to get to the bottom of the tree. When the doors of the lift slid open, my stomach turned into knots.

Claudia waited for us, chuckling. Two vampire guards were with her.

"Did you really think you had any chance of escaping?"

The two guards restrained Eliza while Claudia pushed me back into the elevator. Trying to capitalize on all my martial arts training, I made a move to hit Claudia, but she dodged my blow. One hit from her, and I crashed into the elevator wall and fell to the ground, fading into unconsciousness.

When I woke up, I was in a small, dim room with no

windows, chained to a wall, naked from the waist up. There were various chains and whips and contraptions that made my gut clench arranged in various areas of the room. On one side, a surveillance monitor was mounted on the wall, its screen showing an image of a large bed. Eliza was lying in the middle of it.

On the opposite side, Claudia was seated—looking quite relaxed—on a metal chair sharpening a dagger.

"What do you want from me?"

Claudia looked up. Her eyes lit up.

"Oh, good. You're awake. This means we can now start with your training."

She stood up and walked to me. She began tracing the tip of her dagger over my torso. "After everything I did to please you, you go off and leave me with that bitch?" She motioned toward the flickering screen. "I'm so disappointed with you, Ben."

With a crazed look in her eyes, she used her dagger to make a long, shallow cut in the skin below my left collarbone. I gritted my teeth. I refused to give her the satisfaction of hearing me scream. I didn't even want to let her see me writhe in pain.

She seemed pleased. "You have a high pain threshold. I like that."

"You bitch."

She slapped me, throwing my head grotesquely to the side. Her blow was so strong I was surprised my neck didn't break. I tasted blood on my lips and her eyes popped wide open. Her gaze *alternated manically between my split lip and the cut she had just made on my torso.*

She took a lick of the blood on both my lips and my chest before making another cut, this time a little above my waist.

My breathing grew heavy trying to keep myself from giving her the satisfaction of a reaction as she made one agonizing cut after the other until my upper body became nothing but a bloody mess. The pain was excruciating and I was begging my brain to make me lose consciousness, but my body denied me even that escape.

When she stopped cutting me, I hoped that it meant she was done. Wrong. Claudia grabbed my hair and made me look up at the monitor.

"Keep your eyes on your little friend there. She's a huntress, dedicated to finishing off our kind. I suspected someone was following me back at the beach. How she found me, I'll never know. When I sedated you, I could hear her gasp from a mile away. Silly, insipid little worm. She thought that she was being stealthy, following us all the way here to The Shade, but I let her allow you the illusion of escape to test your loyalty to me." She grinned. "Now, that you've proven yourself disloyal, I can commence with punishing you."

She gave my torso a manic glance. "Oh wait, I already did." To my surprise, she cut her palm and shoved it over my lips, forcing me to gasp when she pinched my nose shut. I had no choice but to let the blood from her palm trickle down my throat. Her grip on my head tightened. "Of course, your punishment is far from over. I said I want you to watch your friend."

I shifted my gaze toward the surveillance monitor. A tall man approached Eliza's unconscious form. She looked so fragile as he lifted her in his arms and pulled her against his body. There was no mistaking the dark expression in his eyes as he looked at her milky white neck. It was ravenous. I wanted to look away when he bared his fangs and bit into Eliza's neck, but Claudia held my head, her blood beginning to travel through my veins. As I was forced to drink Claudia's blood, I was also forced to watch another vampire drain an innocent young woman.

By the time the vampire was done with Eliza, Claudia pulled her palm away from my mouth. She looked at my body, which was, to my surprise, beginning to heal.

I didn't realize fully the extent of her madness until she said, "Perfect. You'll be like new soon, and then I can cut you up all over again."

"Claudia was sadistic and insane," I told Sofia. I no longer wanted to continue the gory details of the torture and humiliation Claudia had inflicted on me, so I simply settled for: "She put me through hell."

Silence followed as both of us got lost in our own thoughts.

"So?" I asked with a bitter chuckle. "Was your experience at The Shade anything like mine?"

"No." Sofia shook her head, her head bowed. "Derek was nothing like Claudia. It was Lucas who tried to make my life there a living hell. If it weren't for Derek, he would've succeeded, but Derek did everything he could to protect me from his older brother."

I found it sickening the way she talked about Derek like he was some sort of hero. Though he might have fooled her, he wasn't fooling me.

Tears moistened her eyes as she was finally able to force herself to look at me. "I'm so sorry, Ben. If I hadn't wandered off that night, you wouldn't have..." She choked on her words, biting on her lower lip. She grabbed my hands and squeezed.

I wanted to comfort her. She couldn't have known. She was a victim too. However, I was too preoccupied mulling over what I hadn't been able to bring myself to tell her.

I couldn't tell her that after what Claudia had put my body through, my sense of touch was so dulled I could barely feel Sofia's hands on mine. I didn't want any more of her pity.

I also couldn't tell her that Derek was the vampire who had killed Eliza, because in spite of everything we'd been through, I was no longer sure of her loyalties. The idea that she could still choose Derek over me terrified me.

CHAPTER 9: DEREK

You shouldn't have let her go.

I tried everything I could to shut out my sister's words, but it was impossible. Sofia was no longer around, and no matter whom I surrounded myself with or what I immersed myself in, I could still feel her absence with every fiber of my being.

Of course, I'd lived long enough to mask what I was going through as I continued my strict schedule of meetings. By the end of the day, word was already out all over the island: *The prince is wide awake. He's done taking a break and is about to get right to the bloody business of keeping The Shade safe.*

I hated to admit it, but Vivienne was right. It was all a ruse, a show I had to put on in order to distract myself from the void that had formed upon Sofia's departure.

After I wrapped up the last meeting of the day, I pulled Cameron to the side. "I can trust you, can't I?"

He nodded. "You know you can."

"I want you to find my older brother. We had a falling out." *He almost killed Sofia.* "It was a pretty big fight and he's running scared of me now. You know how cowardly Lucas can get."

A smirk formed on Cameron's face. It was recognized by a handful of us that Lucas wasn't the kind of *warrior* we'd like to end up on the battlefield with. He'd throw us at the enemy's cannons if it meant he could save his life.

"What do you want me to do, Derek?" Cameron asked.

"I need you to find him. He's hiding on this island somewhere, or maybe he's even out with some of the scouts looking for new slaves. I don't know… I just need to know where he is."

"What do you want me to do once I find him?"

I hesitated, but nodded. "Lock him up. In the Cells." *I can't afford to have him go after her.* "Then report back to me immediately."

"The king isn't going to like that. Neither will your sister."

"Vivienne will understand. She's always been on my side. As for my father, I'll take care of him when he gets here. It's of prime importance right now that I know where Lucas is located at all times."

Cameron nodded. "I'll be on the lookout for him."

Satisfied that the search for my older brother was in capable hands, I retreated to my penthouse for a well-deserved rest. The moment I entered my house, however, I realized that my day was far from over. Ashley, Paige and Rosa, the three girls who, along with Sofia, completed my harem, were waiting for me.

Harem. I grimaced at the word. It was another one of those innovations The Shade had come up with during my four-hundred-year slumber. Keeping a house full of young, gorgeous human slaves was a reckless indulgence the Elite and some of the other Lodgers—naturalized vampire citizens of The Shade—enjoyed. I'd never been a fan, but it was this very indulgence that had brought me Sofia.

I scowled at the three lovely teenagers, standing in the middle of the hall, waiting for my arrival. Seeing them only reminded me of Sofia. *Hell, everything about this place reminds me of Sofia now.*

"Where's Sofia?" It was the blonde, Ashley, who spoke up. Of the three, she'd always been the gutsiest one.

I wanted to just walk past them and head directly for my

room, but they would follow me so I sat on one of the couches in the living room. "I don't know where she is exactly, but she's no longer here." I motioned for them to take seats across from me. The girls exchanged glances as they sat next to each other on the largest couch.

"She escaped?" Ashley asked.

"Yes. Her and that boyfriend of hers... Ben."

"Ben's not her boyfriend." Rosa, the pretty petite one with the short, wavy black hair said. She was the one who always looked like she would die of fright whenever I was around. I had to give kudos to her for speaking up for the first time.

I exhaled, annoyed, before waving a hand in the air. "I don't care."

A lie.

Paige, the sporty brunette, scoffed at me. "Oh, sure. You don't *care* about her. Look, we know Sofia. She would never leave without us. She wouldn't betray us like that."

"But she did, didn't she? She's no longer here."

"What did you do to her?" Ashley asked, her voice mixed with accusation and fear.

"I helped her escape." I grimaced even as I glared at Ashley for daring to question me. "Look. If it's any consolation, she begged me to let you come. I wouldn't hear of it. I couldn't risk The Shade by just letting you loose."

"But you trust Ben enough to let him go?" Paige's voice betrayed her frustration.

I was Derek Novak. I didn't have to answer to three teenage slaves, and yet I found myself explaining to them. "I had no choice. Sofia wouldn't have left without him."

"But she left without *us*," Rosa said.

"This conversation is going nowhere." I rolled my eyes and stood up.

"What are you planning to do with us now?" Ashley's face was pale.

I sat right back in my seat and looked at each one of them. I could do whatever I wanted with them… use them, break them, bed them. No one would think worse of me for it. No one but Sofia.

"I really don't care what happens to any of you. Right now, all I need from you is to make sure that nobody finds out that Ben and Sofia are gone. Nobody. I already warned Sam and Kyle that they are not to breathe a word of this to anyone. As far as everyone at The Shade is concerned, they're still locked up somewhere in this house, or dead. As for the three of you, the only reason you mattered to me in the first place was because you mattered to her."

"What makes you think we no longer matter to her?"

"What don't you get, Ashley?" I snapped at her. "She's no longer here! I could swing you over my back, take you to my bedroom and do the most despicable things to you. She wouldn't know."

A chilling silence followed.

It was Rosa who broke the silence. "But you won't do that, because you still care about what Sofia will think."

"Maybe so, but so what?"

Ashley smirked. She leaned back, shaking her head as she focused her almond-shaped eyes on me. "It's funny."

"Yes? What is?"

"You spent so much time with her, practically demanded her time, and yet you still don't have the slightest clue what kind of girl Sofia is."

I straightened up. "What are you talking about?"

"With people she cares deeply about still here—us, you— Sofia would *want* to come back." Ashley stood up and glared at me. "You'd know that if you actually got to know her all those times you were keeping her in your bedroom."

Ashley stormed out of the room. Paige followed suit. It was Rosa, however, who gave me hope that I could get Sofia back. She gave me a tentative half-smile and said, "Sofia cared deeply about you."

I wanted to believe, to hope, but the ever-present voice of darkness hissed at me. *And look where caring about you got her.*

I shook the thought away, eliminating all hope that she

could once again be in my arms. *Keeping her here would only put her in danger. Just let go of her, Derek.*

Just let go.

Chapter 10: Sofia

Night was the only time Ben and I chose to stay indoors. We'd decided to take a one-bedroom suite at the hotel, considering that as best friends, we'd slept in a single bed dozens of times. For some reason, however, things had changed and sleeping in the same bed felt uncomfortable, like a betrayal of Derek.

Back at The Shade, after Lucas had killed Gwen, Derek had asked me to start sleeping in his bedroom. He was more able to protect me that way. I couldn't even explain why, but it seemed natural. I expected awkwardness, him being an attractive young man and myself being, well, a young woman. I was surprised by how well we adjusted to one another. It was like a dance. We knew how to move around each other. He got me and I liked to think that I got him too.

I couldn't understand why, but something had changed between Ben and me. The rapport we'd had was gone. I assumed that the problem was with me, so I shoved thoughts of my vampire captor out of my head. It was, after all, how Derek had got to me in the first place—when I'd allowed myself to stop pining for Ben.

As I sat on my side of the bed, lightly bouncing over it as I grabbed a pillow, I huffed and gave Ben a small pout.

"What?" he asked.

"I hate this."

"Hate what?"

"This! This tension. Since when are we so on edge around each other?"

The expression in his eyes softened. I knew he couldn't deny that there was some level of awkwardness, because he had barely spoken to me since our trip down memory lane back at the beach. He sat beside me and grinned as he cocked his head. "I don't understand how you could still appear so fair and pink and soft in spite of the fact that we spent the whole day in the sun."

"Fair and pink and soft? You make me sound like a pig."

"No, you're pretty, Sofia. It's just weird how you never

seem to get sunburn."

"That also means I never get that perfect tan you have."

I didn't realize how much I'd missed the arrogant grin on his face. "Yes, yes… The sun does love me. How did you describe me that one time?" He squinted an eye at me. "I believe you called me a Greek god."

I rolled my eyes. "You never do get tired of bringing that up, do you? I was being sarcastic."

"Riiight… You keep telling yourself that." A self-satisfied smile formed on his lips as he lay flat on his back on the bed.

It was a glimpse of the Ben I missed. Fun-loving, easy-going, never one to get hung up over problems. I smiled as I watched him fall asleep, and giggled when he once again began to snore. I rolled to my side, trying to fall asleep.

By the stroke of midnight, I gave up trying. I got up, pulled a robe over my body and took the sealed envelope from the backpack. I was hoping that it came from Derek. After everything Ben had told me about his experience at The Shade, I didn't want him finding out how much I missed Derek. I didn't want to feel guilty that I hadn't had as bad an experience as Ben back at the island.

I walked out onto the terrace, relishing the cool breeze carrying with it the taste of salt from the ocean. I opened the brown envelope and found myself fighting back tears.

The package wasn't from Derek. It was from Corrine, the

witch. She'd become a kind of older sister to me during the time we'd spent together. The package contained the cell phone I'd used to teach Derek how to use mobile phones, my favorite Polaroid snapshot of us together after I showed him how to use a camera, a silver ring studded with what looked like rubies, and a note that said: *The phone and the photo is for you to never forget. The ring is a gift from me. May it help you find your way home. The island is several shades darker without you. We'll miss your light. Love, Corrine.*

I clutched the envelope to my chest. Hardly any time had passed since we'd left The Shade and I already found the ache within me overwhelming. I was supposed to be thankful that I'd made it out of The Shade, but all I could think about was how much I wanted to go back.

"Sofia?"

Ben's voice from behind me caused me to jump back, startled. I wiped the tears away.

"What's that?"

"It's… just… it's nothing."

"How could it be nothing? Let me see." He stepped beside me and gestured for me to hand over the envelope.

"Don't get mad." I handed it over to him, afraid of what his reaction would be—especially over the photo, with me smiling and looking straight at the camera, while Derek's eyes were set on me.

Ben tensed when he saw what was inside. He handed it back to me, as if he was disgusted by it. "Where did you get that?"

"It came with the backpack."

"I don't understand how you can trust him."

"He saved me so many times… I…"

"Don't you get it, Sofia? You wouldn't need saving if it weren't for him!" The outburst was a first in a long time. "It was Derek. He was the vampire who killed Eliza."

His words came like a punch in the gut, knocking the wind out of me. I remembered the night Derek had come to the penthouse, blood dripping from his lips, how menacing he looked…

"You don't seem surprised."

"Some of the other vampires offer up their slaves to him… for him to feed on."

"Did he ever feed on you?"

"No, never."

"So what exactly are you saying, Sofia? As long as you're safe and taken care of, it's fine that he's a murderer who feeds off of other people?"

"No, Ben. It's not like that. You don't know him like I do. You haven't seen him struggle to take control." My reasoning seemed hollow.

"How on earth can you turn a blind eye to these things,

Sofia? Since when did you become the kind of person who stood by, comfortable in some penthouse, sleeping with the enemy while people are being murdered all around you?"

"I never slept with Derek in the way you're implying."

Ben gave a wry laugh. "Right, but that isn't the point, is it? If the vampire prince shows up—right here and right now—takes you in his arms and kisses you, would you resist?"

I opened my mouth to answer, but nothing came out.

"I thought so." Ben smiled bitterly. "You're too blinded by your infatuation with him to see him for what he really is." He eyed the envelope I was still clutching. "He's a monster."

He turned back to the bedroom. "Home is in California with the family who raised you for eight years. You don't need their witch's ring to find your way there. We make the drive back home first thing tomorrow."

That night, Ben called his parents, informing them where we were. The only explanation he gave them was that we'd wanted a taste of independence and decided to run away.

I feared that we would have to tell one lie after another, but I didn't want to worry about it. The only lie that was circling my mind was the one I kept telling myself. I wanted Ben to be wrong about Derek and about how I'd simply turned a blind eye, but I knew he was right.

I didn't know if it was self-preservation or something more than that, but back at The Shade, I'd wrapped myself in this little bubble, secure in Derek's protection and unfounded fondness for me. I'd seen how other human captives were treated by other vampires and never bothered to help. I'd simply thanked the powers that be that it wasn't me. I was selfish and blind. I'd been so wrapped up in my own survival, I'd failed to see the immensity of the darkness that permeated The Shade.

It was natural to hate the island the way Ben did. I'd been held captive. I'd almost been raped and killed. A friend of mine had been murdered. I had every reason to hate The Shade and want to destroy it.

But I didn't. And I couldn't understand why.

Chapter 11: Lucas

Breathless, Claudia and I rolled to our sides on her king-sized canopy bed. I pulled my arm from beneath her bare form so I could reach the table where I'd laid a pack of cigarettes. I propped myself up, leaning my back against the headboard before lighting up a cigarette.

I could feel Claudia's eyes on me. She was the girl I ran to whenever I needed a quick tumble in bed. She'd served her purpose well. Of course, the entire time we were screwing each other, it hadn't been Claudia on my mind. It had been Sofia.

My brother's slave had etched herself permanently on my subconscious from the very moment I'd first laid eyes on her—only to realize that she could never be mine. When I'd finally got a taste of her blood, I was a lost cause. I couldn't get her out of my head. *The fragile little twig.*

"Word's out that Derek has sent Cameron on a full-scale hunt for you. They're hunting you as we speak." Six-hundred-year-old Claudia rolled her seventeen-year-old body over the bed so that she was lying on her stomach. She grabbed the cigarette I'd just lit before I could start smoking it and took a good, long drag.

I glared at her. "You're enjoying this, aren't you?"

She laughed. "You know I am. Can you blame me? You preying on Derek's precious little pet… Derek hunting you down… You, prince of The Shade, the royal highness himself, hiding out with me, ready for my bed whenever I please. How the mighty have fallen."

I scowled, but it wasn't like I was in any position to disagree. Whether I liked it or not, I was at her mercy. I hated owing Claudia anything, but she was the only person among the Elite whose depravity and selfishness could equal—perhaps even exceed—mine. We'd had each other's backs for centuries simply because we allowed each other to indulge our dark sides. Hell, I wasn't even sure if Claudia had a side that wasn't made of pure evil. She wouldn't betray me by handing me over to Derek.

I lit another cigarette and pressed it to my lips.

"Do you really think Derek has it in him to kill you?" Claudia asked.

"He was going to. I could see it in his eyes. The human girl stopped him."

"Oh, that's rich. She saved you. Now you owe her your life."

"I don't owe her anything." I blew out smoke, annoyed. It was me who'd found Sofia. She was supposed to be mine. I had the right to do with her as I pleased.

"If you say so. Be that as it may, you can't keep hiding here forever. What are you planning to do now you're being hunted down?"

"I don't know."

"You could always escape."

"Oh yeah? And go where?" I took another puff from my cigarette. Claudia had already thrown hers away.

"Well, there's only one other coven who has it almost as good as we have."

I scoffed. "No way."

"Where else are you going to go? The Oasis is the only logical option."

I entertained the idea in my mind. I actually found the prospect appealing for two reasons: seeing the legendary Oasis, and finally meeting Borys' right-hand woman, Ingrid. She was rumored to possess beauty unlike any other.

"Though laying eyes on this mysterious pet Borys just added is not without its allure, you must've forgotten who I am, Claudia. I'm Lucas Novak. *Novak.* The Maslens will have my head the moment my feet hit Cairo."

Claudia shrugged. "Well, it really isn't my problem, is it? All I know is that you have to get out of here, because if they find out I'm aiding and abetting a criminal, Derek won't hesitate to rip my heart out."

I gave her a glare. *Claudia... such a sympathetic friend.* I tossed my cigarette into a nearby ashtray and pushed myself on top of her. "Sometimes, I wonder where your loyalties lie, Claudia."

"That's easy." She smirked. "I'm loyal to me."

"Of course you are." I rolled my eyes. "I'll be out of your hair in no time, Claudia, but for now..." I kissed her deeply. She tasted of blood and nicotine. I distracted myself with the pleasures she provided one more time. I still had a couple of days to spare. The real danger was when the impetuous and insane blonde vampire writhing beneath me finally got bored of me.

Until then, she would keep me safe. Until then, escape could wait.

Chapter 12: Derek

I spat on the dirt ground and threw my opponent a disgusted glare. Across from me on the makeshift circle in the training grounds, Xavier Vaughn was trying to catch his breath, his right arm hanging limply at his side, clutching the hilt of his katana like his life depended on it. He was exhausted, bloody, and bruised.

I couldn't stand the sight of him. Before my sleep, he would've bested me in any sword fight nine times out of ten. After four centuries, it took only half a dozen strikes to wear him down.

"We've only been at this for about ten minutes, Vaughn."

The fresh wound my katana had inflicted upon him

quickly closed up and healed.

"I haven't done this in centuries, Novak." Xavier never addressed me as his prince. It was one thing I liked about him. "I'm a little rusty."

"A little? Is that a joke? Where's the warrior I once knew? If you'd fought this way during the Battle of First Blood, we'd all be dead by now."

Amusement showed in the corners of his tired, steel-gray eyes. He raised his katana and lunged forward to attack me.

It took about a minute to slash an ugly wound across his back and have him lying face down on the ground. The blood that spilled from his back tainted the ground, mixing with that of the others who'd fought me before him.

What have they been doing for the past four hundred years? My merciless stare followed Xavier as he dragged himself out of the arena. "Looks like we've got a lot of work to do. Who's next?"

Eli Lazaroff stepped into the arena, looking more like a librarian than a warrior. I honestly felt sorry for one of our Elite's most valuable strategic minds, because as Eli approached me, he was shaking like a leaf.

I flexed my neck muscles before taking a step toward him. That caused him to flinch. That was enough to make me suck up any guilt over what I was about to put him through. Raising my weapon, I dealt him the first blow.

Whether I liked it or not, as ruler of The Shade, I needed to remind my subjects what pain felt like. They needed to remember what it was like to fight for their lives and bleed for a cause.

The year was 1512. The battle would always be remembered as the Battle of First Blood. It was the first battle ever to take place on the island, the day we stopped running. We all agreed that it was time to fight back or die.

We were a sorry bunch, huddled within the caves that would eventually become the Black Heights, home to The Shade's prisoners and slaves.

It'd been two years since I'd been shipwrecked on that island, thinking that I'd lost all of my loved ones to yet another hunter attack. The only companion during my first year marooned on the island was an olive-skinned, brown-eyed, black-haired beauty. Her name was Cora and she was the only reason I was able to keep sane after I'd lost everything worth fighting for. I had no idea then who she was, or how valuable she would eventually be.

Sitting in that cave, I realized that we still had a lot to fight for.

I was seated on the ground, leaning against the cave wall, with Cora sitting right next to me. My father, Gregor, sat opposite us. He sent a ravenous stare Cora's way.

Cora was the only human among a cave full of hungry vampires. None of that fazed her. She just smirked.

Liana Hendry was sitting near the cave entrance. She pulled her knees to her chest, shivering due to the cold. She stared blankly toward the cave opening. Cameron had left the cave with Lucas and Xavier to scout the hunters' location hours ago.

Beside Liana sat Vivienne, looking unnervingly serene, her head on Liana's shoulder. In the depths of her blue-violet eyes were mysteries we could only wonder about, because I couldn't even remember the last time I'd heard my twin speak.

Two or three feet away, Eli was drawing some sort of map on the ground with a stick. So wrapped up was he that he barely noticed how peeved his younger brother, Yuri, looked when Claudia began chatting him up and making suggestive gestures toward him. Yuri eventually snapped at her and it was the first time I'd seen such a murderous glare on her pretty face.

They comprised only some of the twenty vampire clans hidden with me in the mountain caves. Most were terrified by what the dawn would usher in. They had barely made it to the island with the hunters in relentless pursuit. The sun was about to rise and the hunters weren't about to give up until every single one of us was destroyed.

In cases like these, the sun was our greatest adversary. How were we to fight back when we had to keep hidden deep in the darkness of the caves?

The wind howled outside the cave, but then came footsteps approaching. I rose to my feet, gripping the hilt of my sword. I let a short breath out when Cameron, Lucas and Xavier *appeared from the clearing. The grave expressions on their faces told me that I had no reason to be relieved.*

"They're approaching as we speak," Cameron announced.

"How many?"

They exchanged worried glances.

"Four or five hundred," Xavier estimated. "Maybe six."

"How many of us are there?" I directed my question to Eli.

He didn't even look up. "Seventy-six. Seventy-seven, if you include her." *He was referring to Cora.*

I stood to my full height, mustering all the courage I had. "How many of us can fight?"

"You can't seriously be considering this!" Lucas stepped forward. "They outnumber us at least five to one. We have no choice but to run."

"Run? Run where?" I shot back at him. "Lest you forget, this is an island. If we want to reach the ship that got you here, we'd have to walk right into the hunters."

"Most of us aren't trained to fight," Lucas continued to object.

"They might simply burn us." Yuri spoke up.

"That's exactly what they'll do if we just sit here and wait for them."

"What are you saying, boy?" Cameron asked.

"I don't know about you, but I can no longer run. I say we fight for this island. We make a refuge out of it."

The other vampires were beginning to huddle around us,

listening in, curious.

"How do you propose we do that, brother?" Lucas spat the words.

"We'll make an example of these hunters. We'll send out a clear message. Any human who enters this island can never leave again." The moment I said the words, there was shock in Cora's eyes. I tried not to worry about her. A decision had to be made and I was clearly the only one who would make it. There was no going back for me. "We need to fight back."

"And if we don't succeed?" This time, it was my father speaking as he rose to his feet. "What if the sun rises as we fight? It will be the end of all of us."

I shrugged. "I don't know about you, but I'd rather die fighting than running."

And so it happened that at the darkest time of the night, we took the offensive and ran straight to the hunters. Their surprise worked to our advantage, but they knew that there was no way for us to finish the battle before the sun rose. However, as we fought for our lives against the best and most fearsome hunters their order sent our way, our fear of sunlight proved to be unfounded. We fought for hours—for as long as it took to destroy every hunter who dared invade us—but dawn never came.

After the Battle of First Blood, the island became permanently enveloped by darkness. The moon became our sun. It would be years later before we found out why. Even after I found out that Cora was behind it, I couldn't fully understand why she spared our lives even though it meant losing hundreds of hunters.

The others lauded the strange occurrence as a miracle. They believed that the island was truly meant to be our sanctuary, and celebrated me for discovering it and leading them to fight for it.

I didn't see it the same way they did. I saw it as a dark omen.

I would never forget Vivienne and me staring at the starlit sky long into the night while the others slept like babies. The fear in her violet eyes was unmistakable. After years of silence, she stared up at the night sky, grabbed my hand and said, "The darkness is coming."

I didn't ask her what she meant. For many of us, it was the first time we had ever intentionally taken human life. It was the night we drew first blood.

By the time I grew too tired to fight, the ground of the arena was blood red, a stark reminder of the battle we'd fought four hundred years ago. Of all the warriors who stood within that circle, not one was able to hit me, much less wound me. They were the same men and women who'd drawn first blood with me—only this time, they were weaker, prouder, and less resilient. In battle, I barely recognized them anymore.

I threw my weapon on the ground and walked away from the training grounds, only to find Cameron approaching.

"You up for a fight, Hendry?"

"Not today, prince." He shook his head, an amused smile forming on his face. "I came to ask if you still wanted that meeting with the council at the Great Dome."

"Of course." I shrugged. "Why wouldn't I?"

He chuckled.

"If we weren't vampires, you would've already murdered more than two-thirds of the Elite Council"—he smiled—"your majesty."

I fought the urge to laugh. The Elite Council now consisted of a rather pathetic bunch. I just rolled my eyes and went for a quick change before I headed for the dome with Cameron.

"What do we know about Ingrid Maslen?" Something about Borys having a new girl didn't sit right with me. He'd been after Vivienne for such a long time, bent on getting what belonged to him. I couldn't believe that he would just replace Vivienne with someone else, unless there was more to Ingrid Maslen than we knew of.

Cameron shrugged. "I'm not sure she's even been allowed out of The Oasis ever since Borys turned her. She's his best-kept secret."

"Any idea why she is kept under wraps?"

"Just rumors. Some say Ingrid is to The Oasis as Vivienne is to the The Shade."

"She's a seer?"

"Maybe. Why else would Borys be so obsessed with her? We both know how sick that man is—if we could even call him that. He wouldn't turn a human like Ingrid and make her part of his clan unless there was something special about her."

I couldn't help but frown, wondering why it bothered me so much. Borys was no longer after my sister. I should've been happy. Still, something wasn't right. I had more urgent matters for the time being, but someday I would come face to face with Borys Maslen again.

A premonition told me that I was going to rue that day.

Chapter 13: Sofia

Blood was all over the Sun Room. The LED lights mimicking the sun's rays were busted. The only source of light was a flickering fluorescent lamp fighting to stay alight. I was pinned against one wall. I couldn't move. I couldn't hear anything. My sense of touch was gone.

A dark presence entered the room. A shadow. I tried to talk, but my voice came out a rasp.

The shadow approached. Its presence was so strong, so powerful, so dark. It stopped in front of me. Blood began to pool on the ground where the figure stood. I was expecting to see Lucas, and gasped. It was Derek. Blue eyes void of life. Fangs bared. Ready to prey on me. He took a hold of me. His fangs were about to sink into my skin. Then nothing. Nothing but a void and a female voice whispering, "The darkness is coming."

I woke up in the hotel room, sweating, tense and out of breath. I was clutching the sheets for dear life, afraid that if I let go, I might get sucked back into the nightmare. I flinched when the bathroom door opened. I could smell Ben's aftershave mixed with the fragrances of shampoo and soap. I stirred on the bed, trying to shake off the nightmare. I was afraid for myself. I was afraid for Derek.

"Breakfast is ready on the veranda," Ben called. He was rubbing his hair dry, oblivious to my trembling.

I dragged myself out of bed. *I can't keep waking up this way.* I might've left The Shade, but the island and all its horrors were still with me.

I pulled my hair up in a messy bun as I made my way to the veranda. I needed the sunlight. Breakfast consisted of muesli, coffee and fruit salad. I would've preferred some toast with jam and butter, but I wasn't in a picky mood.

Ben joined me not long after I settled down in my seat.

"Mom and Dad are on their way to pick us up. We might end up staying here a couple more days. Apparently, they made a whole fuss with the police when we disappeared." He sat across from me, looking bothered.

I cringed. "I was afraid of that. We'll have to talk to the police, probably even a social worker…"

"So what's our story going to be?" He leaned back in his seat, rolling a grape around on his plate. "We ran away? That's it?"

"I guess we could just keep it simple by keeping our mouths shut. We ran away. Period. No need to give them any details."

"Unless…" Ben began drumming his fingers on the table.

"Unless what?" I pushed my bowl away. It seemed neither one of us had much of an appetite that morning.

"Unless we just tell them the truth. The whole truth."

I knew it was an option, but something inside me was screaming against it. "We can't do that."

"Why not?"

"What are we going to tell them? We were abducted by vampires and taken to an invisible island to be their slaves? We don't even know where The Shade is. They're going to think we're insane."

"So what? We met people there. I'm sure someone out there has reported them missing. How else would we have known about them?"

I shook my head. "We can't. Derek trusted us. We can't betray…"

"So there it is then. The truth. You don't want to talk about The Shade because of *him*. What did he do to you, Sofia? It's like you're possessed by this inexplicable urge to please him."

The words stung. I couldn't look Ben in the eye. I didn't know why. I wished I knew. "It's not just Derek. I'm sorry, Ben, but I just can't. Not this way."

A knock on the door interrupted our conversation. Ben's eyes threatened to burn holes through me, but he stood up and answered the door. From the veranda, I could hear his mother, Amelia, sobbing.

"Where's Sofia, Ben? Is she with you?" Little Abby sounded cautious.

If his father, Lyle, was there, he certainly wasn't talking much. Ben came out to fetch me. "The police are here. They want to ask us some questions."

"And what's our answer going to be?"

He ground his teeth before responding. "We ran away."

They spent a considerable amount of time trying to get us to talk. They kept telling us that we could tell them the truth, that we didn't have to be afraid. They tried their best to pry out information about where we were, how we managed to keep ourselves hidden, how we survived. Ben never even hinted about The Shade. Just like me, he kept silent about it and I was grateful for it. I knew he couldn't understand why I refused to give The Shade away—heck, even I didn't understand—but he supported me and I thought the world of him for it.

The police eventually gave up. Running away wasn't a crime, and unless they were charging us, we had no reason to talk.

It took three days before all the necessary paperwork was done to get Ben and me cleared to go back to California. The physical examinations brought about an onslaught of questions. They didn't find anything wrong with me, but there was no hiding the scars on Ben's body.

I would never forget the look in Amelia's eyes when she saw the scars. It felt like I was being torn apart when she cried, "Who did this? Why won't you tell us who did this?"

It was the first time I'd ever seen Lyle so angry. "Sofia, where were you? What happened to both of you?"

Ben's eyes on me ate away at my conscience. "I'm so sorry," was all I managed to say, head bowed and tears streaming.

I expected Ben to tell them everything, but he held his ground. Lyle and Amelia tried to pry information out of us. They screamed, they begged, they threatened. Neither Ben nor I said anything about the vampires.

Finally, everything came to an end when Ben sighed in exasperation and said, "Can we please just go home? I'm exhausted."

His statement paved the way to the tensest road trip ever. Ben slept through most of the trip. I envied him; as hard as I tried, I was unable to get a wink of sleep throughout the entire drive home.

Their home. Not mine.

It wasn't until we reached their house that I pulled Lyle over to ask him the question that'd been bothering me since I saw them.

"Did my dad know I was gone?" *Did he care?*

The look on Lyle's face was heartbreaking. "The checks came on schedule."

I knew what that meant. It didn't matter if my father knew. As far as Aiden Claremont was concerned, his fatherly obligation toward me started and ended with the quarterly checks he sent the Hudsons.

I didn't know why I was surprised. From the moment my mother had gone insane and he'd shipped her away from home, he'd married his work as the founder of a small home security agency that developed into a larger business. Truth be told, the sums he was sending the Hudsons were just scraps considering what he was actually worth. He was a miserable excuse for a father.

Lyle awkwardly rubbed my back. "The Aiden I used to know adored you."

Yeah? Introduce him to me once you find that version again. I just smiled back at Lyle. It wasn't right to take my frustration out on him. He'd lost a best friend the day I'd lost a father.

Amelia kept me busy with her in the kitchen making dinner for the rest of the evening. Dinner was tense. Abby was the only one in a bubbly mood. We tried to oblige her, but none of us eased the friction.

That night, I tossed and turned in my bed, unable to sleep. I kept my eyes shut. I'd thought of escaping The Shade many times while I was there. At the back of my mind, I'd had some vague idea about exposing The Shade and freeing all its human prisoners. That was what I'd thought I'd be doing now, after leaving the island. Instead, I'd gone back to California, had dinner with the Hudsons and talked—rather uncomfortably—about going back to school.

I'd had to force myself not to laugh when Amelia said she expected Ben and me to return to school immediately. Ben had said nothing. He'd seemed dazed since we got back.

I was convinced that I would spend the rest of the night obsessing about living with the Hudsons for the next few years when I heard a knock. I sat up in my bed and Ben pushed my door open.

"Hey."

"I just..." He seemed genuinely embarrassed. "Do you mind sleeping with me in my bed? I'd rather not be alone."

I needed no further prodding. I got up, grabbed my pillow and blanket and followed Ben. We snuck through the hallway until we reached his bedroom. We snuggled beneath the sheets, but I couldn't shake away the thought that it provided none of the security and comfort that I'd had with Derek.

Even together, Ben and I stayed up way into the night, afraid of the nightmares.

"Mom wants to drive to school tomorrow, see what we have to do to catch up."

"You're actually willing to go through with this high school thing?"

"I think I owe it to my parents—even to myself, I guess— to at least try. Besides, what else are we going to do?"

It was another small glimpse of the Ben I used to know— the Ben who loved his parents and loved being the popular hotshot in high school. To once again see that side of him was the only reason I said, "High school it is then."

There was a long pause, with both of us mulling over our thoughts.

I eventually broke the silence. "Ben?"

"Yeah?"

"Thank you."

He didn't ask why. He knew. "They did something to you at The Shade, Sofia. I don't know what, but I hope you break out of whatever they did and see sense. I'll wait until graduation. After that, I'm going to take revenge on the island, and I'm going to do it whether you're with me or not."

The coldness in his voice terrified me, but not as much as the fact that I suddenly felt an urge to protect The Shade—no matter what.

Ben was right. They must've done something to me at The Shade, because no matter how far away from the island I was, I remained its captive.

The Shade had become a part of me and destroying it felt like destroying myself.

Chapter 14: Derek

The Great Dome was a large, round hall located at the topmost level of the Crimson Fortress' west tower. It earned its name due to the dome-like, cavernous structure of its ceiling. Over the years it had become the main center of all our governmental, judicial and military gatherings.

The dome was designed to show the hierarchy of The Shade's Elite. Across from the large oak doors, right at the front of the room, the balcony had four seats. On a pedestal three feet above the ground was my father the king's seat. To its right, two feet above, was my seat. On either side of mine were Vivienne's and Lucas' seats, situated one foot above the ground.

At the very center of the room was a round stage which served as the stand for whomever was addressing the council or under trial.

On either side of the stand facing the balcony were twenty seats for the Elite's vampire clans. Above and surrounding the council seats were seventy-five seats arranged in an amphitheater style reserved for the Elite. Rarely was anyone who wasn't a member of the Elite brought to the Great Dome—unless to stand trial.

When I'd first paid the dome a visit, it had rarely been used over the years, which left a lot to be said about how the kingdom was being run in my absence.

I tasked Vivienne with the responsibility of modernizing the dome, since we were going to use the place a lot more. Given her keen eye for design and knack for getting things done, it took her five and a half days to accomplish the task.

It was the same basic structure, but brought into the twenty-first century, with flatscreen monitors and updated sound equipment. She refurnished the room—the ancient-looking thrones were replaced with comfortable recliners that still looked elegant and regal. Arguably the best alteration to the hall, however, was replacing the roof with clear glass, so that the moon and stars always shone down on the hall.

After "murdering" the majority of the Elite Council, as Cameron so aptly put it, I perched on my recliner on the balcony, staring up at the dark sky. I was waiting for the council to show up so we could discuss the results of the census.

Eli was in charge of the census and since he was still trying to recover from the physical ordeal I'd put him through, he'd requested that we postpone the meeting for an hour. The request had initially irritated me, but I figured he deserved the break. Not knowing what to do with my time, and not up to spending it at my penthouse dodging questions from the girls, I'd decided to go to the dome ahead of everyone else.

I'd only been there for a couple of minutes when Vivienne showed up.

"Derek."

"You did a great job with this place, Vivienne."

"Yes. You've told me several times." She climbed her way up to the balcony, right up to my level.

I could have sworn I saw a dark gray haze stirring at the center of her pupils. Deeply bothered, I stood up and brushed a hand over her shoulder.

"What happened? What's wrong?"

She looked up at the night sky. The last time I'd seen that same fear in her eyes had been centuries ago after the victory of First Blood. I followed her gaze. All I saw was hundreds of stars illuminating the beautiful night sky.

Vivienne uttered four words that triggered a flood of haunting images—the shipwreck, the lighthouse, the caves, First Blood, the slaves, the wall, the beasts, the uprising, the massacre, the spell and finally, sanctuary. I could hear the screams of the dead crying out from the very foundations upon which The Shade was built. The deafening sound was followed by the guilt I would never in a thousand lifetimes be able to escape.

I shifted my gaze from the vast heavens back to the storms raging behind my sister's eyes. It was only then I realized that when she'd said those four words, she was no longer looking at the sky.

She was looking straight at me.

Her words?

"The darkness is coming."

Chapter 15: Sofia

The darkness is coming.

The words from my recurring nightmares kept echoing in my ears. Eerie and ghostly, haunting me wherever I went. I had no idea who'd spoken, but it had something to do with The Shade, something to do with Derek.

I was sitting cross-legged on one of the cushioned seats inside our school library. My elbows leaned on the dark mahogany table. My fingers drummed on the book I was trying—and failing—to comprehend. Apart from the librarian shuffling her feet over the carpeted floor and the rustling of a page a couple of tables away, the library was quiet.

I used to love the silence. It had once been my refuge. That small corner of our school library was perhaps the only thing I missed about our school. That afternoon, the silence only gave way to the voices that haunted me on a nightly basis.

The curve that formed on my lips was bitter. *What a joke. Darkness can't possibly come to The Shade. The Shade is darkness.* The idea shook me. I had no idea what the nightmares meant or whom the darkness was headed for. I didn't want to know. I just wanted to forget.

Of course, that was impossible.

"I knew I'd find you here." Ben pulled up a seat next to me. He flipped it so that its backrest was leaning on the edge of the table before he straddled it and flashed me a smile.

I tried to smile back, but it seemed I failed miserably, because he asked, "What's wrong? You all right?"

"Yeah. What are you doing here? Aren't you supposed to be at football practice?"

"I'll catch up. I just wanted to tell you that Patrick confirmed that we can resume our martial arts lessons on Friday afternoons next week, so we're headed for the gym then. Don't make any plans."

"Okay. Tanya coming?"

Rumor said that Ben was back together with Tanya, the gorgeous blonde cheerleader.

"No. I just broke it off with her."

I searched myself for a reaction. Glee perhaps? Nothing. "How did she take that?"

"She'll survive."

I stared at the book in front of me. Orwell's *1984*. I felt a lot like the characters in the book, following a routine set out by someone else.

It'd been several weeks since Ben and I had returned to high school. We were beginning to fall back into normalcy. He was the school quarterback, popular and beloved. I was his best friend for reasons no one but Ben understood.

However, something had shifted in the dynamic of our relationship. I used to be so dependent on Ben it was borderline pathetic. I'd practically been his shadow. I'd loved being around him and I'd resented seeing him with other girls—Tanya Wilson included. Now, hearing about his high school flings just made me feel disconnected.

If there was one thing The Shade had changed about me, it had made me independent of Ben. I loved him—he was still my best friend, after all—but I no longer pined for him. I could actually imagine a life without him. I found the realization both fearsome and empowering.

"What are those?" Ben pointed at several pieces of paper scattered over the table. He grabbed one. "College application forms? Harvard?"

I shrugged. "I was thinking of becoming a lawyer. You know that."

"So you're actually considering going to college?"

I wrinkled my nose. "Why wouldn't I? What else would I do? That's what we're doing here, aren't we? Trying to return to normal? That's where all this leads, Ben. We graduate. We go to college."

My statements were received with silence.

"You won't get that football scholarship if you don't go to practice." I grabbed my bag from the floor beside me and took out a pen. I pulled over one of the college application forms and began filling it out. *Take a hint, Ben. Go away.*

Ben grabbed the form, crumpled it and tossed it on the table. "Eliza gave me a name and a number. She was the girl—"

"I know who she is," I interrupted. Just the mention of the name made me feel guilty. I felt like an accessory to a crime that Derek had committed. "What name? What number?"

"The hunters. It's a contact person. His name's Reuben. I think he's my... *our*... ticket in."

I sat up straight, threw the pen I was holding on the table and slammed my book shut. "You can't be serious, Ben.

You're saying you're going to join them?"

"No. I'm saying *we're* going to join them. How else will I exact revenge on The Shade, Sofia? It's not like I can crawl back to the police and change our story."

"Where is this coming from, Ben? We've barely spoken about the island."

"We get nightmares every single night, Sofia. Don't tell me you haven't been thinking about that place."

"Of course I have, but I thought…"

"You thought what? We'd just move on? Come on, Sofia. High school? College? I think we've been so good at pretending to be normal that you got yourself convinced that we're *actually* normal. The Shade stole that from us and they've stolen it from countless others. They have to pay."

I shut my eyes, hoping that if I did, everything else would shut down right along with it. "Ben, believe me when I say that I thought about exposing the island so many times while I was there, but…"

"But what?"

The last time we'd talked about exacting revenge on The Shade was that first night we'd got back from Mexico. I thought about it from time to time, but I couldn't become a hunter, living a life devoted to vengeance.

"I don't think I can live that way, Ben."

"So what? We're just going to keep this up? Pretend that

nothing happened? Go on with life as usual? What about the people you left at The Shade? Ashley, Paige, Rosa. What about Gwen, Sofia?"

At that, I stood up. My knuckles were white from the way I was clutching the edges of the table. "Don't go there, Ben. Not a day has gone by since we left that they haven't crossed my mind."

"Well, maybe it's time to stop thinking about them and start doing something about it. How can you not see that this is the only way?"

"I can't bring myself to accept that it's the *only* way. I do not want to spend my life killing vampires. There's got to be a better way, one that doesn't involve as much bloodshed."

His shoulders straightened as he held his head high. "How can you be so naïve?"

At his question, a slew of memories flooded my mind. Derek and Vivienne embracing after centuries of being apart... Derek playing harmonies on his grand piano... His decision to allow us to escape... His laughter, his embrace, his patience trying to train us girls in combat... the delight in his eyes when I showed him the Sun Room... how much he seemed to crave light...

Perhaps it was just me clinging to this hope that I wasn't wrong about him. I wanted to believe that I saw goodness in Derek Novak, and if the prince and savior of The Shade could still be capable of goodness, then perhaps there was still hope yet—for him and the other vampires.

Or perhaps Ben was right. *How could I be so naïve?*

Chapter 16: Ben

I sat across from her, waiting for her to explain, but she remained silent, a pensive expression in her green eyes as she brushed a stray strand of hair away from her face.

I caught my breath at how beautiful she looked. My best friend was Rose Red come to life. The auburn hair, the pale complexion, the hourglass figure, those legs that went on for days… I'd have to be blind not to see how lovely she was. I'd known she'd grow up to become a stunner from the moment I first laid eyes on her. That was the day her father left her at our house and never returned.

What a damn fool he was.

Her father was just as unaware of her as she seemed to be

of herself. Sofia didn't notice the way men looked at her whenever we were out. It was part of her appeal.

That and the fact that she was mine.

It helped that I was the only person she'd ever truly let in. She kept to herself, her fear of becoming like her mother and her insecurity after being abandoned by her father always looming over her. It made it easy for me to keep her to myself. The guys in school knew that she was off limits. I thought even the girls I dated knew that they were flings and that Sofia was the one. It was never spoken out loud, but we belonged together.

My confidence was my undoing, because during the time we'd spent at The Shade, she'd let someone else in—Derek Novak. He'd managed to get through to her and I couldn't understand how.

All I knew as I sat across that table from her in the library was that I was losing her. *You never know what you've got until it's gone, Ben. You treated her like crap and now you're scrambling to fix things with her.*

"I'm not trying to pressure you, Sofia…" I began to say.

"Really? That's exactly what it feels like."

I wasn't used to her being so assertive around me. She normally always heard me out—yet another thing that had changed about her since we'd left The Shade.

"I can't take this." I got up from my seat. "I'll see you

after practice." Like I always did when forced into situations I had no idea how to handle, I ran.

Had it been any other guy, I would've been happy for her, but this was Derek Novak. He'd killed Eliza, drained her of every drop of blood. No hesitation. No hint of shame. He'd preyed on her remorselessly. I didn't care whether there was still any hope of good in him. Sofia deserved better than him.

And yet it felt as if I were losing her to him.

As I sped through the corridors of our school, weaving past people waving and calling my name on my way to the football team's locker room, anger began to consume me. The island had taken everything away from me. I'd had to break it off with Tanya because I couldn't even make out with her without thinking about Claudia. Even if I could, I doubted I would've felt it. I barely had a sense of touch after what that vampire wench had put me through.

By the time I reached the locker room, I was raging mad. Sofia and I were pretending that we could gain back what we'd lost. That was a lie. There was no going back to the life we had. *Why can't you see that, Sofia?*

"Hey, man. Coach has been looking for you." Connor, one of the guys in the team, approached me. "You okay?"

I brushed past him and went straight to my locker.

"Ben!" another one of the guys hollered as I dialed my

combination. "Heard you broke it off with Tanya. You don't mind if I start hitting on her, do you?"

I grunted in response as I pulled my locker open.

"Whatever. We all know he doesn't give a hoot about Tanya, dude. I think he's finally ready to move on to Rose Red. So, Hudson..." Jed, one of the biggest guys on the team, leaned against the locker next to mine. "Are you finally going to man up and tap Sofia?"

Jokes about me not going after Sofia were standard fare inside the boys' locker room. This time, it grated on my nerves.

Jed prattled on. "I hope Rose Red's worth your wait, Ben, but just one look at her and you got to believe she'll make a good lay."

I ground my teeth in a failed attempt to maintain self-control, but it was a lost cause. I slammed my locker door shut and faced Jed. "Don't talk about her that way."

Jed's face got a violent introduction to my fist. Connor tried to intervene, so I punched him too.

They came at me and I didn't care if they were attacking me or simply trying to hold me back. Every time I threw a hit, it was at Claudia, at Derek and at every other bloodsucker at The Shade. I was hitting them back for taking everything I held dear away from me.

By the end of the whole bout, I was bruised and bloody,

and though I was burning up with anger inside, my body was as numb as my soul was aware.

No matter how I got beat and cut up, my body could barely feel a thing.

CHAPTER 17: SOFIA

"Sofia?"

Still in the library, I looked up to find one of the people I least expected to find there—the football team's linebacker, Connor James. The tall, dark senior had a fresh new shiner on his right cheek.

"Hey," I muttered, not quite sure what to make of him approaching me. "What happened to you?" I pointed with my pen. I'd been absent-mindedly fiddling with it while I read the same paragraph in my book for the fifteenth time.

"This? It's nothing." He looked almost timid. He was usually one of the loudest, most outgoing guys in our class.

Is he blushing? I was beginning to find the encounter

uncomfortable. Connor had barely spoken a word to me before. "Aren't you supposed to be at football practice with Ben? Did something happen?"

He twisted his body to one side, his face showing his discomfort. "That's kind of why I'm here. We had this epic battle at the locker room. Well, Ben's at the clinic. He got banged up pretty bad. Thought you might want to know."

What did you get yourself into, Ben? I gathered up my belongings and stuffed them inside my bag. It'd been years since Ben had gotten himself into a fight. Way back in middle school, one of the guys in class—a bully I always did my best to avoid—had tried to kiss me. The bully came out of the fight with a few scratches and a broken nose. Ben, on the other hand, got a broken arm and rib.

Of course, Ben had milked his injuries for all they were worth and become more popular than ever, but after all the sermons he got from Amelia, Ben never got into a fight again.

That was also when he'd started having martial arts lessons at the local gym. It didn't take long for him to drag me to the Saturday lessons. I obliged him, because I never could say no to him, but I was a pacifist at heart.

As I rushed through the school hallways, I couldn't help but smirk at how useless those classes were to me. *Certainly no use against vampires.* Then again, I'd never had enough presence of mind to use what I'd learned against Derek or Lucas. Stopping in front of the clinic's door, I was bothered by the thought that I'd never fought back. *As much as you chastised yourself to not become the victim, that's still what you were at The Shade.*

I twisted the knob of the clinic door and pushed it open. I let out a gasp. Ben had a large black, purple and blue bruise occupying nearly half of the left side of his face. A deep gash lined the right side of his torso.

"Ben…" It came out in a breathless whisper. I wanted to grab him by both shoulders and shake some sense into him. I made my way to his side and brushed my thumb over the line of his jaw. "What the *hell* were you thinking?" He refused to look me in the eye.

Our school doctor walked in and gave me a curt nod. "Miss Claremont, kindly step aside. This won't take long."

I got out of the doctor's way and watched as he dressed Ben's wound.

"May I ask how you came upon this cut, Mr. Hudson?"

"Coach already told you, Doc. I got into a fight."

"And your teammates cut you?"

"No. One of them tackled me to the ground… don't even remember who… it was so crazy. I was trying to get away from him and my side rubbed against one of the benches. It's just a scratch. Barely even felt it."

Pacifist or not, I felt the urge to sock him in the jaw. The sight of his bare torso and the "scratch" he'd just added to all the scars that were already there made my stomach churn.

"How did you ever get such ugly cuts?" The doctor stepped back after finishing up bandaging the gash on his side. He stared at Ben's body, his face marred with concern. "What happened during your absence, Ben?"

"I'd rather not talk about it." Ben flashed his biggest smile. He grabbed his shirt and pulled it over his body. He got up from the clinic bed, made his way toward me and took my hand. "Come on, Sofia. Let's go home."

I wanted to pull away, but the last thing he needed was to be dragged into a fight with me. I forced a smile at the school doctor as we brushed past him. "Thank you, Doctor."

"Oh, yeah." Ben nodded the doctor's way. "Thanks, Doc."

We were out of the clinic and a good distance headed for the parking lot when I stopped walking and pulled at him to stop.

"What? Let's just go, okay? I don't want to talk about it."

"Since when did you start getting into fights again, Ben?"

"What part of 'I don't want to talk about it' don't you understand, Sofia?"

I pursed my lips and nodded. I pulled my hand from his grasp and began walking. "Let's go then." I didn't miss the wounded look on his face when I passed him.

We reached the black pickup his parents had recently bought him. He'd had his eye on it since summer and apparently Lyle and Amelia had thought that the best time to get it for him was a week after we got back from Mexico.

Ben tossed me the keys. "You drive."

I got in the driver's seat and started the car. I was already backing up when Ben asked a long overdue question.

"Why did you come back with me? Why did you choose me over him?"

"Since when was the choice between you and Derek?"

I flinched when he hit the glove compartment in frustration. "Can you *really* be so dense, Sofia?"

"I came back because it was the sensible thing to do. You have no idea what I went through in there, Ben. There wasn't a day that passed by that I didn't think of escaping. Heck, I even tried as soon as I got the chance."

"You tried to escape?"

"Yes—I thought I already told you that. I got as far as the wall lining the island before two vampire guards caught me."

"What happened?"

"They were going to kill me. One of them was already licking one of my scratches when Derek showed up."

Ben tensed at the mention of Derek, but I ignored him. This was my story to tell and it was he who'd opened up this can of worms. *Suck it up, Ben.*

"He asked who'd had a taste of my blood. One guard admitted to it. Derek ripped the vampire's heart out and let the other one go."

"And you still don't think he's a murderer?"

"I'm not saying what he did was right, but he did what he thought was necessary to protect me. Once a vampire gets a taste of a human's blood, they *will* crave that particular human. Derek knew that as long as I was around, the guard would have an urge to hunt me."

"Then why didn't he do the same thing to his brother? Lucas fed on you, didn't he?"

"He was going to." I recalled the look in both brothers' eyes that night. Derek had been more than willing to end Lucas' life. He would never be able to forgive himself for doing it. "I stopped him."

"You what? Sofia, why? If I could be given the chance to end Claudia's life, I wouldn't hesitate to do it and I wouldn't feel an ounce of guilt about it either."

"Lucas is still Derek's brother. That means something to Derek. Family means *something* to him."

At that, Ben grew silent. He knew why I would respect Derek for valuing family. I stopped at a red light and rubbed my neck with my palm, trying to ease my own tension.

"Derek... did he ever..." Ben hesitated.

"No. He never fed on me. He never had his way with me." I was relieved when the red light went green again. *The sooner we get home, the sooner this conversation is over.* "And for the record, my choice to leave the Shade wasn't about you or him. It was about me. I didn't want to live my life as a slave—Derek's or otherwise. That wasn't a future I wanted for myself. I left the island because I knew that I could carve a better future for myself out here than back there."

"I'm sorry. I didn't know."

"That's because you never asked, Ben."

For the rest of the ride home, both of us remained silent. When we reached the Hudsons' driveway and I finished parking, we lingered inside the pickup, both of us hating the strain between us.

"I feel like I'm losing you, Sofia."

I didn't know what to say to that. It sparked the memories of all those times that I'd wanted him to want me, times I'd daydreamed of being in his arms. *Is it possible that he felt something for me all this time?*

Consumed by the silence, I took his hand and squeezed tightly. "I'm right here." *For now.*

Our fingers intertwined and then his lips were on mine. Gentle. Chaste. Sweet. Numb. I was too surprised to respond and the kiss came to a quick end. Our eyes met for a split second before we both fumbled out of the vehicle and made our way to the door.

Amelia's mouth dropped open when she saw her son. "Ben… what happened?"

"It's nothing, Mom."

Amelia looked at me, as if she were blaming me for the cuts and bruises he'd received.

We entered the house and I let Ben explain to his mother what had happened. He was telling her that either she or Lyle had to go to school and speak to the guidance counselor with him tomorrow when I retired to my room.

I wondered where Lyle and Abby were and remembered that she had a play date. Lyle probably went to pick her up.

I was exhausted—more emotionally than physically. I collapsed on the bed. My phone began vibrating within my bag. I fished for it and found a text message from an unknown number. *For the record, Ben was fighting for you— Connor.*

I wondered if Ben put him up to sending the text. Either way, I was intrigued. *Fighting for me?* I found it confusing that Ben would suddenly—in a span of one day—show that kind of interest in me when he'd never looked at me as anything more than a friend for so long. *Is he just doing this to get me to join him in his quest for revenge?*

I opened my closet for a change of clothes. I'd just finished slipping on a red tank top and buttoning up my shorts when Ben knocked twice and opened my door.

When he stepped inside, I was taken aback by the look he was giving me.

"Ben?"

As soon as I spoke his name, he held my waist and pulled me against him. He kissed me fully this time. I shivered as I responded with gusto.

It wasn't void of passion and no one could ever accuse Ben of not being a good kisser. He was a great kisser in fact—not that I had many others to compare him with. Still, kissing him was just as I'd always imagined it to be. Except I couldn't feel a thing. In fact, the whole time, the one emotion that stood above all was the now-familiar ache of how much I missed Derek.

CHAPTER 18: DEREK

I sat in stunned silence as Eli Lazaroff began reporting the results of the census to everyone present at the dome. Apart from the staggeringly clear picture of the state of the kingdom, Vivienne's presence and Lucas' absence upset me. Vivienne's words still rang in my ears and Lucas was the constant reminder of how I'd lost Sofia.

Eli started with the number of the Elite. "We now number a hundred and ten." He then began listing each vampire clan and where the hundred and ten belonged.

Clans didn't necessarily consist of blood relatives. New members were added when a new vampire was sired by one of the other members of the clan.

When I went to sleep, only sixty-five vampires—including me—had composed the Elite. Through the centuries, forty-five humans had been turned into vampires. As far as I was concerned, that was a huge number. The largest vampire clan was the Vaughns, with Xavier as head of the clan and their representative at the council. Their clan numbered fifteen. On the other hand, the smallest clan was Claudia's. Her clan only had one member—herself.

After his report on the Elite, Eli moved on to talking about the Lodgers, vampire clans who didn't belong to the original twenty clans. They had sworn fealty to The Shade in exchange for the security of becoming one of the island's citizens. The number Eli uttered made my mind reel. "One thousand, three hundred and twenty six."

"What?" I exclaimed, unable to keep myself from reacting. "We didn't even have three hundred when I went to sleep."

"That was four centuries ago, Derek," Vivienne reminded me. "Many have sought refuge at The Shade since."

I kept my mouth shut, but one question kept circling my mind as Eli plodded on with his report. *How much human blood has to be shed to sustain all these vampires?*

"Among the Elite, twenty-five are Knights while among the Lodgers, we have three hundred and fifteen guards and fifty scouts." Guards were warriors who belonged to the Lodgers, while scouts were authorized to leave the island, specifically to retrieve necessary materials from the outside or to take human slaves. Scouts were only allowed to leave the island under the supervision of at least one Knight.

"That concludes my report." Eli gave me a curt nod to indicate he was done.

"Done? And what of the slaves? How many humans are living in The Shade?"

He looked at his feet uncomfortably. "I didn't think they were to be included in the census."

"Why not? Are they not under the kingdom's jurisdiction?"

The silence spoke volumes. After all, why keep track of the population of humans when hundreds of them were lost and replaced on a regular basis?

Xavier said it best when he leaned back in his council seat and nonchalantly shrugged. "Keeping track of the humans is arguably equivalent to keeping track of The Shade's food consumption."

It was a shocking portrayal of how depraved we'd become over the years. A lot of us had begun to see humans as cattle. Guilt knotted in the pit of my stomach, because I'd played a hand in the culture we'd created at The Shade. Thus, though I hated to force the council—or even myself—to get into the nitty-gritty of this logistical nightmare, I couldn't ignore the issue either.

"I want a full accounting of every human who lives at The Shade, starting with those residing at the Black Heights, all the way to the slaves living with vampires." Another figment of our past began to haunt me. "We can't afford another uprising."

"I think there's someone who can help with this." Vivienne spoke up.

I waited for her to speak further. She seemed hesitant.

"Corrine."

I was surprised, but if there was anything we vampires had an abundance of, it was time. "Have her brought here then."

Within minutes, one of the guards was sent to the Sanctuary to escort the witch back to the dome. When Corrine arrived, I shifted uncomfortably in my seat. Her uncanny resemblance to her ancestor, Cora, always knocked some breath out of me.

"What do you want?" she demanded.

"Vivienne says you'll be able to help with a dilemma regarding how many humans are currently residing at The Shade."

Her brow rose. "You want to know because…?"

"It's high time we figured out the actual state of this island and its residents, don't you think?"

This seemed to take the witch by surprise, but she took her place at the stand, straightened to her full height, and began to address the issue at hand.

"The numbers fluctuate—as you might well expect." She glared, as if to accuse every single one of us of the crimes we were guilty of. "However, the number of Naturals doesn't change much. It's the Migrates who come and go depending on you vampires' whims."

"Naturals? Migrates?" From the look on the council's faces, none of them had any idea what Corrine was talking about.

"Of course." Corrine rolled her eyes. "You vampires haven't paid attention to the humans brought here as long as they keep in line. We humans have classified ourselves according to those who were born on this island—the Naturals—and those who were taken from the outside world and brought here—the Migrates."

Growing impatient, I sat up straight and leaned forward. "How many of them are there, Corrine?"

"As of our last tally, the island had seven thousand, five hundred and thirty-two Naturals, all crammed into the Black Heights, and two thousand, three hundred and twenty-nine Migrates living at the Residences along with their vampire masters. Of course, that number has most likely changed. Who knows how many of them have died since the last time we checked?"

The numbers left me shell-shocked as question after

question flooded my mind. *How are we sustaining all these human lives? What are they all doing here on the island? How did their population get so large? What happens to the dead?*

Then the reality hit me full force. *They outnumber us at least five to one. If they ever realize their strength, we're done for.* I stared at the witch, whose loyalties I wasn't certain of. All they had to do was get Corrine on their side for The Shade to meet its end.

CHAPTER 19: LUCAS

Claudia swung the door open and stepped beneath the doorposts of the bedroom she was keeping me in. Feet apart, hands planted on her hips, blonde locks cascading down to her waist, the little spitfire looked incredible.

I smirked. *This is going to be interesting.*

"Your brother is going to drive everyone at The Shade mad!" she exclaimed.

"What's he done now?" Having just stepped out of the shower, I was still rubbing my hair dry with a towel.

"He asked for a census of all the humans in the island."

"What an enormous waste of time."

"That's what I thought. Of course, the mighty Prince

Derek won't hear any of it."

"Any of what?" I chuckled. "Your thoughts?"

She shot me a stern look and I was almost certain that I'd just earned myself a fight, only for her to groan. Her shoulders sagged. "He made us fight him in the arena. It was exhausting. I haven't bled this much in a long time. Makes me hate Cora sometimes."

"What does the great, dead witch have to do with Derek making the Elite fight him?" I found the idea amusing. I'd never thought Derek would go this far to satisfy his bloodlust.

Claudia rubbed her palm against her neck as she walked toward the bed and let her curvy form drop over it. "Cora's the reason he's so powerful. Wasn't it her who made sure Derek's sleep would also strengthen him over time? Damn that witch for falling in love with your brother."

"My brother and the strange effect women can have on him," I bemoaned.

"More like the strange effect he has on women," Claudia sighed, her face softening. I didn't need to be a mind-reader to figure out that a dozen daydreams about my brother had just flashed through her demented head.

I threw the towel on the floor. *If it weren't for Cora, Derek wouldn't be ruling over me.* I frowned. Hard as I tried to deny it, that wasn't the reason I resented Cora.

I leaned on a bedpost watching Claudia reposition herself on my bed. The look she was giving me as she twirled the ends of her long blonde hair clearly indicated what she wanted from me. *They keep choosing Derek over me. Even Claudia.* I resented Cora because I had desired her, but her heart had been Derek's up until her very last breath.

Wanting to get my mind off Cora, I joined Claudia in bed when it seemed something sparked inside Claudia's mind, distracting her from her seductions. I inwardly groaned, because it seemed she was about to once again gripe over my brother. For all her mind games and her hatred toward human men, she still came off as a whiny teenager sometimes, despite the fact that she was fifty years older than I was.

I was relieved when she made no further mention of Derek. Instead, she drew a breath and twisted her neck to the side in order to look at me.

"Why are you still here, Lucas?"

It was hard to keep up with her erratic behavior sometimes. I was about to throw her a suggestive quip when we heard several loud bangs on her front door. A scowl painted her face. "What now?" She made no move to get out of bed and I thought she was going to ignore the knocks when another set of loud bangs made her drag herself out of the bed. She shut the door behind her.

Overcome with curiosity, I followed her. Claudia rarely had any visitors. Apart from myself, most of the Elite tolerated her, but looked down at her. It was what made her penthouse such a great hiding place.

I put my ear to the closed door and listened.

"Hello there, gentlemen," Claudia purred.

"Geez, Claudia. You're no longer a whore. Stop acting like one."

I tried to place the voice. *Yuri Lazaroff.*

"We're here to ask you a few questions. Do you mind?"

Scottish accent. Big ol' Hendry no doubt.

"I don't mind." Her voice was now flat. Yuri had a way of getting to her. "Please make yourself comfortable, Cameron. Go to hell, Yuri."

"That's exactly where I am now, Claudia."

"You two, behave." Cameron sounded like a bedraggled father trying to keep his teenagers in line. "Have you had any contact with Lucas Novak over the past few days?"

"No."

"Sure, you haven't."

Two voices responded. "Shut up, Yuri."

"You don't mind if we search your home then?"

Panic gripped me. I'd always known that I couldn't hide out at Claudia's forever. I just hadn't thought it would be such a close call. I tried to be as quiet and as quick as possible as I made my way back to the bedroom. I made haste getting dressed. I'd barely finished buttoning my jeans when I began to hear footsteps and doors being pushed open.

Claudia was throwing a full-blown outburst. "I'm still part of the Elite. You can't just barge into my home like this."

"Sure we can," Yuri responded. "If you have a problem with this, go ahead and take it up with the prince."

A slew of curses escaped my lips. I took a black hooded jacket from a clothes hook near the door and put it on. From under my bed, I grabbed my emergency backpack.

From the sound of their inquisition, they were seconds from opening the bedroom door. I threw the windows open, no longer caring if they overheard, and jumped out.

I landed flat on my feet. I rushed toward the port. I groaned as I ran, realizing that I couldn't have picked a worse time to leave the island, because no matter where I went, the sun would rise to its peak before I could seek shelter. Still, I wasn't about to place my life at Derek's mercy.

I knew my brother, and I knew the darkness that was within him. I didn't know what Sofia had done to appeal to his humanity, but I wasn't going to stick around and wait for her effect to wear off. Darkness was sure to overtake him and when it did, he wouldn't hesitate to kill me.

As I ran full speed toward escape, it was clear that I would sooner die under the sun's rays than die at my brother's hand. After all, it seemed far nobler to give up one's life to the light than to the dark.

CHAPTER 20: DEREK

The darkness is coming.

Even as the words echoed in my head, it felt like a dark mist was already stirring from the depths of my soul, overtaking all that I was. It triggered so many unwanted memories that the guilt had once again become overwhelming. I wanted to shut it out, but after the council meeting at the Great Dome was dismissed, Vivienne reminded me why I simply couldn't.

I remained in my seat long after the Elite Council left and Vivienne stayed with me.

"It's killing me," I confessed.

She nodded knowingly. I rarely had to explain myself to

Vivienne. She understood. "I can see that. Guilt can be quite an adversary, but it's also your ally."

"How can that be so?"

"It's the only thing that keeps the darkness from completely taking over."

Her words, as they often did, haunted me.

Before she left me on my own, she turned to say, "You need her back. You won't be able to handle all of this without her."

I grimaced. *Sofia's made her choice. Now we both have to live with it.* "I don't want any mention of her. Ever again. She's not coming back. That's it. We have greater things to worry about."

I returned to my penthouse shortly afterwards, consumed by my sister's admonitions. She was the Seer of The Shade. It was hard to ignore her.

On arriving back at my penthouse, everything about it just pointed me right back to the girl who'd made waking up at The Shade after four hundred years bearable.

When I stepped in through the front door, the first sight that welcomed me was Ashley playing a round of cards with Sam and Kyle in the living room. In the kitchen, plates clinked and I caught the scent of dinner cooking. I figured Paige and Rosa were in the kitchen.

Memories of Sofia swam through my mind at the sight of

the girls and the guards. Sam and Kyle stood up on seeing me. Both looked sheepish about being caught playing games with the girls while off duty.

"Your highness," Sam began to explain, "we were just…"

"It's fine." I waved his explanation off. Truth be told, I was trying to reel my anger in.

Ashley gave both guards an odd look, remaining seated on the couch, a full hand of cards still clutched.

Largely due to Sofia, my being prince of The Shade wasn't emphasised within my own home. I'd never interacted much with the girls. As far as I was concerned, they were Sofia's friends, and I didn't need to bother as long as Sofia kept them in line. With Sofia gone, however, I couldn't just leave them cooped up doing nothing. That was just another item in my growing list of things to deal with.

I gave the two guards curious glances. They seemed to have developed quite a rapport with Sofia and the girls. *Maybe I could just give them the girls. At least that would get them all off my back.* I was surprised by my adverse reaction to letting the girls go. *The house would be so empty without them, even if they've managed to get under my skin.*

Irritated, I ignored the people making a hangout of my living room and walked away. Afraid of the darkness, I sought light.

"Where are you going?" Ashley called after me.

"The Sun Room."

The Sun Room was the one room in the penthouse that Sofia had designed herself. I'd mentioned to her once that I missed the sun, so she'd designed a room with a beach mural on one wall and the illusion of sunlight streaming from a sunroof on the ceiling.

When I opened the door, it was largely untouched since the night Lucas had attacked Sofia and drunk her blood. Broken glass glittered all over the floor. Cracks lined the wall I'd thrown Lucas against. Traces of blood still appeared in several areas of the room—some Ben's, some Lucas', some Sofia's, some mine.

It reminded me of one of the darkest periods of The Shade's history. The Uprising. The memory overtook me, and just like that, all the light the Sun Room represented turned into pitch-black night.

The screams were deafening, the sound of cannons alarming. I watched from the top of the fortress as hundreds upon hundreds of the human slaves we'd kept at The Shade to finish the Wall fought for a chance to escape the island, or if not, escape the life we'd forced them into.

"What do we do now?" Lucas hissed as he leaned over the fortress, terror in his eyes.

I swallowed down the guilt. It was the first time I'd ever allowed myself that indulgence. I knew the drastic measure we had to undertake, because none of them could escape. Not a single one.

"We have to kill them all."

I jumped down to the solid ground and with one swing of my sword killed three of the men poised to attack me. They came at us, violent and angry, no longer willing to remain our slaves. We tried to convince ourselves that we had no choice, but at the end of the battle, standing amidst the bloody grave left by our determination to keep our sanctuary safe, I knew that the price I'd paid for The Shade was far too high.

Cora approached me. She was quiet, obviously disturbed.

"How many more must die?" My voice came out broken, blood still dripping from the corners of my lips. "They were innocent."

"No one is innocent." Cora shook her head, her gaze distant. "We're all tainted."

"I can't do this anymore."

Cora grabbed my hand. "You won't ever have to again."

I wondered if what Cora said had been a lie, because as a moment of clarity jolted me back to reality, I was standing in the middle of the Sun Room with Vivienne holding me by the shoulders.

"What have you done, Derek?"

I tasted blood on my lips. "I don't know," I stammered. "I guess I blacked out." Behind Vivienne, Ashley lay limp on the ground, bite marks—mine—on the side of her neck. Sam and Kyle were groaning as they tried to get up from the ground. Newly formed dents were on the walls I'd thrown them against.

As if it weren't already too much to take, Cameron showed up at the door, his eyes widening. "What happened?"

I responded in a menacing hiss. "Why are you here?"

"Lucas. He escaped. Yuri and I tried to stop him. He almost killed Yuri... if I hadn't..."

Cameron's voice faded away as my eyes reverted back to Vivienne's.

"Derek, if Lucas is out there, then..."

I lifted a finger to silence her. I wanted no mention of Sofia. "No, Vivienne." I eyed the bloody mess surrounding me. Guilt gripped me when I saw Ashley on the ground, but the deed had already been done. "Get her the care she needs, take her to her bedroom, I don't care. Just get her out of my sight."

They scrambled to do my bidding. Only Vivienne remained in the room with me afterwards.

"You're not going to go after her? You can't just mean to stay here and..."

Before I could stop myself, the back of my hand met the side of her face and she stumbled to the ground. I immediately regretted hitting her. I wanted to help her up, but something held me back. After waking from the sleep I'd asked Cora to put me under, I'd been reluctant about taking leadership of The Shade once again. That was long gone now.

"I told you never to speak of her."

Her hands cupping her face, my sister looked up at me. Her violet eyes contained no anger, no accusation, no condemnation... just resignation and a deep sadness that made me ache inside.

"It seems the darkness has arrived."

As usual, Vivienne was right.

Chapter 21: Lucas

My escape was narrow, to say the least. The only thing I managed to take with me was my backpack filled with sacks of blood, a change of clothes and my wallet. Upon reaching the port, I immediately went for one of the speedboats. I needed to get out of there before Cameron showed up to rip my heart out—or worse, take me captive so Derek could do the deed.

As the glass-covered tube lifted the speedboat up to open seas, I had to act fast. The moment the boat reached The Shade's boundaries, I would be exposed to daylight. The longer I stayed close to The Shade, however, the greater the chance that the guards could reel me back.

I did a quick inspection of the boat. All I had was a toolbox, a first-aid kit and a rolled-up sheet of canopy used to cover the boat when not in use. That was exactly what I needed. I unrolled the sheet and it became my savior.

It protected me from the sun's rays, but not from its sweltering heat. Floating in the middle of the sea with that sheet over me while the sun beat at me felt like being inside an oven. It was a struggle starting the boat and when I moved the wrong way and exposed my flesh, the sun seemed to burn through my skin down to my very bones.

Rumor was that there was no more painful death than to burn under the rays of the sun. I'd never actually seen a vampire die because of exposure to the sun, but I wasn't about to put it to the test anytime soon. Besides, the few times my flesh was exposed to it were painful enough to convince me that the rumor was true.

I eventually had to stop the boat to wait until the sun had set. I couldn't reach the shore in my condition. It felt like days, but I waited it out.

The sun faded into twilight. Thoughts of Sofia flashed through my mind. I could practically still feel her blood running through me, still taste her sweet blood on my lips. I wanted her so badly just thinking about her made me ache, but she was back at the island. I would seek her out eventually, but I had to set thoughts of her aside for the time being. What I needed to do was make my way to the one person who had any chance of overpowering my younger brother.

Our father. Gregor Novak.

CHAPTER 22: SOFIA

Thoughts of how much I missed Derek quickly faded away when Ben's lips parted from mine. The way he looked at me—like I was precious to him—made me forget any doubt I might have had regarding his intentions. We stared at each other, both shaken, until his cheeks began to flush.

It called my attention to the bruises he'd gotten from his fight. I wondered how he could kiss me and not ache from the way I accidentally touched the bruise on his cheek and the gash on his side.

His eyes settled on my lips, which felt a bit swollen. "Wow, Sofia. You really are Rose Red."

I found the breathlessness in his voice endearing. It made

me feel wanted, desired—something I didn't remember him ever making me feel before. My hands were still clasping his neck. I leaned my forehead against his broad shoulder. Both his hands were on my waist, his thumbs softly brushing over my stomach.

"Rose Red?"

"You know, from the fairy tale." He took a step away from me, winking. "Snow White's sister?"

"Yeah, I know who Rose Red is. How am I Rose Red?"

"Well, isn't she just like Snow White only with red hair?" He showed me a toothy grin. He took my hand and began caressing my arm. "Skin as white as snow…" He planted one soft kiss on my lips, smiling while his lips were still pressed against mine. "Lips blood red…"

I'd never seen this side of him before. My knees buckled.

"I'm not *that* white. My lips aren't *that* red."

His strong hands supported my weight. "Sofia, you're as fair as fair gets, and you should really see your lips after you've just been kissed." He was looking at my mouth as if it were the tastiest treat he'd ever had the pleasure of having.

I couldn't help but smile. *No wonder girls swoon.*

"Ben and Sofia sitting in a tree…"

Ben's eyes widened at Abby's high-pitched sing-song voice. Both our gazes shifted toward the door where the five-year-old was standing.

Mischief was written all over her small face as a smug smile lifted the corners of her lips. She was still wearing the denim skirt and pink button-down blouse she'd gone to school in. Her right hand was planted firmly on her hip, while her left arm hung at her side, one arm of Colin, her stuffed elephant, clutched in her hand. Her blonde curls swayed, her head bobbing as she finished her song: "*K-I-S-S-I-N-G!*"

"You runt." Ben glared at her. "What are you doing here?"

"Oversized meanie." Abby stuck her tongue out at her older brother. "I came to see Sofia just like I always do when I get back from school. What are *you* doing here, Ben?" Her scowl disappeared and her face fell when she got a better look at his face. "What happened to you, Ben? Why do you keep getting beat up?"

"Hey, come on." The expression on his face softened into concern. "Don't cry, Abby. It's nothing. A bunch of guys in school were saying mean things about me and Sofia, so I had to beat them up." He picked her up in his arms and cradled her against him.

"But it looks like *they're* the ones who beat you up, Ben."

"Well, that's only because you haven't seen them yet, you midget."

These were the moments that reminded me why Ben was

such a catch. I was so moved by how sweet he was to Abby that it took several minutes before questions began to flood my mind. *What were the guys saying about Ben and me? Was that what Connor was talking about in his text message? Did Ben put him up to it?* Abby was pushing against the gash on Ben's side. *How could Ben not feel pain over that?*

Ben planted Abby back on the ground. She looked up at him, her curls falling to her back. "Just stop getting beat up, okay? It makes Mommy cry."

At that, Ben and I exchanged glances. I could see the guilt in his eyes, even past the amused tone he took on when he rapped Abby on the head with his knuckles. "Sure, dwarfette."

Abby stomped her foot on the floor. "Hey, I know what I saw." She set her baby blue eyes on me. I swallowed hard. Abby could really be a pain when she wanted to be. "I saw you two kissing!" It was almost as if I had betrayed her. "How could you do that, Sofia?" She wrinkled her nose. "It's so gross. You kissed a giant ogre."

"Hey." Ben frowned.

I couldn't stifle a giggle.

At that moment, Amelia poked her head through the door. "Sofia, if you're not too busy, I'd like help preparing dinner."

I was still grinning as I faced the hallway, but any

amusement faded away when Ben told Abby, "Laugh all you want, midget, but I'm warning you. You can't tell Mom and Dad about Sofia and me. You understand?"

Ouch. I bit my lower lip as I made my way down the stairs and into the kitchen. *Is he ashamed of me? Am I going to end up as his big secret?*

I remained quiet throughout dinner—not that there was much to say, considering it consisted mostly of Lyle scolding Ben over the fight. Amelia, of course, didn't hesitate to put her two cents in. Abby, on the other hand, kept darting her glance from Ben to me. She couldn't stop giggling throughout the whole meal.

After dinner, Amelia tucked Abby into bed and Lyle asked to have a private word with Ben. That left me to clean up the table and do the dishes. I welcomed the solitude. It allowed me to sort through my thoughts.

I was already unloading the dishwasher and putting the dishes in their proper places when Ben's hands found my waist. He pulled me back against him, his lips on the nape of my neck.

I paused. "What is this between us, Ben?"

"What do you mean?"

"This. All the kissing... Rose Red... It's too confusing. It's going too fast. I'm having trouble keeping up."

He moved to my side and leaned against the granite

counter. I couldn't look him in the eye, so I just kept wiping the dishes dry and placing them where they belonged.

"First, we argue in the library and then you get into this big fight—apparently over comments that involved me—and now this. You just broke up with Tanya for crying out loud. I don't want to be your rebound, Ben."

He remained silent as I finished getting the kitchen in order. When everything was done, he grabbed me by the shoulders and made me face him. "You are too important to me to be a rebound. Get that into your head, Sofia. I'm tired of being just your friend and I want to give *us* a real shot."

"Why now?"

"Because as I told you back at the truck, I feel like I'm losing you. I don't want that to happen, Sofia."

It didn't feel like a good enough reason to get into a relationship that had too much potential to leave us both hurt. "I'm scared," I admitted. "What if this doesn't work out?"

"Look, we don't have to rush this. Let's take it slow if we have to." His gaze was hopeful... expectant... desperate. "Let's start with a date, and then see where we go from there."

"One date," I agreed, "but I do have a condition."

"Anything."

"There will be no talk of The Shade."

Just the mention clouded the expression on his face, but he nodded in agreement. "Fine by me."

"And one more thing," I added. "If we do get serious about this, I don't want to be your dirty little secret, Ben. We let Lyle and Amelia know."

It hurt that he didn't seem happy about that, but again, he agreed to my terms. "Of course."

It was awkward when we parted. We didn't talk about it, but for the first time, the idea of sleeping in the same bed with him felt wrong. We said good night and went our separate ways. I spent a good deal of the night debating if I ought to sneak to his room, if only in case of another nightmare.

Just when I had made up my mind to stay alone, my door creaked open. The bed shifted and Ben sat on the edge. He didn't need to explain. I made room for him and snuggled against him. His lips found my forehead. A kiss goodnight.

What Ben and I had used to be simple. We were best friends. We knew where we stood with each other. A couple of kisses, a few suggestive quips and an agreement to have one date had ruined whatever comfort zone he and I had.

Lying next to him that night, all I could think of before I drifted off to sleep was how complicated things were going to become. Still, a smile crept over my lips, because whatever it was that I had with Ben, it felt like a step toward moving on.

It was wishful thinking, because the moment slumber came, the nightmares came with it.

CHAPTER 23: DEREK

After the blackout, the darkness began to consume me and I didn't have enough will left to fight it.

The first step down was when I decided that Sofia was no longer my responsibility.

I asked Cameron and Yuri to meet with me right after I'd attacked Ashley and hit Vivienne. I was in the music room. I kept the lights dim, playing a sad tune on the grand piano. The Knights approached tentatively. Perhaps my face betrayed that I was in no mood for company.

"Find yourselves a seat and tell me what happened. How was it possible that my brother escaped from you both?" I kept playing the sorrowful melody.

Cameron took the lead and made himself comfortable on one of the cushioned benches. Yuri followed soon after. He appeared to be on edge, his fingers twitching. Yuri never seemed to be at ease when he was around me.

"Well? Speak."

"We found Lucas at Claudia's," Cameron obliged. "Apparently, he'd been hiding out with her all this time. He was quick to escape. Most likely heard us coming and jumped out the window right before we arrived."

"I ran after him," Yuri chimed in.

"And Lazaroff was pretty damned fast too. Always has been."

Cameron glared at Yuri, as if to tell the younger vampire to let him do all the talking. Of the three of us, Cameron was the oldest—both in natural and vampire years. He'd shown me more reverence and respect than Yuri ever did, however.

"Yuri caught up with your brother," Cameron continued after a short pause, "but Lucas overpowered him. Had I not caught up, the prince would've ripped Yuri's heart out. When Lucas saw me coming, he made a run for it. By the time I reached the port, he'd already knocked out the guards and escaped on one of the speedboats."

"The speedboats?" I stopped playing. "He didn't take a submarine?"

"The subs are new and far slower than a speedboat. He

wouldn't have known how to run one," Yuri explained. "He hasn't shown any interest in navigating the subs anyway."

"So he went off the island in broad daylight?" I turned on my bench so that I was facing them. "He'll die for sure."

"I wouldn't bet on it." Cameron chuckled. "If there's anything I admire about your brother, it's his will to survive."

Cameron was right. Knowing my brother, he had a plan up his sleeve that would help him survive even the sun. "Why was Yuri there?"

"He was the one who tipped me off that Lucas was at Claudia's."

I eyed Yuri thoughtfully. I didn't know why I was surprised. I'd just thought that after all those centuries, the thing Claudia and Yuri had was over. I'd never understood the dynamic of their relationship or Yuri's outward disdain for, and yet seeming fascination with, Claudia.

"How exactly did you come about this information?"

Yuri gave me a response—a long-winded one, as he was inclined to do. His explanation escaped me, because my mind drifted off to Sofia's welfare. To say that I didn't care what happened to her was a lie. The thought of any danger befalling her sickened me. If Lucas survived—and he most likely would—he would pose a formidable threat to her life. If he wasn't aware that Sofia was no longer at The Shade, he still had plenty of time and means to find out that Sofia was no longer under my protection.

Part of me wanted to heed Vivienne's coaxing to go after her, but I couldn't bring myself to traipse around the mainland in search of some teenager. Sofia had chosen to leave, knowing full well that upon leaving The Shade, she would no longer be under my protection. If Lucas went after her, that was her cross to bear. Not mine. She'd ceased to become my obligation the moment she chose to escape.

"So? What do we do now?" Cameron inquired.

I had to blink several times to snap out of my reverie. "I want Claudia arrested and put on trial."

Yuri's eyes widened. "Sir, with all due respect, no Elite has ever been tried for a crime in all of The Shade's history. It's unheard of."

"It's either put her on trial or kill her for defying me. She spat in my face when she kept my brother from me when I demanded that he be delivered into my hands. I cannot stand for that if I am to rule."

"Derek…" Cameron slightly stood to try and reason with me.

I turned away from them. "Have it done immediately. The trial starts tomorrow." I continued playing the piano.

My next stumble down was when I removed everything that could possibly remind me of Sofia.

I paid Ashley a visit inside the room she shared with the girls not long after Cameron and Yuri left. She was still unconscious.

"Why hasn't she healed? Hasn't she been fed any blood?" I stared at her limp form. I searched for a sense of guilt, but the urge to suck her dry was overwhelming. It was in my nature to kill and the predator in me craved more.

"I fed her my blood, your majesty," Kyle began to explain. "It takes time for it to take effect."

The times I'd had to heal Sofia with my blood, she'd healed instantly. I shrugged it off. Sofia was different. I'd known that from the moment I first saw her. My gut turned at the longing I had for Sofia and the hunger I felt for Ashley.

My eyes focused on the area of Ashley's neck that I'd sunk my teeth into. The pain inside—the hunger—was almost unbearable.

"Get her out of my house." The command came out deep and threatening.

Kyle's eyes fell on me. "Sir?"

"You heard me. Get her out of here. Take her to your house, I don't care. I won't be able to keep myself from devouring her if she's kept here."

Kyle nodded. "The other girls?"

"Take them too. Have Sam take one or both under his

wing. I just want them out of here."

I motioned to leave the room before I lost all self-control. With all the strength I had left, I stopped and gave Kyle one final instruction.

"Destroy the Sun Room. I want it stripped of everything that's in it. Make it a blank canvas once again. I don't want anything in this house to remind me of her."

Vivienne was right. I'd succumbed to the darkness.

As I sat in my place at the Great Dome in preparation for Claudia's trial, the one emotion that still connected me to my humanity was the guilt. It never left me. The temptation to ease my pain by switching off the emotion was strong, but I couldn't do that. I couldn't lose what little was left of my humanity—no matter how painful it was.

Claudia was brought to the stand. To say that she looked unrepentant was an understatement. She glared golden fire at me.

Eli, who was to head the proceedings, shuffled on his feet as he took his place beside Claudia. He kept stealing glances at her, as if he were afraid that she might pounce on him. With Claudia looking like a lioness and Eli a mouse, it seemed possible that Claudia would end up devouring the thin, lanky vampire.

"Let's get this done with, shall we?" My eyes fell on the empty seat where Vivienne was supposed to be. *Where the hell is she?* I made a mental note to seek her out after the trial.

Eli began to make the introductory remarks, announcing the purpose for the trial and what Claudia was being charged with. None of us were sure of what to do. It'd been centuries since a person was last tried at The Shade. This was the first time a member of the Elite had been on trial.

Eli's jaw was twitching when he finished his introductions and turned toward the defendant. "How do you plead?"

"Not guilty." Claudia kept her eyes on me.

My brow rose. "You deny keeping my brother within your home?"

"No."

"Were you aware that I, your prince and superior, gave a command that he be surrendered into my custody?"

"Yes, I was aware."

"Then how are you not guilty? Is it not clear that you defied me?"

"Let's stop playing this charade, your royal highness," she hissed. "All of us know that you left The Shade with no laws before you went on your four-hundred-year retreat. You cannot charge me with a crime when there are no laws to break."

I leaned an elbow over the armrest of the leather recliner. One corner of my lips rose in an amused half-smile. "You see, that's where you're wrong, Claudia. In this island, there is but one law and you broke it. The word of those who rule over you—and in my father's absence, that word is *mine*." I scoped every member of the Elite present in that room. "Mark my words. In The Shade, for as long as I rule, my word is law. Those who defy it will suffer the consequences. Does anyone dare object?"

The silence was electrifying. I was expecting Claudia to stand up for herself, but to my surprise, she cowered back. I smirked. *Even lionesses fear the king of the pride.*

"Is there anyone here who would like to speak on the defendant's behalf?" I called out.

Claudia didn't have an abundance of allies at The Shade, so I was surprised when Yuri stood on her behalf. Of all the people I'd expected to say something to save Claudia's neck, he wasn't one of them.

Yuri took the stand, glaring at Claudia before addressing me. "It's no secret how much this wench and I detest each other. I find it sickening just to stand here alongside her. However, it's also no secret that if there's one citizen on this island who was ever able to stand her, it was your highness' older *brother*, Lucas." He paused for a breath and gave Claudia a pointed look.

Claudia's eyes moistened with tears. I found myself all the more intrigued by Claudia and Yuri's strange relationship.

"We cannot excuse her defiance of your majesty, the

prince, but I stand here appealing to mercy rather than to justice. We became the Elite because we bled together in battle. We stood as brothers and sisters, as a *family* during the worst of times. Lucas was such to Claudia—a friend perhaps, a lover maybe, family at best. Must we punish her for protecting the one person at The Shade she considers her ally?"

My response to Yuri's plea would cause commotion and I knew it. "I find your words moving. However, defiance is defiance and I will not stand for it. Unless someone can give me a more substantial reason to give her reprieve, she will serve as a warning to everyone in the kingdom." I stood to my full height to give my words further emphasis. "I will no longer be defied by *anyone*."

I saw fear in Claudia's eyes. It was rare to see her tremble and I relished every second of it.

"I sentence her to thirty lashes and six months in the Cells effective immediately."

The result was chaos, but the message was loud and clear. The Shade was no longer a lawless kingdom. *I* was the law.

Chapter 24: Sofia

I was running through The Shade's dark, misty woods. I was cut up and bruised. I tasted blood on my lips. Tears streamed down my cheeks. A dark presence was after me. Hope surged within me when I saw the clearing that would lead to my escape. I was going to make it. I sped up.

Any hope was replaced by terror when I fell over the edge of a large, dark pit. My gag reflex was immediately triggered by the stench, the sight, the silence and the sense of being surrounded by death. I was surrounded by countless corpses, some of which were familiar faces. Ashley. Paige. Rosa. Sam. Kyle. Ben. Me.

My entire body was tense. I couldn't move a single muscle, but I was keenly aware of the uncontrollable tremble of my body.

"Sofia?"

Ben's arms wrapped around me from behind, his breath hot and erratic against the back of my neck. I thought for a moment that he was seeking to give me comfort and I leaned back against him. He too was shaking, more profusely than I was.

It had been yet another unrestful night.

I slowly regained control of my own body and after a few minutes, lying there, the tremors of our forms molding against each other, I was able to roll over facing him. I still couldn't shake my dreadful dream, so instead of attempting to soothe him, I drew close, leaning my cheek against his broad shoulder.

It felt like hours before our bodies stopped shaking. His heartbeat against my face slowed down from its quick, erratic beats. I gasped. His hand was over my thigh, hiking up my hips, my nightshift rising along with his palm. He lifted me higher over the bed so that our faces were parallel. His lips were on me. First the corner of my lips, my jaw, my neck, my shoulder... I froze as his hands traveled my body the way Lucas' hands had.

"Ben," I croaked.

His mouth found mine and I could no longer speak, no longer object. Eventually, I pushed him away.

"No. Ben, we can't do this."

His eyes met mine and anger blazed in them. "Do you have any idea how many times she used me?"

Claudia. She was a dark cloud always hanging over him.

"How many times did *he* use you?"

"I told you already: never." I recalled all the nights I'd spent in Derek's bed. "He never even laid a hand on me." I was taken aback by that realization. I couldn't remember a single time that Derek had ever touched me while I was in his bed, at least never in a sensual manner. There had always been this safe distance between us.

But then came the memory of lying on his bed, my hands pinned above my head, Derek holding me down by the wrists. It was the first time he'd ever done something like that to me since the incident at the Sanctuary upon his waking. I had to admit that Derek wasn't as blemish-free as my infatuation wanted to paint him.

"We can't keep doing this." I shook my head and got off the bed.

"Can't keep doing what?"

"Sleeping in the same bed. Not if we want to pursue a relationship. We're treading dangerous waters."

"You never had a problem sleeping in one bed with *him*."

"Where is this coming from?" My hands rose in the air. I shook my head emphatically. "You know what? Forget it.

I'm going to do you a favor and forget this happened. I'm going back to my room."

Outside Ben's window, faint hues of violets and reds signaled the break of dawn. It was the morning of our first date. We'd set our date for the weekend after we'd decided to give our relationship a shot a couple of days ago. This wasn't a great way to kickstart our first date.

I snuck out of his room and returned to mine. Sleep escaped me and I stared outside my window, watching the sun rise.

During breakfast, it was clear from the bags under his eyes that Ben hadn't gotten much sleep either. True to my word, I was determined to forget what had happened earlier that morning, blaming it on whatever nightmares still plagued him. So I smiled at him and playfully punched him on the shoulder before placing a plate of French toast in front of him. He gave me a surprised look, but it seemed he was relieved that there wasn't tension between us.

"You two are up early," Lyle commented as he took a sip of his coffee, his eyes on the news article he was reading on his tablet. "It's a Saturday. You're teenagers. Aren't you supposed to be sleeping in?"

Amelia and Abby were still in bed. They always slept in during weekends.

I just smiled as I dabbed butter and strawberry jam over

my French toast. "Maybe we're not your ordinary teenagers, Lyle."

He gave me a lingering stare, enough to bother me.

I lifted the fork I was holding mid-air. "What?"

He shook his head. "It's nothing."

"Actually," Ben drawled as he poured a generous dollop of maple syrup over his toast, "Sofia just couldn't wait to wake up so she can spend some time with me."

My cheeks reddened. I couldn't ignore the way Lyle shifted his glance from Ben to me and back. Lyle mostly kept to himself. I rarely heard him raise his voice even when he was scolding his children.

"You two ought to be careful," Lyle warned. "Whatever is going on between the two of you"—he set his eyes on Ben— "I think we know that your mother isn't yet ready to consider the idea of you being together. Tread lightly."

"Yeah, Dad. Sure thing." Ben had that deer-caught-in-headlights look about him.

Ben and I exchanged glances. *How does he know?* I mouthed the moment Lyle shifted his focus back to his daily news.

Ben shrugged as he pushed his food around on his plate. Lyle finished the rest of his coffee and replaced his tablet in its case.

"I'm off to work. Enjoy your day, and please don't do

anything you'll regret."

Ben chuckled as he watched his father leave. "He doesn't seem to have anything against us dating. Guess that's a good thing."

"Yeah. I guess."

"That being said…" He gave me a once-over. "Get dressed, Sofia. Don't you have a date today?"

"Psshh." I threw a crumpled paper towel at him. "I was thinking of bailing. A wise man just told me that I should be careful and *tread lightly*." I attempted to mimic the way Lyle said those last two words.

"Right," Ben scoffed. He leaned on the dining table as I got up in order to put aside the dishes. "As if you can bail out on *me*."

I raised a brow at him. "What makes you think I can't?"

He shrugged, feigning self-confidence. "What makes you think you can?" He tilted my chin upward with his forefinger and was about to stoop for a kiss when Amelia walked in, her blonde hair a total mess, looking like she was half-asleep.

"Good morning, Mom," Ben said. Never a morning person, Amelia just grunted and went straight to the fridge. "Sofia and I are going to spend the day out, okay? We'll be home by dinner."

"Uh-huh." Amelia nodded, her head still stuck in the

refrigerator. I was pretty sure none of what Ben had said sank in. She poured herself a glass of orange juice and walked out of the room.

I motioned to pick up the dishes but Ben grabbed my arm. "Leave it. I got you." He grinned, giving my PJs a look. "You really have to get dressed. I can't be seen with you looking like that."

"Is this what you do to all the girls you go out with?" I rolled my eyes.

"Nope." He shook his head. "Only the ones who show up in their PJs."

He escorted me to my room and gave me time to get ready as he himself got dressed. I didn't know what he had in mind for our date, so I spent a good five minutes staring at my closet, wondering what to put on. *Why don't you just go ask him, Sofia? For crying out loud, this is Ben.* Still, I wanted it to feel like a real date—complete with all the hassles of assembling the right outfit.

Since it was a Saturday morning and I was sure Ben wouldn't drag me into a formal gathering, I ended up putting on a baby doll blouse with a white lace tube top and a sheer rose chiffon bottom. I paired it with dark skinny jeans. I considered lifting my hair up into a ponytail, but decided to wear it down and accent it with a crystal headband.

I'd just finished putting on some light makeup when Ben began knocking on my door. I stuffed my phone, makeup and wallet in my handbag and grabbed it. When I opened the door, his eyes lit up.

I'd known him half my life and still found myself mesmerized by a side of him that I'd never been introduced to before.

"So? I guess now you'd be willing to be seen with me?" I teased.

He looked at me from head to foot. "Mmm-hmm. You'll do."

I rolled my eyes and lightly slapped the uninjured side of his face.

"Ow. Fine." He relented. "You look perfect, Sofia."

We made our way to the driveway and got on his truck.

"So?" I asked as I made myself comfortable in the passenger's seat. "What exactly do you have in mind for our first date, Mr. Hudson?"

"Well..." He started the vehicle. He looked genuinely excited. "I figured that we've been having some pretty nasty memories lately, so it might be worth our while to revisit the good ones."

I smiled. "Sounds interesting. Where to then?"

"Just wait and see."

Ten minutes passed before we arrived at our first stop: a

string of outlet stores that I didn't remember visiting before. *What kind of memories would I have in a place like this?*

We stepped out of the truck. Ben held my hand and led me to a toy store. He passed the racks of toys as he strode with purpose toward the back of the shop.

I couldn't bear my curiosity any longer. "Why are we at a toy store, Ben? I've never been here before."

"Neither have I," he admitted, amusement wrinkling the corners of his eyes as he continued to scope out each rack he passed by, his fingers still intertwined with mine. "Ahhh... there it is!"

He stopped at a rack containing an impressively large assortment of water guns. He faced me and smiled. "Do you remember the first time we played together?"

"You call *that* playing together?" I burst into giggles. "You kept squirting me with a water gun... right in the face!"

"It was the first water gun I'd ever received. I was nine years old. I thought it was a pretty cool toy and then you showed up, and you couldn't even sit in one place for even a second... What? It's true! You were all over the place and you kept bugging me with stupid questions." He shrugged. "I was annoyed."

"So your solution was to shoot water at me whenever I opened my mouth to speak."

He leaned his face closer to mine and slitted his eyes at

me. "It shut you up, didn't it?"

"For the record, the questions I was asking weren't stupid. You just didn't know the answers to them."

"Doesn't matter. It was annoying."

I rolled my eyes again. Still, the memories connected to Ben's water gun always put a smile on my face. It was how we'd first begun to bond. He was always chasing after me because I never could stay still. I was always on the hunt for something and Ben was always curious what adventure I was headed off to. Whenever he caught up with me, I'd start blabbering about what I'd discovered or start asking questions that he apparently found annoying. The time had come when just seeing the water gun made me seal my lips shut.

"Whatever happened to that thing?" I wondered out loud.

"I always thought you hid it somewhere."

"I didn't, actually."

"Well, either way, it's lost. That's why we're here. The water gun was a gift from my Uncle Bob, so I called him up and asked him where he got it and well, here we are."

"You're going to replace the gun? Why? So you can squirt me in the face with it?"

He chuckled, his hand on mine tightening as he spoke. "As tempting as that sounds, Sofia, no. I thought it would be fun for us to have a water gun fight by the pool or something in case… you know…"

"In case what?"

"In case we progress to a second date."

Oh, smooth, Ben. Very smooth.

We picked up our choice of hydro-powered weapons, paid for them and headed back for the truck. Before he began driving, he gave me a disclaimer. "Once you see where we're going next, promise not to kill me, all right?"

"I'll try not to resort to violence. Where on earth are you taking me now?"

"You'll see."

When he parked the car in front of our next destination, I was mortified. It was the venue of the most embarrassing moment of my life. I cast him a glare.

"You promised not to kill me."

"I did no such thing."

All I got was that grin of his that helped him charm his way through life.

"Come on, Ben…" I groaned. "How can this place hold any good memories?" We were parked in front of a clothing boutique—my favorite one when I was thirteen—where I'd been caught for shoplifting.

"What? It's the scene of your first crime!"

"How is that a good memory? And for the record, I was framed."

"Yes. You told us that story many, many times. It was Jenna who put the dress in your bag."

"It's true." I crossed my arms over my chest and pouted.

"I'm not refuting that." Ben raised his hands in surrender. "But this place holds a good memory for me, because this is where I first realized that you had a crush on me."

"And how exactly did you come upon that revelation?"

"Weren't you there because you were stalking Jenna and me?"

I covered my face with both palms. "That's so embarrassing. You knew?"

"Of course I knew."

"So all this time, you knew I had a thing for you? How would you even…"

"It doesn't matter how. I just knew." He leaned back in his car seat, his eyes forward.

"But you were never interested in me. Not in that way at least."

He gave a wry laugh. "Never interested in you? Sofia, I had a crush on you from the first time I met you. Do you have any idea how cute you looked when I first shot you in the face with that water gun? I've had a thing for you since then."

"Then why didn't you ever say anything? I had to watch you have all those flings and date all those girls. I don't understand."

"I always thought of you as the girl I would eventually become serious with. The only explanation I can really give you is that I wasn't ready to settle yet. But I know I caused you a lot of pain and there's no excuse for it. I was being a complete jackass."

Then Derek came along and you got a taste of your own medicine? Is that why you're so interested in me all of a sudden? It's definitely not because you want to "settle down".

"Anyway"—Ben drummed his fingers on the steering wheel—"we're here because I thought this would be a great place for you to look for a prom dress."

"Prom dress?"

"Yeah. Come on."

"Do I have to?" I whined.

"You can't go to the prom with me if you don't have a prom dress, Sofia." He took my hand and coaxed me out of the truck. "Besides, it's about time this place gave you a good memory or two."

As we walked toward the boutique's front door, I quipped, "Whoever said I was going to prom with you?"

Chuckles escaped his lips. "Of course you are. That's going to be date number three."

After we picked out my prom dress and his suit, he brought me to our favorite ice cream shop. He knew what to

order me without needing to ask: mint chocolate chip. He
hated that flavor, kept telling me that it tasted like
toothpaste. His favorite was actually strawberry, something
he'd never admitted until high school, because as a boy, he'd
always ordered rocky road. He'd thought strawberry was too
girly because it was pink.

Every venue we visited contained a memory of the eight
years we'd been best friends. It was a reminder of how well
we knew each other, of how well-acquainted we were with
each other's quirks and idiosyncrasies. It was as if he was
reminding me why he still mattered, why *we* mattered.

We sneaked into our middle school and fooled around on
the swings. We reminisced over the first fight he'd ever
gotten into. We would've stayed longer, but the old security
guard—Enrique—chased us out.

We then had lunch at the restaurant where we'd both
worked one summer. The manager who'd looked over us was
still working there. We got free dessert. Finally, we took a
winding stroll through the park near the hospital where Ben
had stayed after he contracted appendicitis.

"You were with me every single day until I got out," Ben
recalled. We were seated on a park bench and he was holding
my hands, playfully tugging at my fingers. "I just want you
to know that I noticed all that, Sofia. I appreciate everything
you've ever done for me."

No words could explain the way this made me feel. There were still so many questions, so many doubts running through my mind, but beyond all the disagreements we'd been having because of The Shade, Ben had been the one constant in my life for the past eight years. He'd been there for me when no one else was. Not even The Shade could take that away.

When Ben leaned over for a kiss, it was the first I'd shared with him where he had me completely. As our mouths explored each other's, not a single fiber of my being was paying attention to Derek Novak. On that particular day, I was Ben's and I was his alone.

Chapter 25: Derek

If my ultimate goal was to forget Sofia Claremont, I'd succeeded the moment Ashley's blood began streaming through my veins. There wasn't a day that passed after I'd fed on her that Ashley wasn't on my mind.

I tried to distract myself at the training grounds or lose myself in my music. Nothing worked. Nothing could distract me from the animalistic hunger for the lovely blonde. I was thankful that I'd had enough sense to have Kyle and Sam take the girls away from me. I had to steer clear of them—of *her*—or I wouldn't be able to control myself. I wouldn't hesitate to once again taste her sweet delicacies.

It was this dilemma over the feisty teenager that brought me to Vivienne's penthouse. Of course, there was also the matter that Vivienne hadn't been showing up at the council meetings since our confrontation at the Sun Room. With an important discussion about to get underway regarding the swelling human population at The Shade, I couldn't afford not to have Vivienne at the meetings.

When I reached her penthouse, I found her inside her greenhouse, lovingly caring for her precious roses, lilies, tulips and orchids.

"It's amazing how life has managed to thrive at The Shade even without the sun." She spoke up the moment she sensed my presence. I leaned against the doorpost, watching her. "Cora's powers will never cease to amaze me."

"Matters of great importance to The Shade are being discussed and you're here growing plants?"

"What have you come here for, brother?" Her response was void of emotion.

"I came to fetch you. Your duty is at the Great Dome, taking part in deciding the fate of the kingdom's human population, not in this greenhouse of yours."

"Is that all you came to say?"

I studied her, wondering if she knew what was going on in my mind even before I spoke. I'd never fully grasped the extent of what my sister was capable of. I wondered if I ever would.

"You are bothered by your desire for Ashley?"

The question was rhetorical so I glared at her, hoping that she would sense my impatience. Nothing. The minutes ticked by and she remained silent. Her focus remained on the plant she was pruning. Her disregard was beginning to vex me.

"I still rule over you, sister. I want your full attention when I am speaking with you."

She dropped her tools and looked straight at me. The moment those violet irises settled on me, I wished I hadn't asked for her full attention. Her gaze was a story of despair—one I wanted to unravel and make right, but felt powerless to do so.

"The one question that comes to mind, my *prince*, is why you're having such a dilemma." Vivienne took a step closer to me. A challenge. "Why not just take her from the guard and do with her as you please? She is nothing but a slave. You have every right to bend her, break her, use her any way you see fit. She's just another human girl. I remember a time when you wouldn't have hesitated to take the life of one such as her. Why do you hesitate now?"

Tension coursed through me as I searched for an answer to her question. A bitter taste caught my tongue as the name came out of my mouth.

"Sofia."

Ashley mattered to Sofia. That's why I don't want to harm her. I resented my sister for her cunning. I'd forbidden her to speak of Sofia and yet, without defying me, she'd still managed to get me to ponder the hold the exquisite redhead had on me.

Her challenge stayed with me as we sat through the council meeting at the Great Dome. She left me with a choice—continue to find turmoil or give in to my predatory nature. Somehow, though the latter seemed inviting, a part of me still fought against it. The part that was aware I *had* a choice, and therefore, a responsibility for the consequences of my decisions.

"Derek!" Vivienne snapped me out of my introspection. "Everyone's here. We're all waiting for you to begin."

As usual, Eli was at the stand, presiding over the session. Apparently, he was already done with the introductions and all eyes were on me to begin speaking.

I straightened in my seat, attempting to focus. "The human population of The Shade is far too great. How did it get this way?"

"With all due respect," Xavier said from his seat, "I don't see why this is a problem. They are not trained to fight. They don't have any weapons or any means to procure them. We can easily quell any attempt they make to defy us. The last human uprising was over four hundred years ago and *that* was a massacre."

"And you would willingly have another massacre? Do we not have enough blood on our hands?" It was Liana, Cameron's wife, who spoke up.

"We're vampires, Liana." Xavier smirked. "Human blood is shed on this island every single day. It is how our kind survives. Let's not pretend to have righteous indignation. We can't afford it."

"We cannot have another uprising." My voice silenced everyone. "We are already threatened by external forces— other vampire covens wanting what we have here at The Shade, the hunters still in relentless pursuit of us. Considering how many humans we've been abducting, it won't take long until the hunters find us out. We cannot risk a rebellion from inside our own walls."

"What does the prince suggest we do then?" Eli leaned over the metal banisters lining the stand.

"For now, the abductions must stop. All scouts are going to be recalled and trained as guards. All human blood we require will come from the humans already on the island. We cannot risk the hunters finding us." Even as the words came out, I was reminded of the risk I'd taken when I let Sofia and her friend escape. *Has she blinded me so much that I've forgotten my duty to protect The Shade at all cost?*

The noise that erupted across the round hall drowned out my thoughts.

"How do we survive then?" a voice cried out. "We must feed."

Ashley flashed through my mind and my gut clenched. *Yes. We must, mustn't we?* "Where do the glasses of blood come from?"

Ever since I woke up, I'd been given a daily ration of blood. It wasn't as succulent as fresh blood pumped straight from a beating heart, but it satisfied a vampire's cravings. I'd never thought to ask where it came from until then.

Again, they closed their mouths to hear me speak. It had always baffled me—how I, younger than most of them in both natural and vampire years, was able to command such respect from the Elite.

This time, however, it wasn't just me who caused their silence. It was my question. "Well? How do we have such a supply of blood?"

Eli's knuckles grew paler on the metal banister. Vivienne more tightly gripped the armrests of her recliner.

"Vivienne?"

She twisted the recliner my way. "The human population is a lot less than it was about half a century ago. There were rumors of rebellion and the humans were growing restless and dissatisfied with their living conditions."

I waved for her to continue speaking.

"Father called for a culling."

From the expression on Vivienne's face, the incident didn't bring forth pleasant memories. I wondered what was going through her mind. *My twin sister, forever an enigma.*

"A culling?"

Eli came to her rescue. "All humans who proved to be of no worth—the weak, the sick, those who could not serve— were slaughtered, their blood drained and preserved in chilling chambers for future consumption."

"Were so many killed that the blood lasts even to this day?"

"A great number were lost, yes." Xavier chuckled. "But we never had much use for the preserved blood when we were always brought a fresh supply from the abductions."

"Well, we have use for it now, don't we?" I challenged him. "My decision stands. There shall be no more abductions. If you must feed, feed on the blood of the dead."

"And when that runs out?" Xavier was never intimidated by me and was not afraid to show it.

Vivienne's jaw twitched when my eyes met hers. She looked at me like she would a dying man, like she was about to lose me. I hardened myself.

"Should the blood run out, perhaps we should see to another culling."

CHAPTER 26: BEN

I couldn't take my eyes off her.

Sofia had me spellbound the moment she walked down the stairs, looking absolutely stunning in the dress we'd picked out during our date. She appeared timid and reserved as my mother and father began taking pictures of us.

My mother hadn't exactly been thrilled to hear that Sofia and I were going to prom together, but we'd explained that neither of us had been dating anyone and since we were best friends, going together would take a lot less effort than scrambling for a date. My mom's shoulders had sagged before she'd kissed me on the cheek and whispered, "If that's what makes you happy, Ben."

And it *did* make me happy. Sofia made me happy.

Ever since our first date, things had been a lot more fun and casual. In order to avoid arguments, we went to great lengths to avoid discussing the future—with me still mulling over joining the hunters and her still opposed to ruining The Shade, something I couldn't understand.

We spent every waking moment together. Since Sofia and I held hands in the hallway and made out whenever we got the chance, it wasn't long before everyone at school got wind of the new couple. Sofia and I were no longer just best friends. In Connor's words, we were "*finally* together". It felt real, or at least I hoped it did.

There were still times I would catch Sofia staring into space, lost in thought. It started with this dark, pensive expression and then something would lift inside her, like a light spreading through her. Her cheeks would take on a rosy glow and her lips would form into a soft smile at some memory I wasn't privy to.

Sometimes, I would be tempted to ask what went through her mind during those moments, but I was afraid. Something told me that those memories had to do with a certain vampire.

The few days I'd spent with them at his penthouse were enough to tell me how she viewed Derek Novak. She never looked at me the way she'd looked at him. She never responded to my touch the way she'd responded to his.

That night of our escape from The Shade… in the woods… it still haunted me. Seeing his lips on hers, his arms around her… I'd known Sofia well enough to know just by the look in her eyes that she'd wanted to stay. No words could explain how grateful and relieved I'd been to find her on the shore with me the next morning. I'd been fully expecting to find myself alone.

As we rode in the limousine to our prom, I was momentarily distracted from Connor's antics—the reason for all the laughter, cheers and guffaws inside the vehicle. Sofia sat by my side, staring out the window. She had that distant gaze, that rosy glow, that smile. Her left hand moved over her knees as if she were playing a tune on a piano.

She had never played an instrument. But Derek did.

I laid my hand over hers. "Hey, you all right?"

She snapped to attention and turned to face me. A flicker of guilt showed in her green eyes before she squeezed my hand and smiled. "Yes. I'm great."

"Be here with me, Sofia." *Not back at The Shade. With him.*

She responded with bewilderment. "I'm here, aren't I?"

Her fingers caressed my jaw. I hated how I barely felt her touch. No other girl had ever made me ache with so much longing. When her soft lips rested on the corner of mine, I took advantage and twisted toward her for a full kiss. If there was one thing that I could completely feel, it was the kisses.

I could sense her surprise. She must've already noticed over the past few days that casual smacks rarely ever satisfied me. I wanted more, demanded more, and it pleased me when she responded, just like now.

Unlike the kisses I had shared with Tanya, Sofia's kiss didn't bring about visions of Claudia.

"Rose Red and Prince Charming are at it again!" Connor announced with a chuckle. He was the first person I had confided in about how I felt for Sofia way back in our freshman year of high school.

I laughed, pulling away from Sofia. The other two couples in the limo had their eyes on us. "Sorry about that." I grinned. Sofia's cheeks took on a crimson blush. "I couldn't help myself."

"Don't worry." Connor waved a hand. "After all these years of trying to convince us that you two are just friends, we can't blame you for making out whenever you get the chance. You have a lot of time to make up for."

"Didn't Snow White end up with Prince Charming?" Alyssa, Connor's date, asked. She gave Sofia a quick glance before looking at me. "Not Rose Red?"

I couldn't blame Alyssa if she detested me. She and Tanya were close friends. What I didn't like was her taking her animosity out on Sofia. I shrugged. "No idea."

"Rose Red ends up with the brother of Prince Charming, actually," Sofia informed us, her teasing eyes set on me. "Do you have a brother hidden somewhere?"

Alyssa crossed her arms over her chest, her disdainful glare fixed on Sofia. "I think there's a variation of the story where Rose Red ends up with the Beast."

Alyssa couldn't have known how close to home her jibes were coming. Annoyed, I tucked strands of Sofia's auburn hair behind her ear. "I can be Prince Charming or his brother... or even the Beast. I'll be whoever I have to be for Sofia to end up with me."

The glow drained out of Sofia's cheeks as her emerald eyes met mine. Questioning. Hesitant. Afraid. I had no idea how to assure her that I was serious about her. *Hopefully, after tonight, she'll know.*

I was relieved when we finally reached the venue, eager to have Sofia to myself. Prom went as well as anyone would expect. I was crowned prom king and had to pry myself away from Sofia for a quick dance with Tanya, who won prom queen.

When I returned for Sofia, she sat at one of the tables, absent-mindedly sketching something on a paper napkin. Connor bumped into me before I could reach her.

"Looks like Rose Red has eyes only for you. A bunch of

guys already asked her to dance and she declined them all."

I reached her table and extended my hand toward her.

"One last dance, Sofia?"

She covered her sketch with her palm, crumpled the paper napkin and stuffed it in the small purse she was carrying. She took my hand and I led her to the dance floor. She rested her hands on my shoulders and my hands found her waist.

"Having a good time?"

"Yes." She nodded.

"Right." I rolled my eyes. "You're lying."

She laughed. "Okay, fine. I never even imagined myself attending prom. You know me. This isn't exactly my scene. Too many people, too much noise."

"Then why'd you come?"

"Because you wanted to be here." She then looked down at her outfit and gave me a pout. "And this dress is too pretty to waste."

"Wanna get out of here?" I suggested.

Her brows furrowed. "You sure you want to go home this early?"

"Who said anything about going home?" I held her hand. "Come on. I have a surprise for you."

We left the hall and made our way to the parking lot where my black pickup was waiting. I'd asked one of the sophomores on the football team to drive it there.

"Where are we going?" she asked.

"You'll see."

It took half an hour to reach Los Angeles. From there, we drove another few miles up the Angeles Crest Highway to a spot overlooking the Los Angeles basin. "This place would actually be better if we came before sunset, but I guess the starry night will have to do."

She chuckled. "I just hope we can still see stars past the smog."

I parked the pickup so that the tail was facing the view of the city. I removed the canopy covering the back and switched on a flashlight to reveal a blanket, a bunch of pillows and a picnic basket. Just seeing that radiant smile on her face made all the effort worth it.

She began fixing the pillows on the edge of the truck so that we could both find a comfortable position. "We're so overdressed for something like this," she commented.

"Who cares? We both look incredible."

"I'll never get used to how modest you are, Ben."

"People who look like me have no need of modesty." I opened the picnic basket and brought out the candles, spreading them along the edge of the truck. I tossed her the matches. "Light them up, beautiful."

By the time she was done lighting the candles, I had already taken out the champagne, the bowl of strawberries and the melted chocolate. She started giggling about something.

When I gave her a questioning look, she explained, "Look at all these candles. I'm just wondering when fire hazards like this started to become romantic."

"So you find this romantic?" I raised a brow at her.

"Yeah, but don't let that go to your head. I'm pretty easy to please."

"Easy? You think it was easy to set all this up? Do you have any idea how difficult it was to put this together and keep it secret from you *and* Mom?"

The delight on her face faded at the mention of my mother.

"Sofia, you do understand why we can't tell my mom yet, right? I don't think we're ready to deal with all the drama that it would cause, and…"

"Yeah, I understand, Ben." She cut me off. "Don't worry about it."

I opened up the champagne and we drank and ate dessert. We eased into a comfortable silence, our focus being the view.

When she finally broke the silence, I wish she hadn't.

"I've been meaning to ask you a question, Ben…"

I sensed her hesitation.

"While you were setting up the food, I tapped you on the

back to get your attention. You didn't respond. That's happened so many times already. When you got beat up, I kept accidentally brushing whatever against your bruises and you never once flinched." Her voice was laced with concern. "Why is that?"

I didn't want to talk about it, didn't want to admit to it, but it was out there. "I think Claudia messed up my nervous system or something. I'm not sure what she did. All I know is that my sense of touch has been dulled."

"Ben... I..."

I didn't want her pity. I'd had enough of feeling sorry for myself. "It's why I want to join the hunters, Sofia. I don't want to go through life pretending that I can go back to normal. Claudia took that away from me."

Her silence was enough of an answer. I doubted anything I could say would convince her that she ought to join the hunters.

One mention of Claudia was enough to ruin my mood. My using my story as leverage to convince Sofia to join the hunters was enough to ruin hers.

"Let's get out of here," I suggested. "I have one surprise left."

"Let's."

We drove back to the city. I had hotel reservations. Without Sofia's knowledge, I'd told my parents that we were going to a slumber party with our friends, so they weren't expecting us home that night.

I didn't know what I was expecting. Perhaps it was a desperate attempt to assure myself that she was mine. I thought that maybe if we slept together, it would be harder for her to leave me.

The moment I opened that hotel room's door, revealing the rose petals scattered all over the bed and the dim lighting, and I saw the expression on her face, I knew I had made a huge mistake.

She shook her head. "I'm not ready for this, Ben. I'm sorry." Her voice revealed that she was close to tears. Her hand was clutching her purse, trembling slightly.

"It's fine. I understand," I lied. "We don't have to do it. It's enough to be able to spend the night with you."

I pulled her to my chest and hugged her. We kissed. Still, I couldn't help but feel like she was slipping out of my grasp.

I spent the night looking at her as she slept. *So peaceful. So beautiful.* I wondered if her calm countenance would eventually become marred by another nightmare. I wondered what horrors her fitful dreams involved. Was I in them? Was *he* in them? I wondered if she still thought about him. I wondered if I had ruined what I was trying to build with her with the stupid stunt I'd tried to pull tonight.

Most of all, I wondered if she would ever truly be mine.

Chapter 27: Sofia

The stadium was beginning to fill up with people. A collective sense of excitement could be felt throughout the bleachers. On one side, several of the school's alumni—former football players themselves—were screaming and hollering, rooting for their team. The cheerleaders were doing what they did best and pulling off a brand-new and rather impressive routine. On the bleachers above us, more than a dozen or so conversations were being exchanged—one of which was Lyle and Amelia's as they gushed over how wonderful it was that Ben was once again back in the game.

Ben was the only reason I was there. I'd never been a fan of the game and I only understood what was going on because of the scoreboard. While others around me were getting impatient for the game to start, I was looking forward to it ending—hopefully with Ben's team coming out as the winners, so that I wouldn't have to deal with him being a sore loser.

"Where's Abby?" Amelia tugged on the sleeve of my cardigan.

"I thought she was with Lyle…" Lyle had carried her to our seats.

"He went out for food. He told me Abby was with you. You were supposed to be watching her."

On the seat beside me, Abby's stuffed elephant, Colin, was seated where the five-year-old was supposed to be. Panic bubbled up inside me. "I'll look for her," I assured Amelia before leaving my seat and weaving through the bleachers in search of the little girl. "Abby!"

"Sofia!" a male voice called out.

I whipped around. I sighed with relief when I saw Abby seated on the lap of Kendra James. Her husband, Mike, was calling my name. They were Connor's parents and close friends of the Hudsons.

"Abby, you scared us to death!" I exclaimed as I neared them.

"I thought you said you asked permission," Kendra scolded Abby in a tone that was too light and sweet to make the kid take it seriously.

Abby flashed her winning smile, her curly blonde ponytail bobbing up and down as she fluttered her eyelashes in a way that reminded me of her older brother. She giggled. "I did. Sofia just didn't hear me."

I rolled my eyes. *The kid could get away with murder if she got any cuter.* Mike and Kendra were particularly fond of Abby, largely because they had four sons, of whom Connor was the youngest, and no daughters. Kendra had been thrilled when Amelia had asked her to become Abby's godmother. They adored the cute little runt and I couldn't blame them. Abby was a charmer just like Ben.

"I think we ought to go back to our seats before your mother has a heart attack, Abby," I coaxed.

"Sorry, Sofia," Mike said. "She saw us and came over. We didn't mean to make you worry."

"Oh, it's fine." I smiled. Of course, the look on Amelia's face when she had asked me about Abby was far from fine. Amelia and I weren't exactly on the best of terms. She hadn't spoken much to me since Ben and I had got back. I extended my hand toward Abby and she begrudgingly took it, but not before receiving a lollipop from Kendra.

"Say thank you, Abby," I said.

Abby tilted her head, some of her curls falling over her face. "Thank you, Kendra."

Of course, the couple found that absolutely "awwww"-worthy. I half-pulled, half-dragged Abby back to our seats, because she kept making friends with the strangers we passed by. She would be easy to kidnap. *Amelia's gonna have to keep a close eye on you, Abby. You're setting yourself up for trouble.*

"Where was she?" Amelia's voice was flat and cold.

"With Mike and Kendra."

"I don't know what it is with you, Sofia, but my kids have a way of getting into trouble whenever they're around you." She began checking on her little girl to make sure she was all right.

"It's not Sofia's fault, Mommy." Abby stood in my defense. "I didn't ask her if I could go."

I couldn't blame Amelia for her concern. I should've paid attention to Abby. The truth was that I was jealous of Ben and Abby for having a mother fawning all over them. The only memories I had of my mother were of her locking me up in the closet when I was naughty. Amelia was nothing like that with her children. She loved them dearly and it showed. I still found it heartbreaking whenever I caught her looking at Ben, her blue eyes glistening with tears. She never showed it to her son, but what had happened to him was tearing her apart.

"The game is about to start in a few minutes." Lyle came to my rescue. "Settle down. It's fine, Sofia."

I smiled and took my seat. My phone vibrated in my purse and I fished it out to check. I found several text messages from Ben, expressing how anxious he felt. It was a big game after all. I messaged him saying he was going to do great.

The teams were called out into the field and as Ben ran out, his eyes caught me amongst the crowd. He winked.

I gave him my best smile and blew him a kiss, hoping that Amelia wouldn't make anything out of it. It was getting harder to hide from Amelia that Ben and I were dating. I knew she noticed the difference in the way Ben and I treated each other around the house. Truth be told, I was beginning to believe that perhaps it was for the best that she didn't know.

After what he'd tried to pull off at the hotel room after prom, I'd taken a serious look at what I had going on with Ben. It felt right and yet wrong at the same time. After everything we'd been through, we owed it to each other to give the romance a chance. But sometimes, I felt as if I was with him because I somehow *owed* it to him to try and make the relationship work.

I knew he wanted me. He was, after all, outspoken about it and never backed away from showing his affections. I, on the other hand, knew that I loved him, but I was still unsure if that love could span anything more than just friendship.

In spite of everything Ben was doing for me, Derek was still the last person on my mind before I drifted off to sleep at night and the first person I thought about when I woke up. I wanted to get him off my mind, but he haunted my every waking moment, and every time I kissed Ben, guilt ate at me.

That same pang of shame and guilt caught up with me as my boyfriend ran to the center of the field. I was the envy of the whole cheerleading squad and a bunch of other girls, but gone were the days when that mattered to me.

I'd now finally got what I'd wanted all throughout high school. I was with Ben and yet something about being together didn't feel right and I wondered if he sensed it too.

The game began and I checked on Abby to make sure she was okay. She was seated on Lyle's lap, clutching Colin the Elephant in her small arms. She seemed to be having the time of her life, her bright eyes sparkling as she watched the game. Amelia looked a lot more relaxed too. I thought it did her good to see Ben back in his game, back in his element.

I leaned back in my seat, not quite sure about what was happening on the field, but a quick look at the scoreboard revealed that no one was winning—not yet.

"Hello, Sofia. May I have a word with you in private?"

I turned my head. My face drained of all blood. Sitting to my right—in Abby's spare seat—was Vivienne Novak.

I screamed, but my reaction was drowned out by a cheer erupting throughout the bleachers. The scoreboard revealed that Ben's team was now in the lead. I had reason to rejoice, but how could I when a vampire was sitting right beside me?

I froze. Try as I might, I couldn't pry my eyes away from her. My breath had stopped. I could neither inhale nor exhale. The crowd began to settle down all around us.

She grabbed my hand and I flinched at her coldness. "Don't be afraid. I mean you no harm, Sofia. I don't have much time. Please. May we talk?"

Beyond the sincerity in her blue-violet eyes, I was moved by an emotion I'd never thought I would see in the princess of The Shade. It was betrayed by the way her hand was trembling over mine and the way her lower lip had the slightest quiver. Fear. She was afraid, and I couldn't help but wonder what someone like her could possibly be afraid of.

For some reason, her fear calmed me, enabling me to breathe again. She was in human territory, *my* turf. She had no power over me here. I shook my head. "I'm not going anywhere alone with you, Vivienne."

"Sofia, is everything all right?" Lyle spoke from behind me, his hand resting on my shoulder.

"Please..." Vivienne's hand clasped tighter around mine and her expression gave way to a whole new emotion: desperation.

I slightly turned my head to address Lyle. "It's fine. She's a girl from school. She came to ask about college applications."

Lyle eyed Vivienne warily, but nodded. "Okay."

I returned my focus on Vivienne. "There's a coffee shop right outside the west exit. I'll meet you there in five minutes."

She nodded and left. It was as if she couldn't wait to get out of there. I watched how she made a pair of jeans, a loose checkered button-down blouse and a baseball cap on her head look sexy and feminine.

A modeling agency could make a fortune out of her. I shook the thought away. *What is she doing here and what could she possibly want from me?*

Five minutes later, after begging a quick leave from Lyle and Amelia, I was fully expecting an answer to that question as I sat across Vivienne inside the crowded coffee shop. I held the latte with both hands, savoring the heat, before taking a sip. I'd just agreed to have coffee with a vampire. *Do you have a death wish or something, Sofia?*

Vivienne's eyes darted from one corner of the room to the other, as if she suspected that someone was following her. She eventually managed to stop fidgeting. "Thanks for agreeing to have a word with me." Her voice was hoarse, as if she hadn't had a drink for a while.

The thought that she was thirsty did little to bring me comfort. I laid down my mug of coffee on the table between us. "What's going on, Vivienne?"

She clasped her palms together and laid them on her lap. She shut her eyes for a few seconds and took a couple of deep breaths before opening them again. "It's nothing. It's just that I haven't been out of The Shade for hundreds of years. I'm a little on edge. Anyway, I don't know how much time I have, but I'm going to answer all the questions you may have for as long as I am able."

Questions about what? I had no idea what she was talking about. *She's speaking like she's going to keel over and die any time now.* Back at The Shade, Vivienne had always seemed calm and poised. She'd had this all-knowing look about her that had made me feel antsy around her, like she could see right through my soul. Seeing her act like a basket of nerves was definitely interesting.

"Could you just tell me why you're here? You're acting weird and it's making me nervous."

A flicker of interest crossed her stunning eyes. "No wonder he was so enamored of you. I came to ask you to come back to The Shade."

My jaw dropped, a dry chuckle coming out of my lips. "You have got to be joking," I said before motioning to rise from my seat.

"Wait. Please. Hear me out."

Vivienne still reeked of fear and desperation, but there was something more, something I couldn't place.

I settled back on the couch. "This better be good."

She fidgeted in her seat and wrinkled her nose as if she was weighing her words. I began drumming my fingers as I waited for her to say something. "Well? I'm waiting."

She blew out a deep sigh before finally finding words. "I didn't expect you to live."

My eyes widened. "That's not exactly a great way to start, Vivienne."

"Maybe so," she agreed, "but it's the truth." She lowered her voice so that only I could hear. "That night, when you and the girls were brought to Derek, just after he woke up, I wasn't expecting him to be able to keep from devouring each and every one of you."

I remembered that night well. How scared I'd been. How I'd held Gwen's hand in hopes of both giving and drawing comfort from her. How I'd somehow caught his attention. How he'd pinned me against a marble pillar.

"If that's what you thought, why would you have brought us to him? You led us to slaughter. That's sick, Vivienne."

"It's the way of The Shade."

"Again, not a very convincing argument for me to go back. What's your point?"

"A prophecy has been spoken about Derek a long time ago. The prophecy says that he will rule and that he will bring our kind true sanctuary."

"Your kind? You mean vampires?" I didn't care to lower my voice. It didn't matter to me who heard. Vivienne really wasn't giving me much reason to protect her.

The surprise on her face showed that she was nowhere near used to my audacity, but she recovered. "Yes. Our kind. Derek asked Cora, a great witch—Corrine's ancestor—to put him under a sleeping spell. He wanted to escape all the things we'd done in order to keep The Shade safe. The guilt was killing him."

"Why? What exactly did your kind do to make him feel so guilty?"

Vivienne shifted in her seat. "That's a question you'd have to ask him yourself."

My shoulders sagged. Her statement made me ache with longing. I smiled bitterly and shook my head. "Go ahead. What were you saying?"

"Derek thought he'd already fulfilled the prophecy when we established The Shade. The island, he thought, was our true sanctuary. Cora knew otherwise. She knew that he wasn't done, so without his knowledge, she tacked on an end to her spell. Derek was to wake once it was time to find the girl who would help him fulfill his destiny."

She paused and looked to me for a reaction, but the words were still sinking in.

"It was Corrine who signaled that he was about to wake and she made it very clear that the girls taken on a certain night were to be reserved for him."

"My birthday." I remembered the way I'd felt that night. Ben had forgotten my birthday and spent most of the day wooing Tanya.

"Yes. Your birthday. Derek hadn't fed on human blood for four centuries. You couldn't possibly understand how difficult it was for him not to feed on you. When he slammed you against that pillar, I thought you were done for."

I remembered Derek's large, virile form pressed against mine, his strong arms holding me up against the pillar, his breath chilling my neck... I'd been terrified.

"But he spared you. I don't know what you told him, but you got to him in a way no other person was ever able to. Not our father nor our brother nor myself nor even Cora was able to get through to him the way you did."

I swallowed hard. I couldn't bring myself to accept what she was implying. "I am not the girl Cora was speaking of, Vivienne."

Vivienne gazed at me with what could almost pass as affection. "Sofia, look me straight in the eye and tell me that you don't feel anything for my twin."

My lips pursed and my jaw twitched. Even if I tried to lie, I wouldn't be able to fool her. There hadn't been a day since I'd left The Shade that I hadn't thought of Derek.

Vivienne's smile was bitter. "I thought so."

I clutched the armrests of the couch and steadied myself on its edge. I wasn't about to let her win just like that. "I care about Derek, Vivienne, but that doesn't mean anything. That doesn't prove that I'm some girl destined to help him fulfill some sort of prophecy." A wry laugh escaped my lips. "Besides, why on earth would I help Derek save your kind? After everything you put me through, after everything you put Ben and so many others through…"

"Because as you said, Sofia, you care about him." Her blue-violet eyes glistened. "He needs you."

She was his twin, she knew him better than I ever had. Her words had weight, but I couldn't wrap my mind around someone like Derek needing someone like me. *Who am I?* Still, her words triggered all the pent-up longing, and I found myself asking, "How is he?"

"The darkness came for him the moment you left. It's taking away the man that he became when you were there."

I could feel my face lose color, and my lips parted as I drew a breath. "The darkness is coming," I muttered under my breath.

It seemed the words meant something to Vivienne, because her eyes flickered with recognition.

"What did you say?"

I shook my head. "Nothing." I wasn't particularly fond of the idea of revealing to her all the nightmares I'd been having.

My phone began to vibrate on the coffee table. I glanced at it, but decided not to check the message. I took another sip of my not-so-hot-anymore latte. I found myself overcome with worry for Derek. *If my nightmares held any meaning, then...* I gulped.

"How are the girls?" Guilt claimed me the moment I thought of Ashley, Paige and Rosa. They were my friends and I'd abandoned them.

When Vivienne told me that Derek had attacked Ashley in the Sun Room, that he'd drunk her blood almost enough to kill her, I had no idea how to recover from both the guilt and the shock. I felt like it was partially my fault, because I'd never done anything to get Ashley and the other girls out of The Shade, but I'd always been secure that Derek would keep them safe. I couldn't even wrap my mind around the idea that Derek could be capable of something like that.

That's nothing like the Derek I knew.

"I don't know how long my brother can keep himself from hunting her." Vivienne kept clasping and unclasping her fingers. "Now that he's had a taste of her blood, I'm pretty sure he's craving her. Even though she's living with Kyle now, she's still too close. He would still be able to sense her."

"Why are you telling me all this, Vivienne?" Tears threatened to spill down my cheeks.

"Remember the night when you arrived? When you were in the dungeon? I told you that you were nothing but a pawn."

I could still remember her exact words and how frightened she'd made me feel. *Understand, girl, that you are nothing here. You're nothing but a pawn, a piece used to make the board move. Your best chance at survival and proving your significance is to win Derek's affections. Considering everything I know about my brother, I'm not sure that's even possible.*

I smiled bitterly. "How could I forget?"

"I was wrong." Vivienne, in all her grace and beauty, looked me in the eye and said, "You're not a pawn, Sofia. You're the queen."

Before I could fully make sense of the words, the vampire's eyes widened with horror, as if she had seen something behind me. I looked back and saw nothing but a group of people having their coffee.

"Vivienne, what's wrong? You've been acting strange ever since..."

"It doesn't matter." She cut me off. "The hunters are here. You need to go back to The Shade, Sofia. There's no other way. You can stay at my home. You won't go back as a slave. I'm going to give you some of my memories along with instructions on how to get to The Shade. They'll know I sent you."

"How on earth are you going to give me your mem—"

She grabbed both my hands and I had to shut my eyes as a deluge of images flooded me. *Vampires being burned at the stakes… A smile and a kiss on the hand from a handsome young man… The same man screaming as he was tortured… A symbol of a hawk branded with burning iron on Derek's bare back…* Images—some sweet, others confusing, most of it horrifying—flashed through my mind in one wave after another until finally, I saw a way back to The Shade and darkness engulfed me.

Snapping out of the influx of memories that didn't belong to me, I opened my eyes to find Lyle in front of me, holding my face with both hands. "Are you all right, Sofia?" I heard panic in his voice. "What did she do to you?"

Behind him, Vivienne's unconscious form lay on the couch across from me. Two men, who looked like paramedics, rushed to her. One of them stabbed her in the arm with a syringe before they carried her out of the coffee shop.

Where are they taking her? I wanted to ask, but Lyle was moving his lips and I couldn't hear what he was saying. I opened my mouth to speak but no words came out. Then my vision blurred before everything faded into black.

CHAPTER 28: DEREK

What the hell am I doing here?

The Black Heights was the last place I'd expected to find myself. I hated the mountain caves and their network of dark tunnels. They brought memories of desperate times.

Still, I followed a guard through well-lit stone corridors to the cell where Claudia was being held. The Cells had changed drastically since the last time I'd visited. Much had been done to develop the caves. Flat, concrete flooring, electricity, doors… those were just some of the modifications that made the place feel more like the interior of an actual building instead of dark, dank caves, void of life and light.

The guard stopped in front of a gate—or at least what

looked like one. White-blue rays formed the bars keeping Claudia prisoner.

"What are those?" I asked, pointing at the bars.

"The structure of these bars is complex, but I do know that they consist partly of UV rays, your highness," the guard responded.

"How many of these types of cells do we have?" I was curious.

"Three. We rarely ever have vampire prisoners."

Of course. The Cells are mainly for humans after all. He pressed a button and the rays retracted. I entered the cell and found Claudia sitting cross-legged on top of the small cot. Her blonde mane made her round face look small. Her blue eyes were set on me. She was wearing a simple white smock—a contrast to her garish outfits. The simple getup and the lack of makeup made her look like a regular teenager. *A seventeen-year-old with old eyes, eyes that have seen too much...*

The bars closed down behind me, imprisoning me with her.

"Just call when you wish to leave, prince."

I nodded and waved him off. I focused on the beautiful blonde before me.

"The almighty prince pays me a visit. What did I do to deserve such an honor?" If she was resentful of me, she was hiding it. Her golden lashes fluttered, a playful grin forming on her lips.

"I wanted to ask you a question."

"Oh?" Her head tilted. "Ask away then."

I hesitated. *Why am I here?*

She stood up and moved toward me, studying me. "You're always so tense, Prince Derek. That's your problem. You don't know how to loosen up like your older brother does." She brushed her fingers over my cheek.

I stepped away from her, revolted by her touch.

"When was the last time you lay with a woman?"

Every night since Sofia left. I'd had Vivienne send me a girl or two to keep me company in my bedroom. Without them, my chambers reeked too much of Sofia. Even with other women to distract me, she was still on my mind.

"I could help loosen you up," Claudia offered.

I pushed her away before she could lay a hand on me. "That's not why I'm here. Sit down, Claudia. I wish to discuss something private with you."

Her brows rose. "Something private." The idea obviously delighted her. "This ought to be interesting." She turned her back on me to return to her cot.

I was surprised to find the back of her smock bloodstained. I grabbed her arm. "The wounds from the lashes… they haven't yet healed? It's been days since…"

She shrugged my hand away and sat back on the cot. "My dear prince," she hissed. "You really should find out what the extents of your punishments are before you dole them out. I was injected with a serum to delay the healing before the lashes were inflicted on me. As long as the serum is in my system, I will not heal."

I swallowed hard.

"Oh, don't worry yourself too much about this." She smiled bitterly. "Someone has been coming to treat the wounds."

"Who?" I didn't know why I'd even asked. I already knew the answer.

"Yuri." A spark of delight appeared in her eyes. "Are you going to punish him for helping me? You really should. His 'treatments' hurt like hell. I'm starting to think he just enjoys hearing me scream with pain."

I had half a mind to ask her about the younger Lazaroff, but decided not to. The thought of exploring Claudia's twisted mind wasn't inviting and it wasn't why I'd come.

"Anyway, do tell me why you're here, Prince Derek. I'm dying to know."

"Ben."

Her eyes flickered with recognition.

"You remember him?"

"Of course. He was special, that one... hard to forget. I

regret ever taking him with me when I visited you, but how could I have known that your fiery little pet once knew him? How is she anyway?"

"I'm assuming that you already had a taste of his blood from the first night you had him with you. Am I correct?"

She nodded.

"How did you manage to drink of him for so long without ending his life? How did you have that kind of control?"

She grew pensive, as if she too were surprised. "Why do you ask?"

"I crave a girl. I've tasted her blood and now I'm desperate to finish the kill."

"Your lovely redhead? Such a beautiful thing to waste on one kill…"

"Answer my question." *First Vivienne. Now Claudia.* The constant mention of Sofia was grating on my nerves.

"Always so feisty." Claudia pouted. "I was never able to control myself from finishing a human off for more than a week or two."

"But he was with you for many weeks. He was brought to The Shade not long after Sofia was." Her name left a bitter taste in my mouth.

"He reminded me of someone. Someone from the past." Something dark and wicked marred Claudia's countenance.

"As I said, he was special. I wanted to keep him for as long as I was able." She shrugged. "Perhaps rage toward a human gives us some form of control."

I shook my head, slowly comprehending. "Not rage, emotion."

"Perhaps. Is that all you came to ask?" She stretched her back and winced. She cast me a fleeting glance—full of rage.

I did this to her.

"Pretty little Sofia." Claudia's gaze was now blank, her words full of venom. "Ben spoke of her in his sleep. What is it with her that has got him and even *you* so wrapped up in her? Do you remember the look in their eyes when they saw each other? The way they embraced each other... so young, so in love... How does that not bother you?"

I swallowed hard. Unwelcome images of Ben and Sofia in each other's arms rushed through my mind. I wondered if Claudia was taunting me, but the anger blazing in her eyes told me that she too was living out the jealousy she'd felt upon seeing them together. Her rage was directed not at me, but at *him,* at *her.*

I remembered that day all too well. Claudia had come to pay me tribute and Sofia had arrived from a walk outside. It was clear to see that she and Ben held affection for each other, so I'd asked Claudia to give Ben to me—for Sofia's sake. I remembered how I'd held Claudia and pulled her body against mine as I gave her my request. I'd used Claudia just to see how Sofia would react to me placing my hands on the sultry, blonde vampire.

I had not imagined it. I knew I'd seen jealousy in Sofia's green gaze.

I didn't know what spirit possessed me to do it, but all I could think of was exacting revenge on Sofia for leaving me. I wanted to make her jealous again. Before I could make sense of what was happening, I had allowed Claudia to pull me down on the cot, her body writhing beneath mine.

For a short span of time, my mind was too consumed by Claudia, Ben and Sofia for it to have room for my craving for Ashley, but I was aware that by sleeping with Claudia, I'd just hit a new low. As I got off her and began putting my clothes back on, I realized that she was sobbing. Her back was turned to me. The fresh wounds that criss-crossed her back made my stomach turn.

Gone was the raging vampire seeking to mete out her revenge on Ben and Sofia. In its place was a broken little girl.

The guilt I felt reminded me of the humanity I still allowed myself to have. In my longing to ease my guilt, I did the worst thing I could do. I told her that I would lessen her sentence for the service she'd afforded me.

The glare she gave me was meant to inflict horrible pain before going for a kill. I realized my mistake immediately, reminded of what she once was. I'd just offered her payment for sex and I knew that she would never forgive me.

Chapter 29: Ben

The moment the team made the final touchdown that won us the game, my eyes flew to the bleachers in search of Sofia. It was a championship game and she knew how much it meant to me. I was looking forward to having my girlfriend run into my arms, congratulate me, press her lips against mine. But she was nowhere to be found. Instead, my mother approached me, carrying Abby in her arms.

"Ben! I'm so proud of you!" she cooed as she pecked me on the cheek.

Abby squealed out a string of cheers that didn't make sense. I figured she was trying to imitate the cheerleaders, but couldn't remember the words, so she made up her own.

"Thanks, Mom, and thank you, Abby." I looked around. "Where's Dad and Sofia?"

My mother rolled her eyes. "Sofia left the stadium with a friend of hers not long after the game began. When she didn't return, your dad went looking for her. I haven't heard from him yet. I'll call him while you go take a shower?"

Something was wrong and I knew it. *No matter how much the whole appeal of football escapes Sofia, she wouldn't walk out on a game she knows is* this *important to me.* "Do you know who this friend of hers is?"

"No, I haven't seen her before. Tall, pretty young woman with black hair."

I searched my mind for anyone who could fit that description and shook my head. "I'll try to call Sofia."

I walked toward the benches where I'd left my phone with one of the junior second-liners. My mom and sister trailed behind me. I dialed Sofia's number. Several rings later, someone picked up.

"Hello?"

It took a couple of seconds before the familiar voice registered. "Dad? Where's Sofia? Is she all right?"

"Yeah. She's fine. We're back home." He tried to lighten his tone. "Did you win the game?"

"Yes, we did. Can I talk to Sofia, please?"

"She's unconscious at the moment, but don't worry.

She's—"

"Unconscious! Why is she unconscious? What happened? I'm gonna be right there."

"Ben." My father's voice was both firm and soothing. "Trust me. She's all right. Take a shower, have a celebratory dinner with your mother and sister. Don't worry about Sofia. She'll be waiting up for you when you return."

"She's my girlfriend, Dad. How can I not worry?"

The shock on my mother's face didn't escape my notice. I didn't care. It was about time she found out. I didn't even wait for a response from my father. I shut my phone and rushed to the locker room to get changed without bothering to explain to my gaping mother.

We were already driving home when she brought up the subject.

"You and Sofia…" Her grip tightened around the steering wheel. "How long have you been together?"

"I saw them kissing," Abby piped up from the backseat.

"Shut up, Abby."

"Don't talk to your sister that way. Answer my question."

I glared at Abby as she stuck her tongue out at me. "We started dating a couple of weeks before prom."

My mother gulped before firing her next question. "Did you sleep together on the night of prom?"

Way to get straight to the point. "No, Mom." I clenched my jaw. "Well, yes, we spent the night together in the same room, but nothing happened."

"She's trouble, Ben."

"See? There it is. That's why we kept it from you, because we knew you'd react this way. You've always been overprotective of me, Mom… and Sofia doesn't need to deal with being rejected by you."

"You don't know her."

"She's my best friend and now she's my girlfriend. I know her far better than you ever will. And if you had bothered to spend time with her over the past eight years, you would know what an incredible person she is. Dad did."

Anger flared in my mother's eyes. "Your father knew?"

"Yes. We didn't tell him. He just knew."

"What if she ends up like her mother, Ben?"

"That's a low blow, Mom. Sofia's nothing like her crazy mother."

Amelia smiled bitterly. "You didn't know Camilla. You never met her. She was just like Sofia. Beautiful, sweet, charming, soft-spoken… They both have this arresting way about them, like they're oblivious to the effect they have on others. Look at what happened to Camilla, Ben. Carted off by her own husband, never to be seen again."

"Sofia's not going to end up that way."

"Go ahead and tell yourself that." My mother stepped on the brakes and I was relieved that we were already home.

I jumped out of the vehicle, eager to get as far away from my mother as possible. I raced to the front door and up the stairs and went right to Sofia's room.

I drew a breath when I saw her lying on the bed, eyes shut. She stirred slightly. I was immediately beside her, climbing on the bed and holding her hand. I slipped my arm beneath her shoulder in order to lift her head over the pillow. The motion caused her pillow to move. I caught sight of something beneath. Curiosity sparked, but Sofia's eyes opened and the moment they fell on me, she had my full attention.

I hated the way she was looking at me. A thousand apologies were in her eyes and I dreaded the reason.

"Sofia… what happened?"

"Vivienne," she gasped.

Vivienne. It took several seconds before it registered who Vivienne was. *The princess of vampires. Derek's sister.* I stared at Sofia, feeling as if she'd just betrayed me. *Why on earth would Vivienne leave The Shade and seek out Sofia?* Fears of losing Sofia began to overwhelm me.

"Why would you be anywhere alone with her, Sofia? What were you thinking?"

"She begged to speak with me."

"Why?"

Sofia licked her lips with hesitation in her eyes. "The hunters have her."

Good riddance then. I looked to Sofia for a trace of victory at the news. Instead, it was as if someone she loved dearly had just died. "Isn't this good news?"

"She's my friend. I'm worried about her." Sofia slowly rose from the bed, sitting on the edge of it, one hand brushing over her forehead. "The idea of what the hunters are going to do to her terrifies me."

A friend? That she would call The Shade's princess a friend was a slap to my face. "What did Vivienne say to you, Sofia?"

Sofia paused. "She was asking me to go back to The Shade."

"She *what*?"

"Ben…"

My eyes grew wide. "Sofia, you're not considering this, are you?"

"This room is suffocating. I need space to think." Sofia got off the bed. "I'm going out for a walk."

"You're not going anywhere, Sofia. We're going to talk about this."

"No, Ben. We're not. Not now at least."

She twisted the doorknob, opened the door and walked

away, leaving me stunned. Half of me wanted to run after her and drag her back, when my father peeked in. "Looks like she's up. Told you there was nothing to worry about."

Nothing to worry about? My dad always had a way of making light of things. I guessed I'd inherited my penchant for avoiding problems from him. "What happened to Sofia, Dad? Why was she unconscious?"

"I don't know." He shrugged. "I found her in a coffee shop with that friend of hers, who was murmuring something while holding Sofia's hands. I approached and suddenly the other girl had some kind of seizure and Sofia lost consciousness. We went to the hospital and they released Sofia, saying she just needs some rest."

"And her *friend?*"

"Didn't think to check on her. Have you talked to Sofia? Did she tell you anything?"

She didn't tell me enough. "Yeah… she says she just needs to take a walk."

"Well, it's probably best to give her some space. And Ben?"

"Yes?"

"What really happened when you disappeared… The day will come when you have to talk about it. I understand the desire to run from it, but with things like this happening, I'm beginning to wonder if…"

"I'm fine, Dad. Sofia's fine."

"All right then. Good night, Ben."

"Good night, Dad."

I was left standing there, not certain what I was supposed to do. Then I remembered how something stashed beneath Sofia's pillow had caught my attention. Giving in to my curious nature, I went to see what she had hidden there and immediately wished I hadn't.

Other than rip me apart, all it did was seal my decision. *I've had enough. I'm going to locate the hunters first thing tomorrow. Either she's with me or she's not.*

Chapter 30: Sofia

A cool breeze carried strands of my hair in the air as I took a stroll along the concrete sidewalks of the suburban neighborhood we lived in. Row upon row of the identical-looking villas completed the subdivision. All the homes looked the same on the outside, but were most likely radically different on the inside.

Sometimes, that's the way it is with people. You think you can tell what they are based on the patterns you see, but when you take a look inside, they're nothing like you expect them to be.

That was how it was with Vivienne. Of course, I'd never really understood her. She was always cold and aloof toward me while I was back at The Shade. It wasn't that she disliked me. She just seemed indifferent, like I wasn't deserving of her time, nor of Derek's.

Then she'd allowed me a peek inside her mind by sharing with me memories from her past, and I knew that I would never see her in the same way again. It was unnerving how much she feared the hunters. *That's why she was acting so strangely. She probably sensed them. And yet she stayed. She risked everything just to convince me to go back to The Shade.*

I still had memories of the night Derek had woken up, how fond they appeared to be of each other. My gut clenched at how Derek would receive the news of Vivienne having been taken by the hunters. I found it even more disturbing to think of what the hunters had in store for her.

It was too much to take in and as I tucked my hands inside the pockets of the hoodie I had on—the one that had Ben's jersey number eight on it—I kept thinking of what was best for Derek.

I meandered throughout the neighborhood, wondering what to do, until my feet finally led me back to the house that had sheltered me for eight years. Seated on the steps leading to its front door, Ben waited for me. When he saw me approaching, he raised his eyes and I knew that I had hurt him deeply.

"Ben..." I took a step toward him and saw what he had clutched in his hands. My heart sank. "I can explain."

"You don't have to." He stood up and handed me the items stashed under my pillow.

He held my shoulders and kissed me on the forehead. "I'm leaving at dawn to find the hunters. If I matter at all to you, you *will* join me. If you don't, then I'll take it as goodbye."

"Ben, don't do this." Tears began to fall from my eyes. I couldn't bear the thought of losing him.

He wiped the tears away with his thumbs, held my waist and pulled me against him before once again claiming my lips—gently at first then becoming rougher, hungrier, more demanding as the kiss went on. I gasped when our lips parted and drew a breath when his gaze fixed on my lips, still throbbing from his kiss.

"An ultimatum, Rose Red. This time, the choice I'm giving you is clear." He glanced bitterly at the items I was clutching. "You're either with him or you're with me."

He left me standing by the front steps. Tears blurred my eyes as I looked at what I was holding. The Polaroid shot Corrine had sent me—the one with Derek's eyes on me—and a sketchbook filled with page after page of the likeness of the vampire who still held me captive.

I was overcome by exhaustion. I'd been a fool to think I could send out applications to colleges and move on with my life as if The Shade had never happened. I was tired of Ben and his ultimatum and all the pressure he was putting on me. Most of all, I was tired of feeling guilty over the fact that I wanted to go back to The Shade—if only to see Derek again.

In many ways, Vivienne's disappearance and Ben's ultimatum pushed me over to Derek's side of the fence. I questioned my sanity even as I returned to my bedroom and packed a bag. I'd accomplished what had never been done before. I'd escaped The Shade and here I was going right back to it.

And yet peace that transcended all understanding—peace that I hadn't experienced since leaving The Shade—enveloped me the moment I made my decision to go back.

It made no sense, but it felt right. I smiled as I packed the last few belongings I had that were precious enough to take with me to The Shade. I checked the clock mounted on the wall. It was close to midnight. If I wanted to follow the path Vivienne set out for me, I didn't have much time.

I sneaked into Ben's bedroom. I had no choice but to take the keys to his truck. It was the only way I could reach the rendezvous point in time. I snuck in only to find him wide awake. He took one look at what I was wearing and knew that I'd already made my choice.

"Ben…" The words came out broken.

"Are you sure this is what you want?"

"I'm sorry, Ben."

"The key to the truck is in my jeans' pocket."

I was surprised that he would help me, but I saw it for what it was. It was him letting go and supporting me in my decision even when it hurt him.

At that point, no matter how confident I was that I was making the right decision, it felt painful.

"Ben..."

"Don't, Sofia. Just go."

Tears moistened my eyes as I fished the key out of his pocket. "I'm going to text you where I parked it. I..."

"I guess Alyssa was right. Rose Red really does end up with the Beast."

His words cut deep, but they failed to deter me. "Take comfort in knowing that the Beast turned out to be not much of a Beast after all."

I got silence as a response. I moved toward the door. "I hope you know how much you mean to me, how much I love you. I hope you know that you will always be my best friend."

"That's what hurts the most, Sofia... knowing that I will always be *nothing but* your best friend."

I was beginning to choke with tears so I hurried toward the door, unwilling to break down in front of him.

I still had one favor to ask before going my way. I knew I didn't have the right to ask it of him, but I felt obliged to.

For Vivienne's sake. "When you reach the hunters, Ben, do me a favor. Please find Vivienne. And try to make sure they don't harm her."

Ben's response was bone-chilling. "Don't count on it. I couldn't care less how much they make her suffer."

I turned his way. His face was enveloped by shadows. Darkness loomed in his eyes. My heart went out to him as I shuddered at what The Shade had turned him into. "You're better than that, Ben. You have no idea who Vivienne Novak is and if you can't believe in her, believe in me. There's good in her, so please, if there's anything you can do to help her..."

"Goodbye, Sofia."

Sadness weighed heavily on me as I nodded and replied, "Goodbye, Ben."

Finally, I left, sensing with deep sorrow that it might be the last time I would see Ben again.

Over than an hour later, I had driven myself to a secluded area of LA's Santa Monica beach. I left the truck and walked a few minutes along the beach. I soon spotted a familiar face walking toward me. *Kyle.*

"Sofia!" he exclaimed as he pulled me in for a friendly embrace. "I was beginning to think you weren't going to come. Is Vivienne with you?"

I shook my head. "The hunters have taken her."

His face fell and fear was in his eyes. "I have no idea how the prince is going to take that."

"I guess we'll find out." I smiled bitterly.

He took my bag and sheepishly smiled at me as he lifted a syringe to my neck. "You know the drill."

I rolled my eyes. "Fine."

The truth was that Vivienne's memories told me exactly where The Shade was, a memory of its location circled on a map, one of the greatest secrets of The Shade. It was a sign of the trust Vivienne had placed in me, a gesture I could not take lightly.

So for the third time, a vampire stuck a syringe into my neck. As the sedative lured me to unconsciousness, I allowed myself a small smile. It felt like I was about to go home.

Chapter 31: Derek

I was at the training grounds. Xavier, who had become significantly better with the sword after the daily training regimen I'd put him through, had just made a slice in my shoulder. My wound was healing when I was gripped by a sick feeling inside, accompanied by the urge to find out where my sister was.

"You do realize that the hunters and perhaps the other covens are now equipped with guns and not swords, right?" Xavier asked. "Why do we have to fight using *these*?" He raised his sword as I straightened to my full height.

"Agility. Strength. The honor of looking your opponents in the eye before you wound them. Sword fights aren't for cowards," I explained, still occupied by an urge to find Vivienne.

"Honor?" He raised one brow. "Is that what we call it now?" He positioned himself for another round. "Perhaps you mean *horror*."

With my opponent poised for another fight, I backed down for the first time.

"Tired, Novak?"

I scoffed. "Far from it. I just can't seem to get my thoughts away from Vivienne." *Among others...* My hunger for Ashley was far from satiated and she never strayed far from my thoughts.

"Vivienne? Why?"

It was no secret that Xavier had many times tried to woo my twin and had been humiliated by her rejection.

"I don't know. I haven't seen her in days."

Not since I issued the command that will pave a way to another human culling.

From behind Xavier, Liana Hendry approached. One look at her worried, grief-stricken amber gold eyes told me a story. *Something's wrong. Something's very, very wrong.*

She stopped along the boundary of the circle Xavier and I were standing within.

"Liana," I called to my sister's closest friend. "Is something wrong? Has something happened to Vivienne?"

It wasn't a secret that Vivienne and I often sensed when something happened to the other. The last time I'd felt this way was when Borys Maslen had held her captive. It took days before she was returned to us and she'd never breathed a word to anyone—save for Liana, who was the only person privy to her soft whispers.

Liana drew a short breath before shifting her weight on the gravel. "I fear she might have been taken by the hunters."

Her words were a dagger struck through my heart and twisted. Breath came in heavy pants. Fear I hadn't thought I would ever again feel enveloped me. The thought of what they were putting Vivienne through in order to discover the secrets of The Shade sent dizziness coursing through my body.

"Derek, I tried to talk her out of it, but you know her. Once she sets her mind to something…"

"How did this happen?"

"She left the island to go look for Sofia."

My head was spinning. "Why would she…" I paused, knowing full well. *Vivienne sought out Sofia for me.*

"She told me she would send word at a certain hour if no harm has come her way. She told me even before going that she feared getting caught by the hunters, and…"

"And yet she still went." *What caused you to have the sudden desire to die, Vivienne?* "How was she to send word?"

"She procured a phone from Corrine. Its signals penetrate the shield provided by the witch's spell."

The protective spell keeping the island secret blocked any communication going in and out of the island.

"Corrine knew of her plans?"

Liana shook her head. "The witch rarely meddles with our personal affairs."

She meddled with Sofia. "When was Vivienne supposed to contact you?"

"Hours ago."

"*Hours* ago? And you thought to tell me just now?"

"I was hoping that something else caused her delay."

The back of my hand crashed against Liana's cheek, causing her collapse to the gravel beneath us.

"Derek!" Xavier rushed to her side.

"It's fine," Liana assured him as he helped her up.

"We're going to find my sister. We're going to scour all the cities of all the nations of the world if we have to. I won't rest until she's safe back here."

"Go against the hunters?" Xavier's muscles stiffened. "That's suicide and you know it. You're going to kill us all if you go out hunting for her."

"I fought all those years and shed that much blood for one reason alone: to save my family! Where are they? Do you see any of them now? None of them surround me! Losing

Vivienne robs me of all purpose!"

"If the hunters truly have her, then she's as good as dead, Derek."

Xavier spoke truth, but I was not ready to hear it. I lunged forward, throwing my full weight at him, causing us both to fall to the ground.

"Derek! Stop it!" Liana cried out.

I pinned Xavier to the ground with my knees holding down his arms while I assaulted his face with one punch after another. Liana tried to stop me from behind, ripping my shirt, but my elbow hit her abdomen, knocking her out of breath.

I had no idea how many punches I threw and how long I punished a comrade for a crime he had no part in committing, but by the time Cameron arrived, grabbed a fistful of my hair and hit me in the face, Xavier's face was already a bloody mess.

"All of us care about her!" Cameron shouted. "Do *not* punish your own people for her loss!"

Loss. The thought that I'd lost Vivienne was too much to accept. I let out a blood-curdling scream as I rose to my feet, unbidden tears rushing down my cheeks. I couldn't stand being around them and sought retreat in my sister's villa.

As expected, it was empty. She never kept slaves in her home and she hated having guards around, claiming that she was capable of protecting herself. My sister enjoyed her solitude. *How could I not have noticed she'd been gone?*

I made my way to her greenhouse, her favorite place in the world, a place where life thrived even when death surrounded us. The moment I entered it, I crumpled to the ground, hands fisting in my hair as I gave in to dark possibilities.

My sister would take everything they threw her way to protect the island. They would make every effort to break her and they were going to fail. Their failure would be paid for at an excruciating price by the person I would give my life to protect.

The night had never felt as dark as it did as I sat on the floor of Vivienne's greenhouse, mourning her loss. I had no inkling of how many hours I spent there. It felt like days. At first I still hoped that Vivienne would walk in unharmed. I fooled myself that her footsteps were gracing the hardwood floors outside. At some point, however, denial gave way to reality and, inevitably, to anger. *Someone is to blame for what happened to Vivienne.*

Only one name came to mind. Only one name was deserving of punishment for my sister's demise. *Sofia.*

Rage I hadn't felt in hundreds of years consumed me and for the first time in a long time, I switched off all guilt in order to give in to the monster I'd become. I was going to make Sofia pay.

I was going to punish the people she cared for. *Ashley... then Paige... then Rosa.* I lost no time in satiating the hunger that had been begging for days.

It didn't take long for me to go from Vivienne's penthouse to Kyle's much smaller residence. He would be at the port—on watch duty with Sam. I wanted to fight them in order to get to Ashley, but she would have to do. I broke down the door.

"Ashley!" I screamed. "Ashley!"

I sensed her fear. Her pulse raced, her heart doubling its beat. *That's right. Be afraid. Be very afraid.* Outside the windows of the small receiving room I was standing in, her form ran along a glass-covered walkway. I smirked. I didn't intend to prolong the chase. I wanted her and I was going to have her.

Lightning speed carried me from where I stood to where she was running. I pinned her against a wall, one hand gripping her jaw, the other grabbing her hair until she gasped in pain. I tilted her head to one side so that her neck would be exposed for me to sink my teeth into. With her bare neck right in front of me, I didn't have even an ounce of hesitation before taking a bite and drinking deep. She screamed, pleading for me to stop. That only fuelled the fire my sister's loss had sparked within me.

I drank until I was approaching her death. I stopped. Claudia was right. Rage gave us control. Ashley was barely conscious when I slung her limp form over my shoulder. I was going to prolong her suffering.

Within minutes, we were back in the penthouse and I pinned her face down on the bed. During her struggle, my claws had ripped through the back of her dress. My eyes widened in both horror and delight when I saw a hawk tattooed on her lower back—the mark of a hunter. I pulled her blonde locks to the side as I leaned over to whisper to her ear. "I had no idea you were one of them. Revenge is going to be sweet."

Weak from the blood loss, all she could do was whimper beneath me. Straddling her hips, I was on the verge of biting into her flesh once again when the bedroom door opened behind me.

I turned around to find the person I least expected.

Sofia.

Chapter 32: Sofia

The first thing I noticed upon swinging the door open was the symbol of a hawk on Derek's back—below his right shoulder. Vivienne's memories proved accurate and for a split second I stood mesmerized.

It wasn't until he turned toward me that I realized what he was doing. The blood on the neck of the unconscious young woman made me faint with shock.

My cheeks drained of blood as I leant against the doorpost for support. "Derek, how could you…" My voice trailed off when I saw the way he was looking at me—as if I were a ghost, a ghost that he loathed.

A deep, heart-wrenching growl came from his lips and

within seconds, he had me against his bedroom wall, his hips supporting my weight, his left hand gripping my right arm and keeping it pressed against the wall while his right hand held my neck.

"How did you get back here?" he hissed.

History was repeating itself: the predatory glare in his steely blue eyes, the chill of his breath, the helplessness and vulnerability, how small and fragile I felt jammed between his body and the wall... It'd all been done before, but this time, I wasn't the same girl. I was no longer a scared, whimpering victim trembling beneath his touch.

"This isn't you, Derek." It was a soft whisper, but not lacking in conviction. I gently wrapped my fingers around the wrist of the hand he had over my throat.

The muscles of his jaw twitched at my touch. He looked murderous and yet severely conflicted. His grip tightened, threatening to choke me.

"Choose your words well, because they might be your last. How did you find your way back here?"

I kept my hand on his wrist, my fingers caressing his skin. "Vivienne showed me the way."

The haze in his eyes cleared and the darkness lifted to once again show me a spark of his bright blue gaze. He stepped away from me, pulling his wrist away from my touch as if it burned him. "How did she..."

His question faded into the background the moment I saw a wooden stake clutched by two trembling hands rise in the air, poised to stab Derek in the back, right through his heart.

"Ashley? No!"

I pushed Derek to the side and he actually budged, perhaps more out of surprise rather than my strength.

The wooden stake Ashley meant for him dug into my shoulder.

I screamed in pain the moment my flesh tore and blood rushed out. I clasped the stake. The throbbing pain made my head spin.

Ashley's eyes grew wide. "Oh God, no! Sofia!"

I looked up, only to watch with horror as Derek approached her. The stake had come from his personal stock. Each of us had one. He'd taught us how to kill a vampire before I left The Shade. I remembered him warning us that if we ever used it against him, he would kill us himself.

When his hands rose in the air, poised to hold her by the neck, I gasped. He was about to break her neck.

"Derek, don't."

His one hand grabbed a fistful of her blonde hair while the other gripped her jaw tightly. "She was about to kill me."

"She was defending me, for Christ's sake!"

I drew a breath when he pulled her head back and his

hand closed tighter over her jaw.

"She's a hunter."

The stake in my shoulder was agony, but I could not survive seeing Derek kill a dear friend right in front of me. Desperate, I staggered forward and gently held his wrist. "Please."

He pushed my hand away and sent me tumbling to the floor. To my relief, Derek threw Ashley toward the direction of the bed. *Not very gentle, but at least she'll live.* She fell to the bed face forward. I saw the hawk on her lower back. Hers was a tattoo and not an iron brand like Derek's but it was the exact same symbol. *The hawk... what does it mean?*

Derek knelt on the floor in front of me. His jaw locked when he saw the blood gushing from my shoulder. "This will hurt."

Before I could react, he pulled the stake out in one quick motion. I cried out, certain that I would faint, but I wasn't given that reprieve.

I wished that I could shut down my senses, but *awareness* sometimes felt like a curse I would forever have to deal with.

"You have a punctured ligament and a displaced shoulder," Derek informed me upon closer inspection. "I'll need to put your shoulder in place before healing you."

He pulled my shoulder in place with one strong thrust. I bit my lip until it hurt, refusing to scream. Seemingly satisfied, Derek stood up and headed for the bed. Ashley moved away until her back hit the headboard. Derek glared at her but relief washed over both of us when he turned to face me again, retrieving a Swiss knife from his pocket. I knew what it was for.

"No. I don't want to drink your blood."

"Why the hell not?" He cut a gash in his palm anyway and shoved his hand in front of my face. "Drink, Sofia." He sounded more authoritarian than ever before.

I sealed my lips shut as I glared at him. It was my act of defiance. It was my way of telling him that I wasn't back at The Shade to be his slave.

"You're trying my patience." He withdrew his hand and looked at me as if I was the most exasperating creature he'd ever laid eyes on. "Whose blood do you want to drink then? Or would you rather just bleed to death? If it's the latter, you might as well just let me feed on you. That way, your death could at least satisfy my hunger."

Derek was making no effort to hide his irritation. He gulped at the sight of my blood, and I wondered how much self-control it was taking not to taste it.

"Help Ashley first."

Blood was still trickling from Ashley's neck and she looked pale as a ghost. The expression on her face made it clear how horrified she was by the idea of drinking Derek's blood.

"You're joking."

I shook my head. I kept one hand on my wound, applying pressure to it.

He muttered several curses under his breath before grabbing me by my uninjured arm and pulling me up to a standing position. The blood rush made me too dizzy to stand on my own and I fell against him. He half-carried, half-dragged me to the bed, sitting me none too gently on its edge before shoving his palm toward Ashley.

"Drink," he ordered her. "Make it quick. Sofia's losing a lot of blood."

Ashley gave him a murderous look before holding his wrist and fingers with each hand. Then she drank. The pink returned to Ashley's skin, a contrast from the pale white it had been only seconds ago.

The bite marks on her neck weren't closing yet. "Why isn't she healing?"

"She is," Derek assured me as he pulled his palm away. The gash on his palm was already closing. "She takes more time to heal than you."

"Why?"

"I haven't the slightest clue." He took out the Swiss knife and cut another gash in the same palm. "Your turn." He offered his hand up to me. "Now drink."

I grumbled as I took his hand in mine. Amusement flickered in his eyes once I started drinking his blood.

"Stubborn girl."

It took half a minute of drinking before my punctured ligament repaired itself. The wound was just about to close when Kyle showed up by the door. He had a smile on his face. He was most likely expecting that I'd had a joyous reunion with Derek. His smile faded away, a pained expression replacing it when he saw Ashley, in her state of disarray, inside the room.

"Take her to the Cells," Derek commanded. "She will stand trial in front of the council tomorrow for attempting to kill me."

Kyle's eyes grew wide. "Of course, your highness." He approached Ashley and gently helped her up. I noticed the pain in his eyes when he saw the bite marks on her neck.

"Wait." I could feel Derek's frustrated glare on me as I stood up. Ignoring him, I rushed to Ashley and embraced her, water moistening my eyes. I wanted to reassure her, but I was at a loss for words.

She was stiff against my embrace, refusing to return the gesture. "Now you return?"

"I couldn't stay away even if I wanted to," I whispered back.

We pulled away from each other. She looked at me coldly,

her expression far too close to hatred. Unnerved, I shifted my gaze toward Derek. "Let her put on something warm first. It's cold there." I could almost feel the chill of waking up in the dungeons.

Derek gave it some thought. He looked annoyed but gave Kyle a curt nod. "See it done."

They both left the room. That left me with Derek and all the unanswered questions between us. Even with my back to him, I could feel his eyes on me. Just being in the same room with Derek caused a wave of unfamiliar sensations to course through my veins. My breathing grew heavy as he approached. When his large hands on my waist pulled my back against him, his breath chilling the nape of my neck, breathing proved to be quite a task.

"You're here."

"Is that a good thing?"

"You tell me."

All of it was too much to handle. I'd been pining for him since I left the island. I hadn't known what to expect upon returning, but I certainly hadn't expected to find Derek about to murder one of my friends. His hands on me, holding me, his lips brushing the back of my neck, breathing my scent in… it was all too much in too little time.

"Do me a favor, Sofia." His voice broke through my silence. "I don't know if you can, but please, for a few hours… try to forget what you just saw. Forget what just happened. If only for a short time, be with me. *Please.*" In a choked, husky voice, he admitted, "I missed you so much."

His plea gave me the escape I needed from all the thoughts plaguing me. One emotion came to the forefront and that was the deep longing to be in his arms. I took his hands from my waist and wrapped his strong arms around me.

"Are you still the man I left behind, Derek?" I dared to ask.

His arms around me tightened, clinging to me. "No."

My heart dropped. I hadn't expected him to be so blunt. "Then who are you?"

His lips pressed against the back of my head before he held me by the shoulders and forced me to face him. Behind his blue eyes, I saw a galaxy of questions unanswered, doubts unsettled, guilt and shame deeply felt.

"Who do you want me to be, Sofia?"

I saw so much anguish in his handsome face, I could barely comprehend his question. At that moment, he wasn't the prince of The Shade, the strong and powerful Derek Novak. The man who stood before me was wearied by the daily battles he was fighting. He was a broken being, trembling beneath my touch. He bowed his head, his forehead pressing against mine as I ran my hands over his muscular arms.

"I want you to be *you*, Derek."

We both began to sway gently to music I couldn't hear, but knew was playing inside his mind. His hands engulfed my waist as he led me into a dance. We were trying to return to the way we used to be, dancing to music that only he could hear.

When his lips found mine, however, the pain in my heart was too much to contend with and I couldn't help but step away from him. "I can't do this. I'm sorry."

"Don't be." He shook his head. "I understand."

He looked at me with longing that seemed to dwarf the longing I felt for him. Intense. Consuming. Painful. I wanted to explain that I shied away from his touch not because I didn't want to be with him, but because I couldn't just turn a blind eye to what I had walked in on him doing.

"I'm going to win you back, Sofia."

I planted a gentle kiss on his cheek. "I don't understand why, but somehow… you never quite lost me."

Chapter 33: Derek

Seated on the edge of my bed, waiting for Sofia to emerge from the bathroom, I wondered if she had any idea how much her words meant to me.

You never lost me.

It was an admission that after everything that had happened, after everything she'd seen, she was still mine. It eclipsed Vivienne's disappearance, something that ought to make me feel guilty. However, all I felt was gratefulness that Sofia was back at The Shade with me. Not long before she arrived, I'd been hell bent on punishing her for being the reason behind my losing Vivienne. Now that she was here, everything inside me was screaming to atone for the things

I'd been doing since she left.

The bathroom door opened and she emerged wearing a towel around her slender form, her long auburn hair still dripping wet. I caught my breath. *Is she really so oblivious to the effect she has on me?*

"I can't find the hair dryer."

I frowned. "I had it removed." *Along with everything that reminded me of you.*

Her nose wrinkled. "I'll have to towel-dry then."

She headed for the bed and picked up the clothes she'd laid out over it before she went for her bath. Her proximity was testing all my self-control. Reminding me of how comfortable we used to be around each other, she went straight to the walk-in closet to get dressed. It didn't take long for her to reappear, wearing a red button-down blouse over tight jeans, combing her hair with her fingers. As she came closer, her eyes rose to meet mine and she took a seat next to me.

She sighed heavily. "What now, Derek Novak?"

Unable to keep my hands away from her, I ran my palm from her knee cap to her thigh while I brushed her still-wet hair away from her face. "I don't know. I'm honestly still trying to figure out if you're really here or if this is all just a dream."

She held the back of the hand I was using to caress her

face, as if relishing my touch. "Vivienne convinced me to come."

Though it was painful to hear her say my twin's name, it didn't have the infuriating effect I thought it should've. Having Sofia around made everything that was going on feel so much lighter, so much easier to bear.

Sofia must've noticed my unease, because her free hand squeezed the hand I had over her thigh.

"I'm so sorry, Derek. I know how much she meant to you."

"I don't know if she's still alive or not. Either way, I'm going to make the hunters pay."

Her cheeks paled. "This cycle of vengeance between hunters and vampires… will it ever end?"

I withdrew from her touch, running one hand through my hair and fisting the other over my knee. "You can't talk me out of this, Sofia. Vivienne is too precious for me not to avenge her."

"I'm not trying to talk you out of anything, Derek. I doubt that I could make you do anything you don't want to do."

I held back the urge to scoff. "You underestimate yourself, Sofia. You've consistently been able to make me do things I wouldn't normally do."

She chuckled. "Oh yeah? Like what?"

"I just spared Ashley's life, didn't I?"

She fell silent at the mention of her friend. My gut clenched at the thought of what I'd been doing when Sofia walked in on me.

I brushed my thumb over her lightly freckled cheekbone. Her cheeks once again blushed red the moment I touched her. "I still can't believe that you came back."

"Vivienne made quite a compelling case."

"Tell me what happened, Sofia. Between you and Vivienne."

"Could we talk somewhere else? Please? I look around here and all I can think of is..." She paused.

Ashley. I nodded and rose from the bed. She took my hand as we walked out of the room. "Where do you want to go?" I asked when we reached the living room.

"The Sun Room maybe?" She eyed me hopefully.

My heart broke as I told her the truth. "I had it destroyed and stripped to a blank room."

"Why?"

"It reminded me too much of you. I thought I'd never get you back, Sofia. I wanted to forget."

She paused, disappointed, before asking, "Did it work? Did you forget?"

"I couldn't no matter how I tried."

"Good." She gave me one curt nod. "You should never

forget me."

Something akin to delight sparked in her eyes when she saw my smile. To my surprise she threw herself at me and pressed her lips against mine. I was frozen with shock for a few seconds, just enjoying her lips on mine, before I wrapped my arms around her waist and lifted her up so she wouldn't have to stand on her tiptoes. I returned her kiss with fervor, releasing all the pent-up longing I had for her. I began walking forward until I had her backed up against a wall, my hands beginning to move along her waist, her hips and her thighs.

By the time she pulled away from me, we were both panting for breath.

"What was that?" I asked in between breaths.

"I couldn't help it. You shouldn't have kissed me before I left The Shade. I've wanted the taste of your lips on mine from the moment I woke up on that damn shore in Cancun," she admitted, her cheeks flushed pink, her lips swollen red. "I'm sorry."

"Don't apologize. You can kiss me anytime you want."

She bit her lip and grinned. "Anytime?"

I smirked and nodded. To my surprise, she pushed me back and placed her feet back on the floor. "It's so hard to think straight when I'm around you!"

I fought the urge to laugh when she hit me on the

shoulder, wincing when she felt more pain than she had inflicted.

"Have you gone mad, Sofia?"

"I'm *supposed* to be mad. After what I saw, after what you did… You attacked Ashley. It took me weeks to finish the Sun Room and you destroyed my masterpiece in a span of a few days." She hit me again. She looked adorable. "I should be *flaming* mad."

"And I'm assuming that this is you being *not* mad?"

She began pacing the floor in front of me as she shook her head. "I'm not mad, but I should be."

"Why aren't you?"

She stopped pacing, heaved one deep sigh and stared at me with burning emerald eyes. "Because it's you. How can I get mad at you when you're standing right there looking like *that,* distracting me?"

I began chuckling. "I'm distracting you from being mad at me?"

She pouted before a giggle escaped her lips. She'd been back only a short while and she'd already gotten me to laugh and smile more than I had during the whole time she was away. In that short span of time, she'd managed to make me forget the pressures weighing down on me.

I cupped her cheeks with both hands. "I adore you, Sofia Claremont." I placed a gentle kiss on her forehead, breathing out when her arms snaked around my waist.

She buried her face against my chest. "Let's just get out of here."

"Lead the way."

We left the penthouse and meandered through the woods, enjoying the silence and the privacy. We were silent for the most part, until I found the guts to ask her the question that had been weighing on my mind.

"What did my twin tell you to make you come back here?"

"We were at Ben's championship game. Football. Vivienne arrived and asked me to talk to her."

The mention of her best friend made a sick feeling settle in the pit of my stomach. The idea that she had been with him the whole time introduced me to an emotion I felt only with Sofia: jealousy.

"We met up at a nearby coffee shop and Vivienne told me that I needed to come back here, that you needed me. She told me that you were headed for a dark path."

"That's it?"

Sofia hesitated and then nodded. "That was the gist of it."

It felt like she was holding something back. "And that's what got you to come back? Because she said I needed you?"

She stopped walking, her eyes focused on the dirt as she leaned one hand against a sycamore tree. "I guess you could say I came back because I was hoping it was true. The fact that it was Vivienne of all people who came to convince me meant a lot. I don't think she was one of my biggest fans."

I smiled bitterly. "You don't know my sister. She thought very highly of you." Vivienne had believed she was important enough to sacrifice herself to the hunters for. I wasn't about to take that sacrifice lightly.

"I know her more than you think." Sofia went on with her story as we continued our aimless walk through the woods. "Just before the hunters arrived, I think she sensed it. She did something to me. I'm not entirely sure what, but she said something about sharing memories with me and showing me the way back here. And then she held me and the memories just came."

"She shared her memories with you?"

Sofia nodded. "I know it sounds crazy, but it's the truth."

"I don't question that you're telling the truth. I'm just surprised that she would risk doing it to a human. Transferring of memories has been known to leave recipients in a coma. The human brain simply can't handle the sudden influx of information. The human subconscious wasn't made to contain and absorb the memories of others."

"I passed out after she did it." Sofia shrugged. "I saw the hunters take her away before blacking out."

Silence followed, neither of us knowing what to say. We

just walked, relishing each other's company. Enveloped by the darkness of night, I put my hands in my jeans pockets and asked her a much lighter question.

"What was the sun like?"

She smiled at the memory. "Warm. Hot. Everything the moon isn't. Our first few days back in Cancun, Ben and I couldn't stay out of the sun."

Ben again. Jealousy reared its ugly head once again. "What became of him?" I dared ask.

"I'd rather not talk about him if you don't mind."

I nodded.

The rest of our walk continued in silence until a familiar sight came into view.

"The Sanctuary!" Sofia exclaimed, excitement lighting up her eyes as she bounded forward. "I want to see Corrine!"

The Sanctuary, befitting its name, was located in the southwest of the island. The white marble structure with its large round pillars and domed roof had originally been built to honor and house Cora, and later became home to every other witch who succeeded her. One of its chambers had also served as my mausoleum during my four-century slumber. Surrounding the structure were lush gardens, complete with a labyrinth, a gazebo and a fountain.

When Corrine saw Sofia, delight showed in her eyes, but she didn't seem the least bit surprised.

"Sofia!" she exclaimed. "It's good to have you back."

It was one of the few times I remembered seeing Corrine smile.

She gave me a curt nod. "Prince."

Sofia's hands found mine. "I'd like to speak with Corrine privately."

"Of course. Go ahead. I don't mind." *Liar.* I minded. I found myself alone, sitting on a bench by the fountain, waiting for what felt like hours.

The Sanctuary's pure white marble façade glowed under the light of a full moon. It was quite a sight to see, but the price paid for such a lavish structure lessened its value in my eyes. *Here at The Shade, everything beautiful and worthwhile comes at a price.*

I'd already been there for what felt like an eternity, so seeing Sofia walk along the stone pathway leading to the gazebo was a relief. Sofia locked arms with Corrine as the older woman spoke to her. I could only guess what they were talking about. Seeing them walk side by side brought about a strange nostalgia, largely due to Corrine's uncanny resemblance to her ancestor, Cora. It felt like I was watching two of the most important women in my life conversing with each other.

Sofia's emerald gaze found me. She nodded and thanked Corrine, who gave me a quick, harried glance before heading back indoors.

Finally. I stood up and approached her. The moment we reached each other, she took my hand and held it tight. We walked forward in silence, away from the Sanctuary, and headed for the woods that would eventually lead to the Vale, the island's town.

Illuminated by the moonlight, she was a vision to behold. Her eyes were downcast. She stopped walking and made me face her with a squeeze of her hand.

"Your few hours are over. We have a lot to talk about."

Chapter 34: Sofia

Walking back through the woods, along the familiar gravel pathway that led from the Sanctuary to the Vale, I was bothered by the things Vivienne had told me about Derek veering towards his dark side. I'd witnessed that firsthand. The conversation I'd had with Corrine further heightened my anxiety over Derek—how he seemed to be gearing up for war, the census, the ban on all further abductions…

I didn't know what to make of all the things I'd been told. *What impact did Vivienne think I could have here?*

My eyes were beginning to moisten with tears as I looked up at Derek. I needed to talk about what had happened. I wanted to understand him again, because the time I'd spent away from The Shade felt like a rift between us.

"Where do you want to begin?" He sounded nervous.

"Ashley… you were about to…" I choked.

His gaze left me. He said nothing.

"Vivienne told me that you attacked Ashley in the Sun Room."

His eyes darkened and once again focused on mine. Something had triggered his ire and he walked forward until he backed me up against the trunk of a giant willow tree. "*Vivienne* is why I did it. When I heard that the hunters had my sister and that you were the reason she left The Shade, I couldn't understand it. I couldn't understand why she risked her own life just to get you back here."

I swallowed. I didn't know how to respond to that. *I don't understand either. Not completely.* "I don't see how that justifies what you did to Ashley."

"I'm a *vampire,* Sofia. The only reason I was trying to control my impulse to kill Ashley after having fed on her was because she mattered to you. After I lost Vivienne because of you, I wanted to punish you. You weren't here, so I punished someone you cared about instead."

His reasoning made me reel with anger. I couldn't believe that he thought that was reason enough to harm a defenseless innocent. Unable to control my rage, I gave in to instinct and did the unthinkable.

I gave him the most defiant glare I could manage. "I'm here now, am I not? *I'm* the reason the hunters have your sister." Trembling, I loosened the top two buttons of my blouse and pulled my right sleeve down my shoulder.

"Sofia? What are you doing?" His voice sounded choked, his eyes wide.

I gathered my hair over my left shoulder and tilted my head so that my neck was exposed. His body tensed as his fists clenched when he realized what I was doing.

"Sofia…"

"Well? What are you waiting for, Derek? Drink. *I'm* the one you want to punish, right? Claim justice for Vivienne!"

The silence was electric as I stood before him.

His move.

My heart dropped when he pushed me backwards, pinning me against the tree. His right hand gripped my jaw, forcing my face to an angle that allowed him more access to my neck. I gasped and my eyes fell into a distant stare, not daring to look his way.

"You should know better than to provoke a vampire," he growled at me. His fangs came out, white teeth glimmering under the moon's light. He was taking me up on my challenge.

"I'm not provoking a vampire," I scoffed at him. *My move.* "I'm provoking *you*. Go ahead. Show me how much of the Derek I knew is lost to me."

The short gasp that escaped his lips told me that I'd gotten through to him. Fangs retracted and fingers painfully gripping my jaw loosened before he stepped away from me.

I'd gotten a major win, but the match wasn't over. I laid both palms on his chest and pushed him back. "Why do you stop? Who am I that you would spare me and not spare Ashley?" The questions came out in a rush and I emphasized each one with a push. "Had I been here, would you have done to me what you did to her? Would you have taken enough blood to lead me almost to the brink of unconsciousness? Would you have carried me to your bed and made me suffer while I lay there helpless? Would you have treated me the same way?"

"No! I wouldn't have!" He gripped me by the wrists to keep me from hitting him. Chills ran down my spine when I saw how he was looking at me. "I can't even bear the thought of doing to you what I did to her."

"Then how were you able to bear doing it to her?"

He looked away. His reason sounded pathetic. I knew it and he knew it. "I wasn't able to control myself."

I shook my head as I tried to get away from his grasp. "That's crap and you know it. I was with you for *months*. So were Ashley, Paige and Rosa. You never once touched us or brought harm to us. Don't tell me you can't control yourself,

Derek. Just don't."

I motioned to walk away, but he kept his death grip on my wrists.

"Let go," I hissed.

"No," he insisted. "You're coming with me."

The last thing I wanted was to go anywhere with him. At that point, I wanted to be alone to sort through the conflicting emotions that were driving me crazy around him.

But no. Despite my protests, he carried me in his arms and sped forward. I'd never quite got used to the lightning speed by which he travelled, but that was the least of my concerns, because when we stopped, I screamed with fright.

We were standing on top of one of the Crimson Fortress' towering walls. A mighty wind blew against us and the crash of the ocean waves on solid rock below was terrifying. I couldn't tell for sure but it looked like Derek was about to jump from the top of the wall to the boulders below.

"What do you think you're doing?" I screamed, clinging around his neck. "Where are you taking me?"

"I'm taking you to my sanctuary. Hold on tight."

Before I could even breathe a word of protest, he took the leap, plunging us both on a hundred-foot free fall down to the ragged cliffs below. The one thought on my mind as I clung to him for dear life was: *Derek Novak has lost his mind.*

CHAPTER 35: BEN

Leaving my family was one of the hardest things I'd ever had to do, but my path had been set the moment I woke up on the shores of Cancun the morning after our escape from The Shade. No matter how much I tried to go back to a normal life, all I could think about was vengeance.

Sofia was the last thread of hope I had, but as she walked away from me that night, it felt like everything had been robbed from me and I only had The Shade to blame.

Not long after Sofia left, I grabbed the bag I'd packed the night before and got out of my bed. My heart weighing heavily on me and a lump forming in my throat, I snuck into Abby's room first. I smiled upon seeing her pink, star-shaped night light and the way she was clinging to her stuffed animal, Colin. At her age, she still sucked her thumb when she slept. I approached her bed and twisted a tendril of her blonde hair with my forefinger. "I'll miss you, dwarfette."

I kicked myself for being so dramatic. It wasn't like the hunters were going to take me captive and keep me from ever seeing my family again, but I knew that the choice I was making was going to break my family's heart. My next stop was my parents' bedroom. I snuck a peek at them cuddled in their bed, a reminder of how in love they still were with each other after all those years—something I felt I could never have now that Sofia had left me. I slipped through the door and snuck inside the room, careful to be as quiet as I possibly could. I saw my dad's car keys above their drawers and took them. I took one last look at my parents and whispered, "I'm sorry."

I headed to the car and made the drive to the airport. I had no idea where to go or what to do. All I had was a name and a number and I was prepared to fly to any destination I was asked to go to.

Once I got to the LAX airport, I headed for the nearest coffee shop and ordered an overpriced cup of coffee. Seated on one of the plush couches, I finally found the guts to call the number that Eliza had given me.

"Here goes nothing," I muttered as I dialed the number.

"Hello?" a deep, gravelly voice answered.

"Hello. Is this Reuben?"

"Who wants to know?"

"I'm Ben Hudson. A girl named Eliza referred me to you." I paused, wondering to myself if I sounded crazy. "I want to join the hunters."

"Eliza?" There was a pause. The only sound was his heavy breathing. "Perfect. We're looking forward to meeting you, Ben. I was hoping you'd get in touch with us."

He was hoping? How would he even know I exist? "Great."

"Where are you?"

"At LAX."

"That won't do. One of our men will have a private plane waiting at Van Nuys Airport in three hours. Does that suit you?"

"Yes." I nodded. "Of course."

"See you soon, Ben."

I hung up and frowned, confused by the conversation. I took a sip of coffee and set it on the table before returning to the car. It didn't take long for me to reach the city limits of LA and get to Van Nuys, where private, chartered and small commercial aircraft flew.

I had arrived early, so I was waiting a while before a tall, lean man approached me. Tattoos crawled up his arms and his head was completely shaven.

"Are you Ben Hudson?" he asked.

"That would be me."

"I'm Fly. Ready to go?"

I nodded and he motioned for me to follow him to the tarmac where a private plane was already waiting. I was impressed upon seeing the jet's comfortable interior; white leather reclining seats, a large flatscreen television and a small bar were the first things to catch my eye.

"We'll get cleared to fly in a few minutes or so. Make yourself comfortable," Fly told me before motioning to go to the cabin.

About three hours into the flight, I walked up to the cockpit to ask Fly where we were headed for.

"All you need to know is that we're going to Hawk Headquarters. Anything beyond that will be revealed to you in time."

I returned to my seat and looked out the window. We were about to land. On the ground below I could make out a large private estate somewhere in the country. Acres upon acres of orchards bordered one side of the estate, while a vineyard snaked around the other. Rows of villas lined one area of the estate while an interconnection of buildings with one big dome in the middle represented what I assumed was the center. It wasn't long before we touched down on the estate's runway.

The moment I got off the plane and stepped onto the tarmac, I was greeted by a petite young woman with short, blue-streaked black hair and a wide smile.

"You must be Ben Hudson!" she exclaimed. "We're so excited that you're finally here! I'm Zinnia Wolfe."

I noticed the small scar on her left cheek as we shook hands. I thought to ask about it, but decided not to. I was somewhat bewildered by the warm welcome. *Why are they expecting me? Why do they even know me?* "I'd introduce myself, but it seems you already know me."

"Well…" She shrugged one shoulder. "Who doesn't?"

I motioned to get my bags but she shook her head.

"Don't worry about your luggage. We'll have it brought to your room later."

We began walking side by side toward Hawk Headquarters.

"After Vivienne Novak was captured, you and Sofia have been the talk of the town."

Alarms went off at that statement and I stopped in my tracks before we could reach a block section of the estate. It had steel-gray exteriors and large glass windows from floor to ceiling. I gave the building a wary glance.

Who are these people? What have I gotten myself into?

"How do you know about Sofia?" The name caused an ache to settle in my chest.

Zinnia smiled, long dark lashes fluttering over her big hazelnut-brown eyes. "I think I've said too much…" Her pupils rolled to the edge of her upper eyelids as she chastised herself. "I do that a lot."

"Well?" I asked, unwilling to let her off the hook.

"All I know is that you and Sofia Claremont have been on our watch list for quite some time now." Her hip swayed to one side, her weight falling on one leg. "Especially after you disappeared and magically showed up again, some of our best hunters were deployed to keep you under surveillance twenty-four seven."

"Why?" I stepped forward, fists balled, brows furrowed. "How did we even get on your watch list?"

"I honestly don't know. Good thing you are both on the watch list though, because we never would've caught Vivienne Novak if you weren't." She had a way of talking about issues as if the best way to tackle it was to laugh about it. She reminded me a lot of myself—my *former* self.

"So if you were keeping Sofia and me under your watch, you know where she is right now?"

Zinnia shook her head. "Unfortunately, we were too preoccupied with getting Vivienne here. By the time we got hunters to go back to keep an eye on you, Sofia was gone and you were already driving for LAX."

I gave her my most menacing stare, annoyed that she was

unable to give me more information.

"Are you always so serious and intense?" She playfully chucked a fist over my jaw. "Relax, handsome. Reuben will answer all your questions later."

Serious and intense. I'd never thought anyone would ever describe me that way. *Ease up, Ben. You got this.* "Fine." I relented, one side of my lips curving up in a smile. "So when exactly will I meet Reuben? I get the impression he's the hunters' almighty leader?"

"I wouldn't say almighty, but yeah, he's pretty close." She chuckled. "And yes, he gets to call the shots. Here at US headquarters at least."

"US headquarters?" I asked. "So there are other headquarters? Outside the country?"

Zinnia's nose wrinkled. "I think I'm going to get myself in trouble if I keep on answering your questions, so please stop asking them. I've already told you too much."

"So what exactly are *you* for, Zinnia?"

"I'm your welcoming committee. I'm going to take you to your room in the dormitories. And until Reuben's ready to see you, I'm the person you go to in case you need anything."

"Anything?" I squinted suggestively at her as glass doors slid open in front of us, allowing us entrance to the large private estate.

She gave me a curious look as we headed for a door. She came up with a metallic card and swiped it over the lock. A beep followed and we were through. "Something tells me that you're a lot of trouble, Hudson."

"You have no idea."

"Then we're going to get along just fine."

We took turns past several corridors before leading to one that showed a massive glass-covered atrium. Men and women wearing identical black jumpsuits underwent martial arts training.

Judo.

"The atrium serves as one of the academy's many training areas. Those are some of the new recruits."

"Academy?"

"Everyone who wants to become a hunter has to go through the academy first. Aside from basic combat training, it's the organization's primary way of allocating recruits. Your skills are evaluated and after you go through at least a year's training, you are assigned to a position within the organization."

I was stunned at the level of organization the hunters had. I'd always pictured the hunters as some clandestine group who lived in basements, hunting and killing off vampires. What I'd got instead seemed like a worldwide organization of highly trained vampire killers.

Zinnia and I stepped into an elevator with large glass windows that still allowed us a view of the atrium. I held the metal banister that lined the walls of the elevator as it rose three floors above ground. We walked out of the lift and Zinnia led me through a maze of corridors and walkways connecting one building to another until we reached the dormitory.

She stopped in front of a door that had a brass number eight identifying the room.

"This is one of the suites. They're for guests. Once you're an official recruit, you're going to be transferred to one of the regular dorm rooms." She opened the door. "For now, you'll just have to bear with this one."

Stepping into the suite, I was quite impressed. The cool blue and white tones and the dark wood paneling gave the room a bright, airy feel, especially through the full-length glass windows that covered one side of the wall. A wide flatscreen TV, a plush semi-circular couch, a great view of what looked like a sprawling vineyard outside, and modern art decorating the walls gave a clear impression: *Hunters have some filthy rich backers.*

Zinnia began pointing out the rest of the room's amenities. "Bedroom's over there. Terrace. Kitchen, not that you'll need to cook. You can have lunch with the rest of us at the mess hall later. Anything you need, you can just call me."

She took my hand, retrieved a pen from her jacket pocket and scribbled her number on my palm. She'd barely finished writing the last digit on my palm when someone knocked on the door.

"Who on earth could that be?" she muttered.

She headed off to open the door while I made myself comfortable on the living room couch. Zinnia exchanged words with a man with a deep, gravelly voice. I couldn't hear much, although I did make out the man saying:

"I figured it's best to just get it over with as soon as possible. Time is of the essence."

I tuned them out while they finished their conversation. I focused on the view outside. *I wonder how Sofia is doing.* I shut the unwelcome thought out. I still found her betrayal painful.

I didn't realize how impossible forgetting Sofia would be—even for just that morning—until Zinnia came back from the door and said, "Ben, I guess you won't have to wait long. This is Mr. Reuben Lincoln, otherwise known as the Boss."

Amusement laced her voice, but not a trace of it could be found in his face or mine. My blood began to boil at the sight of the man who called himself Reuben.

"It's been a long time, Ben."

"Too long," I responded through gritted teeth, glaring at

the hand he was extending towards me.

His presence answered many of my questions, but it also added dozens more. Standing in front of me—tall, suave, imposing and with green eyes that reminded me of the girl I'd loved and lost—was Sofia's father.

Aiden Claremont.

Chapter 36: Derek

When my feet landed on one of the boulders outside the fortress, Sofia's slender form trembling in my arms was the first thing that registered in my mind.

Her arms clung tight around me, her hands gripping my hair. Her face was nuzzled against my neck, her erratic breathing hot against my skin. I leaned my head backwards to get a better look at her face and found her eyes shut tight with terror. She was biting on her lip so hard, I was afraid she might draw blood.

As if everything about you isn't already temptation enough… The last thing I need is to get another whiff of your blood.

I couldn't help but smile at how badly her knees were

shaking as I placed her on her feet. She opened her eyes, her breaths raspy, as she took in her surroundings. When she saw the smile on my face, she let go of me and pushed me on the shoulder. I chuckled. That seemed to annoy her.

"Are you crazy? If you want to commit suicide by jumping off a cliff, you can't take me along for the ride!"

Her outburst only amused me further. "First of all"—I pointed at the wall—"that's not a cliff. Second, didn't I tell you I was going to take you to my sanctuary? The leap was a shortcut. Third, you're alive, aren't you?"

"Barely!" Her rosy red lips formed into a pout as she crossed her arms over her stomach, her hands clinging to her elbows. Her eyes moist, she looked like she was about to cry. She glared at me. "Stop laughing. I'm still mad at you."

I made an attempt to keep a straight face. It was never my intention to make light of the outburst she threw at me back at the woods. Truth be told, the encounter was still gnawing at me.

However, I took one look at the blush on her cheeks and the way she was hugging herself and I just couldn't help myself. It was too precious a sight not to at least grin at. She slapped my arm—something teenage girls seemed to enjoy. This time, however, her mouth twitched. She rolled her eyes and then there it was. She gave in. Lighting up her face was that radiant smile of hers.

I hadn't realized how much I'd missed that momentary flicker of delight on her face whenever she looked at me until then. We locked eyes for a split second before she stomped her foot on the stone ledge we were standing on.

"I'm supposed to be mad at you."

"You can get mad again later. Plenty of time for that. For now, come with me." I held the hand she'd used to assault me and began to assist her as we navigated past the jagged boulders. "The lighthouse isn't far from here."

"The lighthouse?"

"It's the only establishment on the island located outside the fortress. Apart from me, I think only Vivienne knows it still exists."

I jumped down a particularly high boulder onto the rocky path below. I held Sofia by the waist and helped her down. I was grateful that the full moon was giving enough illumination for her to see where we were going. Living on an island with no mornings did have its disadvantages.

As her feet once again settled on the ground, she gave me an odd look. Sympathetic. Then a small smile appeared on her lips. Affectionate.

I swallowed hard, wondering what it was that she saw in me. *How can you look at me that way, Sofia?* I shifted my gaze forward, focused on the trail ahead. Her hold on my hand tightened as we moved forward on a narrow stony path that

268

was much easier to walk on than the slippery boulders we'd left behind. I could only guess what was going through her mind.

"It would be much easier if you just sped us right to your lighthouse, you know," she whispered. "Since you're so fond of shortcuts…"

"And miss out on this?"

"This?"

I squeezed her hand, enjoying the warmth it exuded. I looked at her and gave her a short, pointed nod. "This."

That smile. That blush. *The things you do to me. The things you make me do.*

We continued the walk in silence. It didn't take long for us to reach the lighthouse. The sight of it made me ache with all the memories linked to it.

I woke up clinging to a plank of wood. Recollections of the explosions, the burning fire, the screams and the chaos revisited me. The ship was gone. The last thing I remembered was the look of horror in my sister's eyes before someone had knocked me unconscious and thrown me overboard.

The sea was much calmer, rocking me in its waves as if it were trying to soothe me of all the lives it had swallowed the night before. I looked at the horizon and shuddered. The sun will rise soon.

I scoped my surroundings and saw it. A lighthouse among jagged boulders. The only shelter that could shield me from the burning sun. It was at least a mile's swim. I didn't have much time. I pushed away the plank that was keeping me afloat, hurriedly making my way to the shore. By the time I reached it, the first rays of dawn were beginning to show and I could feel its weakening effect.

I was about to speed toward the lighthouse when I heard it. A whimper followed by a loud, chilling growl. Despite my need to find shelter, I couldn't ignore the sound. Behind a large rock was a semi-unconscious woman slowly coming to her senses. Just a few steps away from her was a black panther, ready to devour her.

Instinct took over. I lunged for the beast before it could pounce. The panther's teeth sank into my biceps and tore out my flesh. I screamed in pain. The sun was hampering my healing. I had to finish the fight soon. Blood flowed from the panther's teeth as its sharp claws tore through my chest. With a growl of my own, I pushed against its chest and ripped its heart out. Standing over the beast's lifeless form, I threw its heart onto the ground and faced the stranger.

She stared at me with unveiled hatred—something that surprised me considering I'd just saved her life. I pushed away any doubts. I didn't have time to make introductions or figure out why she was looking me with so much anger. The sun was rising and I had to shelter myself with darkness. I sped towards the lighthouse, leaving her by the shore. I soon reached the top of the lighthouse. After pulling heavy drapes over its windows, I sought refuge in the octagonal room's most shadowy corners.

The wounds still weren't healing. Blood covered my clothes and my hands. I trembled as I wondered how my body would recover from the harm even the smallest of the sun's rays did to a creature of darkness like me.

I barely heard the footsteps that approached me. Tentative footsteps.

"You're a vampire," a sultry, female voice said.

"Yes. I am." I hated to admit the truth. I had been a hunter—the best one they'd ever had. Now, I'd become their hunted and in their hatred of the creature that I'd become, they'd destroyed my family.

She stopped in front of me and lifted her hand toward me. She was holding something in her hand. A wooden stake. She placed its point against my heart. I looked up, straight into her eyes. Big brown ones, peering through long thick lashes. She was an exotic beauty, olive-skinned, beautiful heart-shaped face, full lips, long wavy brown hair...

"You're a hunter," I said. It was rhetorical. I wondered what was keeping her from driving the stake right through my heart. Is it because I just saved her life from that panther? She didn't even seem grateful for it back at the shore.

"You're cursed."

"That I am." I scoffed.

She pushed the stake forward, just enough to break my skin and draw blood. "You just killed a panther with your bare hands. What's keeping you from killing me?"

"I've never killed a human being in my life. I'm not about to start today. If your conscience can take ending my life, then go ahead and be done with it."

Back when I was a hunter, I wouldn't have given a moment's thought before ending a vampire's life—and I'd ended many. I saw them as cursed, remorseless, wicked creatures who took life without inhibition—the same way one of their kind had taken my mother's life. I saw vampires as immortals dead to their conscience. I'd never thought they were capable of emotion until I became one of them.

I looked into this young woman's brown eyes and wondered what all the vampires I'd murdered had felt when they looked into my eyes. Had they felt as I felt at that moment? Had they anticipated the moment the stake would drive through their heart? Were they begging to be freed from their accursed immortality?

It felt like an eternity before our eyes unlocked and she sank into the ground, pulling the stake from my chest. She watched as the wound caused by her stake healed.

"I'm not a hunter," she admitted.

I smirked. "I can see that. If you were a hunter, I'd be dead by now."

"You're not what they say you are, not what I expected you to be."

I couldn't find a proper response to that statement, so I

introduced myself instead. "I'm Derek Novak."

She stared at me for a couple of minutes before finally deciding that I deserved a name to call her by.

"You can call me Cora."

The lighthouse became my refuge through all the terror and bloodshed that happened in that forsaken island in its first hundred years. The people who entered it were the people I trusted enough to completely let into my life. Only two had made it within its walls. Cora and Vivienne.

That night, a third person was about to enter my sanctuary. As I gently laid a hand on the small of Sofia's back, guiding her up the winding staircase that would lead to its topmost room, I realized that I was something that I hadn't been in a very long time: terrified.

Chapter 37: Sofia

I raised the lantern Derek had given me over my head as we continued to climb to the top of the lighthouse. I could swear that the hand Derek laid on my back was shaking.

Derek Novak? Nervous? Will wonders never cease?

As we neared our destination, it was obvious that this place held a lot of meaning to Derek and I was excited to find out why, but there was also a sense of foreboding, as if the lighthouse housed something dark and disturbing.

I was relieved—and out of breath—when we finally reached the top. Derek, who'd been behind me the whole time, took the lead for the last few steps. He retrieved a metal skeleton key from his jeans' side pocket and unlocked the arched rosewood door.

His hand was already on the latch, but he took several breaths before finally pushing the door open.

"Derek?" I asked as I stepped beside him. "Are you all right?"

It was the first time since I got back that I'd been struck by his appearance. He towered at least half a foot over me. His hair was as black as night, his skin as pale as snow. His blue eyes changed shades with his mood. This time, they were a deep dark shade of blue as if a storm was brewing in them, with his pupils as the storm's center.

He faced me and gave me one small smile. Bitter. Heartbroken. Disturbed. Afraid. He didn't say anything. He just stepped aside to give me a better view of the room.

The octagonal room had four large windows on every other wall. Each window had heavy red drapes drawn to the sides, allowing us a view of the starry night skies. From our vantage point, it was clear to see where the night stopped and where the day began. Miles away from us was a bright, sunny day where the light cast by the lighthouse's lantern was wholly unnecessary.

I turned around to find Derek standing at the very center of the room. His eyes were beginning to moisten and I realized that I'd never seen him cry. "Vivienne. She maintained the room all these years."

I took small steps over the hardwood floor as I perused the rest of the room. Framed photos were all over the walls. Unlit candles surrounded the room. A sectional velvet couch was on one side, right in front of a fireplace mounted on one windowless wall. A coffee table was set up in front of the couch and over it was a large leather-bound book that looked like it belonged in the fifteenth century.

To me, the room was a well-decorated place that provided the perfect retreat to anyone who wanted to get away from the confines of The Shade. To Derek, however, it looked like the room meant so much more.

I stopped in front of him and looked up at his face, breathtaken by the intensity of his emotion. "What is this place, Derek?"

"I told you… it's my sanctuary." One side of his lips curved up as he led me toward the couch. He sat down and pulled me to sit beside him. He sat up straight, leaning his elbows on his knees as he took the book on top of the coffee table and placed it on his lap.

"If you're going to stay here, you need to know about The Shade and everything it cost to make it what it is now." He paused, a pensive expression coming over his face. "More than that, I need you to know me. *Everything* about me."

And that, I realized, was the reason he was so terrified.

CHAPTER 38: DEREK

I opened the leather-bound book that showed pages upon pages of inked letters. "These pages contain the chronicles of The Shade's history," I explained. "It is basically a record of how The Shade came to be." I gently closed it and handed it to her. "The book cannot leave the lighthouse, so if you want to read it, you have to come here."

The thought of her reading the deepest secrets of The Shade made my stomach turn. Just thinking of how she would look at me after reading those pages broke me. A tear ran down my cheek before I could stop it.

"Derek..." She brushed her soft fingers over my cheekbone, using her thumb to wipe the tear away.

I couldn't bear to look at her. "If you think what I did to Ashley was bad, Sofia, you'll find that I've done a lot of worse things to protect my family and The Shade." I returned my gaze to the book on her lap. "Read, Sofia."

She opened the book to the first page. I flinched as she began to read out loud.

It felt like we spent hours inside the lighthouse as she read page after page after page, gasping at certain parts, tearing up at others. At some points, she would look up at me, a million questions in her eyes, as if wondering how I was able to live with myself having committed such atrocities.

I couldn't live with myself, Sofia. That's why I asked Cora to put me in a sleep that I could never wake up from. I still don't understand why she broke her promise and made me wake up four hundred years later. I wanted to explain, but I kept my mouth shut through the whole thing.

At times, she would pause and stare at me with what I thought was admiration. I was fooling myself to even entertain the notion that she could admire me after reading about the grisly history of The Shade. *The shipwreck, the lighthouse, the caves, First Blood, the slaves, the Wall, the beasts...*

When she began reading about the uprising and the subsequent massacre, tears began trickling down her face and she started sobbing. I was convinced at that moment: *That's it. I've lost her.* She stopped reading and continued to cry, mourning the loss of all those slaves who dared rise up against us.

I sat still, my fingers brushing her hair as I waited for her sobs to subside. When the sound became unbearable, I withdrew my touch. I barely managed to say the words, my own guilt choking me.

"I guess now you know exactly what I am."

She took hold of my hand and pressed its palm over the side of her face, her fingers caressing the back of my hand. "I think I've always known exactly what you are, Derek. The thing is… I don't think *you* do."

I had no idea what she meant, but if her touch wasn't already healing balm in itself, her seeming acceptance of me caused me to hope again.

She shut the book and tossed it back to its place on the coffee table. "I'm horrified," she admitted. "I can't fully understand how you were capable of making those choices…"

My lips twitched. I felt like shrinking under the weight of her stare, knowing that her admonitions were gentle compared to what I deserved.

"… but I've seen firsthand that you are better than the choices you sometimes make. I don't think that the man portrayed in those pages is the same man who woke up in *my* time."

I looked into her eyes and saw sincerity and hope... hope that I could still have some good in me. At that moment, I adored her more than I ever had any other woman in my lifetime. I doubt she had any idea what her words did to me when she said, "You can be better than this."

When she leaned closer and her lips touched mine, I couldn't bring myself to believe it. I held her waist and drew her closer, practically carrying her so I could plant her on my lap as I once again partook of the pleasures her sweet lips provided.

That night, at the lighthouse, everything else faded away and my entire world became Sofia Claremont.

CHAPTER 39: BEN

I sat rigid on the circular couch, staring at the charismatic, confident man calling himself Reuben Lincoln. Zinnia was sitting on the same couch, a bright curious look in her eyes as she shifted glances between us. Reuben, on the other hand, was sitting across from me on a leather recliner, his posture relaxed as he leaned against the seat's backrest, his elbows propped up on the recliner's armrests.

"You look like you've seen a ghost, Mr. Hudson," he noted.

"That's because I just have." Bitterness was in my voice. That I could still be hurt on her behalf as I stared at the father who had abandoned her for eight years was a cold reminder that Sofia still meant more to me than I was comfortable admitting. "You're Aiden Claremont."

I was expecting him to deny it, so I was surprised when a smirk showed on his face and he said, "I figured you would recognize me. You were old enough to remember."

"Remember what? That you abandoned your own daughter?"

Zinnia shifted uncomfortably in her seat. I wondered if she even knew that their revered leader was actually Sofia's father.

"I really don't have to answer to you, Ben." He retrieved a cigar from the back pocket of his suit and took out a lighter. He was about to light it when he looked at me. "Do you mind?"

"Yes. I mind."

He scoffed. "Good thing I don't give a rat's ass." He lit the cigar and took a puff. "I was only asking out of courtesy."

"How courteous of you," I responded through gritted teeth. "So you're Reuben Lincoln now?"

"To the hunters, yes. That's how I'm known. To the rest of the world, I'm still Aiden Claremont."

"Which of the two identities is the real you?"

"Both." He gave it a moment's thought. "Neither." He shrugged. "Does it matter?"

"Sofia needed you."

His lips tightened as he placed his cigar on a nearby ash tray. He glared at me with intensity that I'd never seen in Sofia's green eyes. "As I said, I don't need to answer to you, boy. Let's cut to the chase. Why do you want to become a hunter? Why are you here, Mr. Hudson? How did you come to know Eliza? And how was she able to tell you about me?"

At the mention of the name, Zinnia gasped. Her brown eyes burned through me with anticipation. "She was my older sister."

I looked at her in surprise. "I'm sorry."

Tears blurred her hazelnut irises. "She's gone?"

I nodded solemnly. "I barely knew her, but she felt like a kindred soul. She could've tried to escape without me, but she risked helping me out. I truly am sorry, Zinnia."

"We all lost someone to the vampires. If not, we were— like you—victims ourselves. That's why we're hunters," Zinnia said through sobs.

"Eliza was always hard to keep a rein on. She was so eager to prove herself to us and was far too impulsive, acting before thinking things through. We sent her to Cancun mainly to get her out of here. It was supposed to be a treat, a vacation. The last time we heard from her, she was asking for backup because she'd discovered a vampire from the Novak coven. We told her to wait for us, but I guess she took matters into her own hands. We haven't heard from her since that night."

I steeled myself and set aside what personal biases I had against Reuben. This was business. I began to unbutton my shirt as I spoke. "I want revenge on the vampire who did this to me." I showed them the scars on my torso. "Eliza was captured by that same vampire. She tried to help me escape, but we were caught. The vampire's name is Claudia."

Reuben's ears perked up. "Claudia? She belongs to the Novak coven just like Eliza messaged us?"

"Yeah, I guess. Derek Novak was their prince or something. He was the one who killed Eliza. Claudia offered her to him as some sort of tribute."

My voice trailed off, realizing that they were staring at me.

I began to question my judgment in revealing so much. *I barely know these people.*

"We want you to tell us everything you know about their coven, *especially* where they are. You're the first person in hundreds of years to ever have been captured by the Novak coven and come out alive. Most of them just disappear, no bodies even, never to be heard of again." Reuben sat on the edge of his seat. "Go ahead, Ben. Tell us what you know."

I shook my head. "No. I've already said enough. Incidentally, I don't trust you, *Aiden*. Not after what you did to Sofia. I'm not telling you anything until I get answers."

The man gave me a murderous glare. "Look, boy. I'm here for one reason and one reason alone and that is to find

Sofia. I don't care what you think of me. The last time you and my daughter disappeared, I practically turned the world upside down trying to look for her. I arrived at one dead end after another, and then you two little juveniles show up out of thin air, giving authorities this crap story about running away—no explanations, no records, nothing." He began swearing loudly. "And now she's gone again right after a private conversation with Vivienne Novak!" Another swear word escaped his lips. "Vivienne Novak! After centuries of not even seeing a trace of her or anybody from her clan, she shows up and she goes after my daughter. If you don't want Sofia to end up the way Eliza did, you're going to tell me everything you know."

He looked nothing short of intimidating and Zinnia looked terrified of him, but his outburst only made me relax. It just showed me how important I was to them. I leaned back on the couch and cocked my head to the side. "Don't you have Vivienne in your custody? Why don't you just ask her what you want to know?"

"You've obviously never tried to break a vampire," Zinnia muttered.

I raised one shoulder. "I'm willing to learn."

"Now's not the time." Reuben was reeling in his anger. "Tell me where my daughter is."

"She returned to The Shade."

"The Shade?" they both asked in unison.

Not wanting to tell them anything about the island, I said the words that left a bitter taste in my mouth.

"Sofia is Derek Novak's lover."

Silence followed as the statement sank in. My eyes remained locked on Reuben as the blood rushed to his face, his knuckles growing white from clutching the armrests. "*Lover?*" The way he said the word made it sound foul and disgusting. "How could something like this happen? How does my own *daughter* fall prey to a Novak?"

I was surprised by the anguish I saw in his face. The anger increased how menacing he looked, yet a deep sadness was mingled with the fury.

"I was trying to protect her, keep her hidden from vampires and hunters and all this bloodshed. What they'd do to her should they find out that I'm her father..." He rose from his seat and began pacing the hardwood floor in front of us. It did little to ease the tension.

I couldn't keep myself from speaking my mind. "Protect her? What the hell are you talking about? You abandoned her!"

"To keep her away from all this! She was safer without me."

"Safer?" I scoffed. "Really? You mean like she is now? Safe as that vampire prince's slave?"

"Slave? I was under the impression that she went of her own free will." Something dark flickered in Reuben's eyes.

I knew then that Reuben would burn down the entire world to keep Sofia away from Derek Novak.

That was what earned him my trust. That was what made him my ally.

I drew a deep breath. "You don't know Sofia. She's naïve. She trusts people too much. You must've heard about what was happening when the hunters came to take Vivienne from Sofia. It was almost like the vampire was hypnotizing Sofia. I don't know... they did something to Sofia on that island. She's fiercely loyal to Derek for reasons I can't even comprehend. After we got back from The Shade, I tried to reason with her as best as I could, but it was of no use. He *had* her. I don't know if there's anything we can do about that."

Fierce determination deepened the lines in his face as he sat back on the recliner. "We're going to get my daughter out of there, and you're going to tell me *everything* you know about The Shade."

CHAPTER 40: DEREK

1509

A light drizzle had begun over the thatched roofs and stone walls of our small village. The fresh air of the countryside was a welcome change to the city atmosphere I'd grown accustomed to since joining the hunters. However, even the comforting sight of our beloved and closely-knit farming community failed to ease the heavy burden I brought home with me.

Though our neighbors greeted me with nods and smiles, they were wary of me, some even fearful. After our mother had been murdered inside our own home two years ago, I'd been written off as mad because I was convinced that a vampire had taken my mother's life. It didn't take long until I couldn't bear working our farmlands anymore. I had to get away. Rumors were circulating about an order known as "the Hawk". They were hunters, determined to rid the world of vampires. I'd found them and I'd joined them.

Of the several times I'd gone home since I joined the hunters, this homecoming proved the most difficult, because along with it came a mission I was afraid I didn't have in me to accomplish.

Upon reaching the thatched roof and brick walls that made up our home, the first person I wanted to see was my twin. Vivienne had joined me during my first year of becoming a hunter. She hadn't become one herself, but she'd assisted me in more ways than one, given her premonitions. She'd eventually had to go home, however, due to an illness. Expecting her to greet me, I was surprised to find our older brother instead.

It was midday, yet it was obvious that Lucas had been drinking. He had his arm around a giggling, sparsely clothed bar wench and a flask of wine in one hand.

"Where's Vivienne?" I asked him.

He blinked several times. "Derek?"

I brushed past him and entered the house. "Vivienne!"

"She's not here." Lucas swallowed hard.

"Where is she? What happened?" My pulse began to race, my heartbeat doubled.

He rubbed the back of his neck with a hand and motioned to his wench to go away. Even in his drunken stupor, guilt was evident.

"What have you done?"

"I haven't done anything! Derek, you must understand... There was nothing we could do about it..."

"Do about what? Understand what? Where the hell is Vivienne?"

"Lord Maslen asked for her. She was brought to their estate only this morning."

Blood pounded in my veins. Lord Maslen was baron of the lands we were living in. His eldest son, Borys, had had his eye on Vivienne for years. She'd told me many times that she couldn't stand him. It made me sick to my stomach thinking of what they could possibly want from Vivienne.

"You know what trouble we could get into if we defy the Maslens. How were we to say no?"

"It's easy, Lucas. You just utter the word. No." I stared at my older brother in disbelief. It was amazing to me what kind of a spineless coward he always proved to be.

"As if that would've done any good! These are the Maslens we're speaking of. They could have our heads. It's not like we can just withhold Vivienne from them."

"Why the bloody hell not? She's our sister! She's not some piece of property they can have at their whim. We're not their slaves!"

"They have all the power."

"Only the power that we give them, Lucas. No more than that."

"It's not that simple." Lucas shifted uncomfortably on his feet.

"She's Borys' betrothed. She's come of age. They said it was time to give Borys what was his."

"Betrothed?" I spat a slew of curses.

"Without our knowledge—and even without hers—Father promised Vivienne to Borys Maslen in exchange for a generous dowry."

I froze. When our mother had died, we were deep in debt and about to lose the farm. I'd tried to contribute by working as a bard at the local tavern. Vivienne worked as an apprentice for a local merchant. Even Lucas did more than his typical bare minimum with his chores at the farm. Even with all of us pulling our own weight, we were still about to lose the farm. Then suddenly, Father had come by a huge sum of money to pay off our debts. He'd refused to let us know where the money came from. Now I knew where he'd gotten it. He'd sold his own daughter to that demon.

"Derek, we had no choice."

"To hell with that. There is always a choice." I stormed out, determined to find my father. I knew that there was only one place to look. Muscles flexed, fists balled and ready to make a hit, I marched through the muddy roads of our village. I wanted to strangle my father.

Fear and worry grated at me. The uncertainty of what my sister was going through in Borys Maslen's hands was overwhelming my senses. Passersby in my path quickly stepped aside. Even at eighteen, I'd already grown a reputation and my *demeanor as I charged toward the village tavern was far from welcoming.*

I pushed the tavern's door open and immediately laid eyes upon our father. When I found him, tipsy and laughing with some of his comrades, I saw red. I lunged for him, tackled him to the ground and began hitting him on the face.

"How dare you do that to your own daughter! How could you send Vivienne there!"

I'd already thrown several blows when my father was able to hit me back. With a few swift moves, he managed to roll me over so that he had me pinned to the ground.

"Watch who you pick fights with, boy." He spat blood on the floor beside me. "Your sister belongs to Borys Maslen now. There are far worse places to be for a young woman. Being the wife of a future baron—a very wealthy one at that—isn't such a bad thing, is it now?"

I stared up at my father, fighting back the tears. "You say that because you don't know Borys Maslen. You just gave your daughter up to the devil."

At that, my father only laughed at me. "Why so tightly wound up, son?" He lightly slapped my cheeks as he staggered upwards, letting go of me. "The lad may be a self-absorbed brat, but he's no devil. Have a drink, Derek. It might loosen you up."

As I rose to my feet, I made a promise to myself that I was going to rescue Vivienne from the Maslens. I couldn't explain to my father why the thought of Vivienne being with the likes of

Borys Maslen made my stomach turn. He would only laugh at me and brand me a fool just like he had the last time I'd tried to tell him about my theories on how our mother died.

I couldn't tell my own father that he'd just given his daughter up to a vampire. A vampire I was assigned to kill.

I'd rescued her from Borys Maslen five hundred years ago. And yet I wasn't able to save her now. I was well aware of what hunters did to vampires once they were caught. No vampire had ever returned. No matter how much I wanted to believe that Vivienne was alive, I had to let go.

Nothing I could say could rationally defend the idea of gathering our forces to get my sister back. Even Xavier and Liana, two of Vivienne's closest friends, kept telling me that the hunters never kept a vampire alive for long. I would only risk the lives of many of our kind if I went ahead and stormed the hunters—wherever they were—in a vain attempt to rescue Vivienne.

She was gone. And I needed to accept that.

As was customary for those among us who had fallen to the hunters, we held a memorial ceremony in the town square. It'd been centuries since The Shade had suffered such a loss and for that loss to be Vivienne Novak was grief felt deeply by every citizen of The Shade.

It was Liana who took care of all the preparations. I wanted no part in it. Just thinking about the loss was already too painful. Our father sent word that he couldn't arrive. Other matters seemed to always get ahead of his family. I even expected Lucas to show up, but I knew that he was too much of a coward to ever show his face to me. Not even his own sister's death—if he even knew about it—could make him risk his own life.

I couldn't shake off the anger as everyone present was given lanterns to release into the cold night air. *I should've been there. I could've saved her.* But I hadn't been there. I'd been so busy protecting The Shade, I'd been unable to protect my sister.

As I stared at the lantern in my hand, I couldn't help but feel a pang of pain at what it represented. Vivienne had always been particularly fond of lanterns. It felt like letting go of the lantern would mean letting go of her.

Sofia was standing a few steps away from me, her eyes downcast as she held the lantern in her hands. She whispered something toward the lantern. I strained to hear what she was saying:

"Wherever you are, Vivienne, I hope you're all right."

After we let go of the lanterns, I couldn't keep my eyes off of Sofia. I had no idea what I would've done without her. Over the past few days, she'd once again taken on the guise of my slave, even though she was anything but. She was the only person keeping me sane.

I bridged the gap between us and admired the mixture of sorrow and fascination on her face as the lanterns rose up into the starlit sky. Noticing my eyes on her, she looked at me and gave me a smile. Her delicate fingers brushed against my arm before her hand found mine. She squeezed tight—her way of saying she was there for me.

Indifferent to anyone around us, I placed my arm around her shoulder and pressed my lips against her temple. I whispered into her ear, "I can't begin to explain to you how much it means to me that you're here."

She gently caressed my hand before her eyes focused on the lanterns rising up to dot the night sky. "I'm sorry you lost Vivienne, Derek."

Lost Vivienne. The words were painful. The thought of being alone that night seemed more than I could bear. "Stay with me tonight, Sofia."

With Lucas no longer a threat, she'd been staying in one of the spare bedrooms in my apartment since she arrived. Paige and Rosa had already moved back into my penthouse to accompany her. They'd been asking me about what was to happen to Ashley, but I couldn't even bring myself to think of the girl.

"Derek…" Her face paled at what I was suggesting—that she stay in my bedroom like she used to.

The hesitation was understandable. The girls were giving her a hard time over her loyalty to me, but I wanted to be around her. I craved her warmth. She was a healing balm to the wound Vivienne's disappearance had left behind.

"Sofia, please." I could've just demanded it of her. I was still prince of The Shade and in the eyes of everyone else, she was still my slave, but her approval of me mattered—perhaps more than it should. Nothing pleased me more than the idea of her being with me out of her own choice.

She turned her gaze from the night sky to me before exhaling. She nodded. "Okay."

The memorial dragged on. Pleasant words were given in memory of Vivienne. When I was asked to speak, I refused. I didn't want to even think about the loss I was suffering, much less talk about it. I didn't stick around for condolences.

That night, the only source of solace was Sofia. Her kisses, her whispers of comfort, her smile, her arms around me and the warmth she exuded... For the first time in a long time, I allowed myself to become vulnerable in front of someone else. Holding Sofia in my arms, I broke down, and she didn't say anything to console me. She didn't have to. She just held me close.

When sleep finally stole her away, I stared at her peaceful, sleeping form and allowed myself to entertain a thought of Vivienne—just enough so I could thank my dear sister for paying the ultimate price in order to give me Sofia.

Chapter 41: Sofia

I woke up to find him staring at me. Waking up next to him felt right in a way it never had waking up next to Ben. I eased myself into his arms. I'd found his chest comfortable enough to be my pillow during the night. I smiled. It was the first time I could remember that a nightmare hadn't woken me up in the middle of the night.

"I'm sorry you had to see me that way." I never thought I'd see him look so embarrassed.

It took a moment to register what he was apologizing for. I shook my head and snuggled closer to him. "Don't be, Derek. You never have to pretend around me."

I could swear his heart quickened a beat. His arms around

me tightened. We lay there comfortably for a few more minutes before we fell into routine as we both got dressed. I'd forgotten how naturally it came to us. We just knew how to move, how to act, when to stay out of each other's private spaces and when to move in.

Something, however, had changed in our routine. After we got dressed, I often went to the kitchen to prepare my breakfast. Often, a glass of blood would already be waiting for him on the dining table. That much didn't change. What changed, however, was the fact that he actually started talking to me—and not just about mundane things, but about how he was going to spend the day, what his plans were for The Shade, things that I never was privy to when I was still his "personal slave".

"I'll be at the training grounds today," he informed me. "The training must go on for the vampires of The Shade."

"Corrine told me about the draft." The topic left a bitter taste in my mouth. "She said you wanted all vampires to be battle-ready. Why?"

"We've grown weak. Should the hunters attack us, we won't stand a chance. I can only imagine the technological advancements they've developed over the years. They're leaps and bounds ahead of four hundred years ago."

"Maybe so, but how on earth will the hunters even find the island, Derek?"

"It's just a matter of time, Sofia. Our defenses grow weaker by the minute. I'm surprised we were able to keep the secret this long."

I stared at the piece of toast I'd just dabbed with jam and butter before finally admitting something that'd been bugging me. "Ben joined the hunters, Derek. He wanted me to go with him, but I didn't."

Derek stiffened. He took a drink from his glass of blood before raising his eyes to mine. "Why didn't you?"

Because of you. I shrugged. "It didn't feel right."

It seemed he wanted to ask another question, but thought better of it. Instead, he nodded. "I have to go soon. What will you be doing?"

"I want to visit Ashley at the Cells. I'm thinking of visiting the Catacombs too."

Blue eyes widened in surprise. "The Catacombs?"

"Is that going to be a problem?"

He paused and gave it some thought. "No. I'll find you there later. I'll make sure a guard accompanies you."

"When is this trial with Ashley going to happen, Derek? You can't keep putting this off."

His face grew grim. "She's a hunter, Sofia."

"What?" I frowned. "How would you…"

"The tattoo on her back. The hawk. It's the mark of a hunter."

"But…"

"Look. I'll strike you a deal. If you can get her to cooperate and give us all the information she knows about the hunters, then I'll release her."

"That's not fair, Derek. She was defending me after you…"

"Don't go there, Sofia." His tone was stern, making it clear to me that I was about to cross a line. "I know what I did, and I regret it deeply, but I am prince of The Shade. She was going to kill me. She almost killed *you*. My offer to release her is more generous than you give me credit for."

I was taken aback. It was the first time I could remember him pulling rank on me. My familiarity with him often made me forget who he was. Whenever anyone at The Shade treated him with deference, I found it downright weird. The idea of calling him 'your highness' or even 'prince' seemed ridiculous to me, but sitting there, it hit me full force: the vampires recognized Derek as their prince.

Words Ben had spoken to me while we were still here at The Shade haunted me. *Don't be a fool, Sofia. We need to get out of here before he decides that he's tired of you and kills us both.*

My insecurities began to resurface. *Who do I think I am?*

The thought of Derek realizing that he didn't need me gnawed at me even as I made my way to the Cells. The deal

I'd struck with Derek weighed on me.

I stepped into Ashley's cell to find her sitting on the edge of her cot, looking distraught. She raised her eyes to me, probably expecting Paige, Rosa or one of the guards. Her face fell when she saw me.

"Oh. It's you."

My stomach turned. Since my arrival, the girls had been giving me a cold shoulder. Even Sam and Kyle were, at best, being polite to me. I couldn't blame them. We were friends and I'd left them at The Shade without even saying goodbye. To top that, I hadn't done a thing to help them out while I was outside The Shade. We'd planned an escape together so many times, with promises that once one of us got out, we would rescue the others. I hadn't done that. Even above all of that, upon my return, I'd walked in on Derek with a barely conscious Ashley on his bed and still I'd managed to forgive him. That last part, I believe, was what they saw as the ultimate betrayal.

They had reason to hate me. That explained the heavy feeling I had upon approaching Ashley. The last time I'd visited her, she hadn't been very accommodating—especially when she found out that I was once again staying with Derek.

"How can you stand being around him?" she'd asked me.

I didn't know how to answer. It felt pathetic when I

replied, "I see him differently, Ashley. There's hope for him yet. I don't want to give up on him."

After that, Ashley had asked me to leave.

Truth be told, I wasn't happy about being seen as Derek's slave, but Derek made it clear to me that it was the only way. After Derek went to painstaking lengths to keep my escape a secret, most of the vampires didn't even know that I had been gone.

"The only way I can protect you is to keep you under my wing. They won't touch you if they know you're mine. On your own, all you are is bait," he told me, and as much as I protested against it, I knew that in The Shade, the only way I could be safe was under his care.

I tried to explain to Paige and Rosa why I couldn't give away information about The Shade after our escape, but my words were empty in light of the trauma Derek had put them through while I was gone. In their eyes, I was siding with the enemy. I wished they'd remember everything Derek did to protect us before everything went south.

Entering Ashley's cell a second time, I realized that I hadn't had many girl friends growing up. Everything had always revolved around Ben and the Hudsons. Even as a child, I'd preferred to be alone on my crazy adventures rather than stay with girls my age. They bored me to death. That was why I valued the girls so much, and now that they held this big grudge against me, I realized how much I'd missed them.

"Hi, Ashley." I tentatively approached her. I crossed my fingers, hoping that she would cooperate.

"What are you doing here, Sofia?"

I sat beside her on the cot. She inched away from me. "How've you been?" I started. Suddenly, my throat felt dry and I had no idea what to tell her. "Have they been treating you well?"

She scoffed. "As well as they could a prisoner, I guess. How long am I going to stay here?" Her lips quivered, her form trembling. "When is this trial even going to be? The anticipation is killing me."

"I don't think there's going to be a trial."

"What? Why?"

"Derek's offered a deal. He's willing to release you."

"Oh yeah? In exchange for what?"

"Information."

Ashley's eyes widened. "I can't believe you. You come here as his lackey, trying to pry information from me? After what he did? Whatever happened to us looking after each other, huh?"

"That's why I came here, Ashley. To look out for you. Would you prefer that he come instead? Knowing how much he craves you?"

The idea obviously scared her. She shook her head. "What do you want to know?"

"The tattoo on your back… it means you're a hunter?"

Her jaw clenched. "Yeah. So what?" She began to twirl the ends of her blonde hair, something she did when she was anxious.

"Vivienne was captured by the hunters."

"Derek's sister?"

I nodded. "She went out of The Shade to get me to come back."

"Why? Why would she risk that? They're safe in this island bubble of theirs. Why would she go through all that to get *you* back? Why are you so important to these people, Sofia?"

Vivienne's words flashed through my mind. *You're not a pawn. You're the queen.* "Ash, I understand your hatred of the vampires. I saw it in Ben's eyes. In a way, I shared that hatred too. They took away so much from us. Derek tried to kill you and whatever excuse he has isn't reason enough for what he did, but we're here and there's no changing that."

"You're not answering my question, Sofia. Why are you here? Why would their princess risk being captured by the hunters to get you back?"

I told her what Vivienne had told me back at the coffee shop. The prophecy and the role she felt I played in it. This was the part that I'd kept from Derek. Just saying it out loud to Ashley made me feel conceited. *Do I really believe that I'm that important? That I could make a difference here?*

By the time I finished, Ashley's face softened. "And you believe her?"

"At first, I didn't, then she gave me some of her memories, random ones that told me her story and the things she went through to protect this island. Then when I got here, Derek showed me the history of The Shade… the price *they* paid to have what they have. And I know for sure that Vivienne was sincere." I inhaled and exhaled, hoping that I was somehow getting through to Ashley. "I'm not asking you to forgive him, Ashley. He put you through too much for that. I'm asking you to trust me, because we were friends. We *are* friends, and things weren't so bad when we were here, and…"

To my surprise, Ashley pulled me in for an embrace. She whispered into my ear, "I knew you'd come back, Sofia. I wished you'd come back to get us out of here, so it was disappointing to find out that you came back mostly for *him*. That still doesn't mean that we didn't miss you. And if I have to stay in this black hole of an island, I'd rather that you're here than not." She chuckled. "After all, I was a lot safer from him when you were here."

I smiled at her, hoping this was a road to reconciliation.

When she stopped hugging me, I was relieved to find a smile on her face too.

"What do you want to know, Sofia? If it gets me out of here, then I'll tell you."

"We want to know any information you have about the hunters. You were one of them."

"There's not much I can tell you, but what I do know for sure is that if the hunters have had her for more than twenty-four hours, she's done for. They never keep vampires alive for too long."

"What reason would they have for keeping one alive?"

Ashley shrugged. "To get information out of her. I'd imagine that Vivienne would be a pretty huge catch, considering that she's princess of this island. They'd probably be torturing her by now."

"How can we find her?"

A sad smile formed on her face. "You're asking about the location of the hunters' headquarters. I'd tell you, Sofia, but I don't know. Look, I belong to generation upon generation of hunters. I couldn't even track how far back our family has belonged to the order. Our parents raised us to hate vampires, and it worked with my brother, but it never worked with me. I couldn't wrap my head around the idea of hating creatures who harmed some ancestor of mine and now several generations after, I'm still supposed to hate them?" Ashley heaved a deep sigh. "I didn't want to live the life they were living, so when they sent my brother and I to the hunters for training, I begged him to not tell Mom and Dad that I didn't go. I got a tattoo of the hawk just so I could show it to them when they asked about the training, but I never once set foot at the hunters' headquarters, so I don't know where it is or how things are run there."

"How were you going to get there in the first place?"

"We were sent to a runway where we were to be picked up by a hunter via a private plane. That's all the information we were given."

I nodded. "Okay. That's all I have to ask now, Ash. I believe Derek will have one of the other vampires ask you further questions. I'm hoping he'll release you soon." I grabbed her hand and squeezed, relieved that she didn't pull away.

"Thanks, Sofia."

I shook my head. "I'm just glad to have you back."

When I left her cell, I felt pretty good. Even though Ashley didn't have any helpful information, she had been willing to tell me what she knew—that had to be enough for Derek.

But something else was grating at me. Derek had pulled rank on me earlier. He was prince of The Shade and he had every right to do what he wished. Still, that didn't mean he was right. Ashley was only one of the human beings who had suffered abuse under Derek's hands. As my feet led me to the Catacombs, I shuddered at the kind of atrocities I was about to find.

Derek had revealed to me back at the lighthouse what The Shade was and how it came to be. *I'm about to find out what The Shade is and what it could become.*

Chapter 42: Ben

The air in Reuben's office smelled of mint with hints of rum and tobacco. The carpeted floor and the white-washed walls, with a few select paintings adorning them, provided a minimalistic feel to the large office interior. At the center was a large glass desk—one Reuben, Zinnia and I surrounded as they once again pushed me for information regarding The Shade.

"That's it? That's all you know?" To say that Reuben looked displeased was a huge understatement. "There's got to be more you can tell us."

"I told you everything I know." I shrugged. *Apparently, I don't know all that much.* Most of my time spent at The

Shade had been inside Claudia's home—in her bedroom or in one of her dungeons. The only time I'd gone out was to be brought to Derek's house. I knew the way to the port but how to get out of the island and how to go back there was beyond me. Reuben was livid.

"Basically, you don't know anything. I don't care what's on the island or how it remains invisible and protected. What I care about is how to get there."

Reuben Lincoln was not a patient man—especially regarding his daughter.

"Well, what about Vivienne? Didn't you get any information from her?" I gave Zinnia a pointed look.

Since I arrived, she'd been with me every day, making sure that I was properly briefed and subjected to the right levels of training. Given my background in martial arts and my time spent at The Shade, I was already several levels ahead of recruits who came before me.

Zinnia shook her head. "She won't talk."

"She's a Novak. She won't break easily. Her twin brother is the stuff of legends." Reuben spoke as if he were thinking out loud. "Derek Novak was a force to be reckoned with while he was one of us. He is even more of a threat now that he's a vampire—a five-hundred-year-old vampire. If we think the Maslens are a threat, he is even more so now."

"The Maslens?"

"A clan leading the largest vampire coven we know of," Zinnia explained. "We'd been tracking them for years. Just like the Novaks, they're hard to find."

"From what you tell us, it seems the Novaks have done even better than the Maslens all these years…" The wheels in Reuben's mind were turning. "How were they able to stay under our radar for this long? There's got to be a loophole somewhere." Something sparked in his eyes and a flicker of hope began to show. "The witch… the one protecting the island… what's her name again?"

"Corrine."

"That's it. That's how they did it. Zinnia, I want all the information you can get on the witches working with the hunters in the 1500's. Specifically find out which witch was sent to find the Novaks before the shipwreck. And make sure all the information you gather is properly chronicled."

Zinnia nodded and left the office. Reuben turned toward me. "As for you, perhaps the fact that you've been to The Shade can better equip you to get information from Vivienne Novak. Come with me."

As we weaved through its network of corridors and halls, the sheer size of the estate and its lavishness overwhelmed me. I was already astounded by the things I'd seen at The Shade, but even the island seemed primitive compared to what the hunters had. Zinnia had made me realize just how much of a threat the hunters really were to the vampires.

"We've eliminated many vampire covens over the years. A lot of them are in hiding. The best defense vampires have against us is to not be found," she'd explained. "That's what the Novaks seem to do best. The last we heard of them was four centuries ago. Before that, everyone we sent to find them never came back. We sent some of our best hunters—some of whom Derek Novak worked with when he was still a hunter. None of them returned."

Her words rang in my ears. I was overwhelmed by my own desire to take The Shade down, so when Reuben stopped walking, I was surprised to see something other than determination in his eyes. Sorrow. Pain. Longing.

"You knew my daughter well, didn't you, Hudson?"

I nodded. "We were best friends for years."

"What could've caused her to fall for a monster like Derek Novak?"

Seeing the heartbreak in his eyes was the first time I could remember seeing Reuben as Aiden Claremont, someone who cared about Sofia. It hurt to have no answer to his question. "I don't know. Hopefully, someday, you'll get to ask her."

His eyes darkened. "Find out what Vivienne did to her. I want her back."

I nodded. It took several more minutes before we finally arrived at the most secured and heavily guarded area in the mansion, Vivienne's holding cell. We first entered what looked like an interrogation room. Through a tinted one-way window, Vivienne was chained to the wall, her back against it, her legs sprawled on the ground. Her gaze was distant. Bloody cuts—very similar to the ones Claudia had inflicted upon me—were all over her arms, neck and face.

"She was being tortured."

"As I said"—Reuben took a deep breath—"it's not easy to break a vampire." He pointed toward a door that would lead me to her. "Go ahead."

I swallowed hard, not exactly sure what I was supposed to say or do to the vampire. I made my way to the room and shut the door behind me. I pulled a metal chair toward her and sat in front of her. Only when I was seated did she raise her eyes to me. Horror filled those blue-violet eyes the moment she recognized me.

"Ben?"

"Hello, Vivienne." I was surprised to be met with such fear.

"What are you doing here? Where's Sofia?" Worry creased the lines in her face.

Her mouth was bleeding. They'd pulled out her fangs. I wondered why she wasn't healing. Claudia always healed instantly whenever she accidentally cut herself tormenting me.

"Ben... You have to tell me where Sofia is."

The worry she had over my best friend was unnerving. "Sofia is of no concern to you."

"She's supposed to be with Derek." Her voice was childlike, but what she said was the last thing I wanted to hear.

I lunged her way and gripped her chin, forcing her to look me in the eye. The light blues and purples of her eyes turned into a deep violet and I was taken aback when I saw fear in their depths. "What do you mean she's *supposed* to be with Derek?"

I wanted to see a spark of Claudia in her. I wanted to find the madness that I'd seen in my captor—a cold, heartless bitch one moment and a broken, whimpering child the next. Looking straight into Vivienne's face, however, not a single trace of Claudia could be found. Instead, I found purpose and a deep sorrow.

"I never thought I would see my brother fall in love. He was too broken, too jaded... but he loves her and she loves him. And I don't think they even fully realize it yet."

Her words were acid to my still-fresh wounds. Before I could think straight, I backhanded her across the face. She crashed to the floor. All those times I'd hit Claudia, she'd just laughed at me.

I rose to my feet and stood over Vivienne as she began

coughing blood. Guilt took a hold of me and I began justifying my actions. She was a vampire. She wasn't some random innocent. I had every right—even a responsibility—to break her.

I tried to shut away Sofia's words. *Please find Vivienne. And make sure they don't harm her.* I steeled myself against my own conscience. Vivienne had information I needed and I was going to do everything possible to get it from her.

"How do we get to The Shade, Vivienne?"

"Why don't you just ask Sofia? I showed her the way to The Shade. She knows everything that needs to be known."

I pictured Vivienne as Claudia—her dark hair becoming a blonde mass of curls, her heart-shaped face turning into Claudia's round one, her hourglass form transforming into Claudia's lithe figure. *They're all the same,* I told myself before kicking her in the gut.

She coughed before looking up at me. A faint smile crossed her face. "Sofia went back, didn't she? She returned to him?"

My fists clenched and I was about to hit her, but then a tear ran down her eye. No matter what justification I had, no matter what torments Claudia had put me through, Vivienne was a helpless, broken woman, and I was beating her up for crimes that she hadn't committed.

"Please." Tears were streaming down Vivienne's face as

she tried to lift herself up from the floor. "Enough."

I sat in front of her and once again gripped her jaw.

She moaned at the sudden action. She'd probably been undergoing torture since they brought her here. Any move caused her pain.

"Only you can end this, Vivienne. Just tell us what we want to know. Tell us where The Shade is. Then all this will be over."

"Tell me, Ben. If you knew that a group of thugs were intent on murdering your family and destroying your home, what could they possibly do to you that would make you give them your family's address?"

My mouth twitched.

"Exactly. I could never give up my family, Ben."

I eased my grip on her jaw, unable to accept that a vampire could care for anyone other than themselves. Claudia had made it hard for me to believe that family could mean anything to them.

"Sofia is my family, Vivienne. You took her away from me. If you had hold of someone who brainwashed your family into agreeing to slavery, what would you do to that person to get your family back?"

"Sofia returned to The Shade out of her own free will and we both know it."

The truth of Vivienne's words stung. I reluctantly let go

of her jaw. I couldn't even look at her, but I felt her eyes on me, searching me.

"You loved her, didn't you?"

"She was supposed to be mine. She wasn't supposed to choose him."

Vivienne lifted a trembling hand and brushed the tips of her fingers over the fine ends of my hair. "I'm sorry, Ben. For everything The Shade cost you. But we were only doing what we needed to do in order to survive."

"Don't tell me that. What Claudia put me through had nothing to do with survival."

"You're right. It had everything to do with revenge. You reminded her of the man who once abused her."

"I was not that man."

She nodded. "And I am not Claudia."

The point was a blow in the gut, but it was well taken. I finally looked her in the eye. To my surprise, after a couple of seconds, the violets of her irises had swirled into a bright blue. When her irises returned to their original blue-violet color, she stared at me as if I'd been made brand new. "Ben…"

I flinched when her thumb gently caressed the line of my jaw. I grabbed her wrist and pulled her hand away from me. "What is it? What did you see?"

A lone tear fell from the corner of her eye to the tip of her

317

chin before falling to the ground.

"You have no idea how much you mean to her. One day, Ben, you're going to look beyond yourself and you're going to see Sofia as she is. Once you see the world through her eyes, you will understand. You could be great, Ben. And for all it's worth, I thank you."

"What? What are you say—"

The door to the room slammed open and Reuben stepped in. "Enough," he bellowed. "It's clear we're not going to get anything from her. We're going to make arrangements for an execution as soon as possible."

Relief washed over Vivienne's countenance. Guilt washed over mine. Her last words haunted me for the rest of the day. *What was she thanking me for?*

I mentioned it to Zinnia later that day.

"She was probably just deranged, Ben. Forget what she said."

I shook my head. "You can't just forget when someone says something like that to you—especially when that someone is the Seer of The Shade."

Chapter 43: Sofia

The Black Heights was a huge mountain range that spread out in the north of the island. Within it was an intricate network of caves containing the Cells in the west and the Catacombs, home to the humans not under the care of a vampire, in the east.

As I made my way from west to east of the Black Heights, the encounter I'd had with Ashley weighed heavily on me. I could no longer turn a blind eye to what was happening at The Shade. I'd been blinded by my affection for Derek, but it could not remain so.

I passed by the entrance of the cave network and headed for the cave opening that led to the Catacombs. I was surprised to find Derek leaning against a solid rock wall, waiting for me.

"I told you I'd send a guard, but I figured I'd send myself instead. Xavier can take care of the training. After all, he's better with guns than I am."

I narrowed my eyes at him, and then forced a smile. "Of course."

"Did it go well with Ashley?"

"She agreed to your terms. You'll release her immediately?"

He called after a nearby guard. "See to it that one of the human prisoners is released and sent to my home. Her name is Ashley. Make sure that she is properly guarded. I want her under close watch."

I waited until the guard left before I spoke my mind. "Is that really necessary? Having her watched like a hawk?"

"She *is* a hawk."

I wasn't amused. "Let's just go."

We passed through a long and narrow tunnel lit up with small incandescent bulbs that lined its rocky walls. I had to control my breathing in order to overcome my fear of enclosed spaces. I felt Derek's hand on my waist.

"You seem so tense, Sofia."

I didn't know if it was him or the claustrophobia, but either way, I just wanted to get past the tunnel. When I saw a clearing ahead, a sigh of relief escaped my lips. I was about to speed up my pace toward the clearing, but Derek grabbed my arm and spun me around to face him.

"You all right?"

"I just have a lot on my mind."

He sensed the tense formality with which I was addressing him. He put a foot forward, asserting his dominance. "What's wrong, Sofia?"

How could I explain to him the struggle to trust what I felt about him in spite of what I saw around me? If I was to stick with him, if I was the girl spoken of in the prophecy, something had to change. I was nowhere near prepared to discuss that with Derek, so I just tried to relax and smile at him. I shook my head.

"I'm okay, Derek. I just want to get out of this tunnel. Closed spaces unnerve me."

He narrowed his eyes before nodding. "Let's get out of here then." His hand rested on the small of my back, nudging me forward—closer and closer to the small opening that led to the Catacombs.

All I knew about the Catacombs was that it was home to the humans. I was nowhere near prepared for what I saw upon stepping into the clearing. Right in front of me was a thriving community, with people milling all around a giant round pit, the bottom of which I couldn't quite see as I leaned over the wooden banister that lined the sides of the pit.

The pit had several levels with cave entrances that led to other areas of the Catacombs. Allowing travel from one level to the other were ladders on the walls, while bridges were constructed to go from one side of the pit to the next. I looked up and estimated at least two other levels on top of us. I could barely even count the levels below us.

Immediately beneath us, I noticed two children—a boy and a girl. Redheads with big brown eyes. The boy looked older than the girl. He was comforting her. I assumed they were brother and sister. It was the first time I'd ever seen children at The Shade.

Derek was standing right next to me, also leaning against the banister. He stared at them, fascination in his eyes.

"I had no idea the Catacombs looked like this," he admitted.

"You've never been here before?" I asked, finding it strange that the prince of The Shade never bothered to visit such an important part of his kingdom. *Does he not rule over the humans too? Doesn't he care at all?*

He shook his head. "No. I never had a reason to."

Never had a reason to? Aren't these people your subjects just as much as the vampires?

"Sofia?" a familiar voice from a level above called to me.

I followed the sound of the voice and saw Corrine. She caught sight of Derek and seemed to be holding her breath.

"You brought *him?*"

Derek tensed up. It was no secret to me that he and Corrine weren't exactly the best of friends and it always surprised me how vocal Corrine was about her disdain toward him.

"Wait for me. I'm going to be right down."

Corrine disappeared and Derek looked at me. "So it was the witch who gave you the idea of coming here?"

"When I came to visit her, she told me that I should come here—to get a clear picture of how the Naturals live."

"The Naturals and the Migrates." He said each word with bitterness—even a hint of spite. I couldn't help but wonder why. I caught sight once again of the children on the level below. Both had their big brown eyes on us. The little girl clung tightly to her brother. I realized that they were both looking at Derek. They were terrified. The boy whispered something into the girl's ear and they backed away slowly before turning back and running into a tunnel.

"You should've said that his royal highness was coming. We could've prepared a warm welcome of sorts. The Elite rarely visit the Catacombs."

I did a one-eighty and found Corrine standing behind us.

Derek was more reluctant to face the beautiful witch. He

slowly twisted around before glaring at Corrine.

"Hello to you, too."

They dueled with glares before both directed their attention toward me.

"So you finally decided to visit the Catacombs," Corrine chastised.

"Well, there was Vivienne's memorial. I was adjusting to being back... I..."

"Hush, Sofia. You ramble when you're trying to defend yourself." Corrine eyed me before once again giving Derek a wary glance. "Follow me. There's someone I'd like for you to meet."

As Corrine led us along the round ledge we were standing on, I could sense Derek's discomfort. I wondered if it was difficult for him to be around all those humans. I instinctively grabbed his hand and squeezed. His grip on my hand tightened. I looked around me at the place shrouded with darkness.

"How is everyone able to cope without sunlight?" During the months I'd stayed with Derek before leaving The Shade, we were given doses of Vitamin D along with other nutrients—I wondered if all humans were given this treatment.

"Most of the people who live here at the Catacombs were born here," Corrine explained. "It's hard to miss something they never actually had. They get Vitamin D from supplements. The lack of sunlight does weaken them in ways that artificial nutrients could never make up for. The average life span of the humans on this island is not long."

I glanced at Derek, remembering the Sun Room and everything it took just to give him a glimpse of the sun. The lavishness of his penthouse seemed an extravagance compared to the drab living conditions of The Shade's human slaves.

Corrine went down a spiral wooden staircase leading to the level below. We followed. I could sense curious eyes on us as we trailed behind Corrine who didn't even bother to check if we were still following her.

"A vampire and his Migrate," a young woman whispered to an elderly one with graying hair.

"Beautiful young woman," the older woman responded. "Poor thing."

Derek's grip on my hand tightened just enough for me to sense his tension, but not enough for it to be painful.

We kept following Corrine as she took a turn toward a tunnel—wider than the one we'd entered. It was the same tunnel the children had retreated to. We passed several arched doorways. I strained to see what was through them, but only saw darkness. Corrine kept walking until she stopped in front of one of these entrances. We walked in and found the two children we saw earlier bundled up with their mother—a beautiful woman with dark auburn hair and a sad smile. Sorrow filled her eyes. Inside what I assumed was their home were three cots, very similar to the ones found in the Cells. An old table was positioned in one corner of the room, upon which a single candle flickered.

Corrine must've noticed me staring at the candle. "Not all the areas of the Catacombs have electricity—even though The Shade's power plant wouldn't even exist without human labor. Those who don't have electricity get a ration of candles every week—candles that *humans* also make." Her eyes were on Derek.

I glanced between my two companions and shifted my weight from one foot to the other. "How do they generate electricity?"

Derek answered me this time. "An effort was made to make sure that The Shade was as self-sufficient as possible. The island has its own power plant, farms, factories, made possible by humans who live on the island."

"When the island is in need of certain expertise," Corrine added, "the vampires abduct someone who has it. No human abducted has ever been able to leave the island. Until Ben and you."

At this, I gave Derek a grateful glance. He didn't even look my way. Corrine shrugged it off and stepped into the room. The auburn-haired woman was whispering consolations to her children before she looked up at us. Fear was in her eyes—magnified tenfold when she saw Derek standing by the door.

"Corrine..." She shook her head, her lips trembling. "Please..."

"Don't worry, Lily. He's not here for you or the children."

Derek flinched. He let go of my hand. I looked up at him and brushed a hand over his elbow before following Corrine inside. He remained by the door.

"I'm Sofia," I introduced myself, my eyes on the two little children.

"Lily." She smiled faintly, but she still looked shaken, her eyes flitting from me to Derek. "These are my children. Rob and Madeline."

"How old are they?" I asked.

She didn't seem to appreciate my interest in her children. Most mothers I knew—Amelia for one—pounced on the chance to talk about their kids. Not Lily. She put her arms around her children and gulped before answering, "Rob is seven. Madeline is five."

"Relax, honey. She's the girl I was telling you about," Corrine tried to soothe her. The information made Lily even more nervous. Her eyes fell on Derek.

"That means he's…"

Corrine nodded. "Derek Novak."

Tears began to show in Lily's eyes. "I can't lose my children!"

"Why would you lose your children, Lily? No one's going to take them from…"

I was silenced by the look of pity she gave me and then her kids. "You don't understand, Sofia. You're a Migrate. You weren't born here. You don't know what it's like. I fear for my children, because just like my husband was, they're beautiful. Beauty isn't something you want your children to have. Not here at The Shade. Beauty assures death."

I gave Corrine a questioning look, not quite sure what to make of what I'd just been told. *Lily's husband… was?*

"After the prince ordered a halt to all human abductions, one of the vampires saw Lily's husband working in a factory. She took a liking to him and took him as her slave. He was returned to Lily a few days later as a corpse. Lily's eldest son, Gavin, has taken his father's place at the factory." Corrine gently brushed her hand over Lily's hair. "No one's going to take Rob and Madeline from you. Not today. Rest assured for now."

Lily nodded, but not without glancing once again at Derek.

I looked at the two children again. Lily was right. They

were beautiful. As the information sank in, breathing became quite a task. *This is wrong. This isn't how it's supposed to be.* I grabbed Lily's hand.

"I'm going to do whatever I can to make sure that no one ever lays a hand on your children, Lily."

"Thank you." She embraced me.

I tensed at the words she whispered into my ear. She voiced my worst fear.

"Don't be naïve, Sofia. Vampires always tire of their pets. The prince will eventually tire of you. What then?"

CHAPTER 44: DEREK

Standing there, listening to the woman express her fear for her children's safety, I remembered why I never bothered to visit the Catacombs. The place made me feel helpless to do anything about the plight of the humans living on the island.

We were vampires. We fed on blood to survive. That was our curse.

Rob and Madeline. They were indeed beautiful children, who would one day grow up to become gorgeous. Lily had a reason to be afraid. *Hell, she should also fear for herself.* I noted how lovely she looked.

She pulled Sofia in for an embrace and whispered something in Sofia's ear. Sofia stiffened against Lily. She pulled away from the young woman and flinched when Corrine laid a hand on her shoulder. My brows furrowed.

"It was nice to meet you, Lily." Sofia's voice was hoarse and broken.

A lump formed in my throat when she turned around and looked at me with such a pained expression I had to take a step backward. Fear, deep sorrow and a million doubts—none of which I felt capable of easing—mingled in her glistening green eyes.

Silently, Sofia strode toward me. She didn't even glance my way. She brushed past me, her slender fingers forming fists as she walked. Corrine and I followed after her.

"What do you seek to accomplish by encouraging her to come here and meet these people?" I asked the witch, my voice strained.

"If this is to be her home, she cannot be blind as to what happens within its walls." Corrine was speaking in riddles as she always did, but I knew her words were full of purpose. She spoke with wisdom no one else had. "What she does after this will mark the difference between who she is and who you are."

Through gritted teeth, I responded, "And what exactly do you mean by that, witch?"

"You were able to stand by and watch thousands of humans slaughtered over the span of centuries. We're about to find out if she can do the same."

Her words were a blow in the gut—one that made my blood pound as it rushed to my head. "What then? What's the point, Corrine?" Sofia walked several paces ahead of us. Watching the sway of her hips and the grace she had about her, I found the idea of losing her sickening. *Is that the witch's intent? For me to lose Sofia?*

"Vivienne's prophecy about you can never be fulfilled unless the young woman Cora spoke about does her part. If that young woman is Sofia, she cannot accomplish what she has been tasked to do with her eyes blinded by affection for you."

My mind began to reel. *What is she talking about?* "Cora spoke about a young woman?"

"I've said enough."

"No, you haven't, Corrine. You said too much and too little all at the same time. You can't just say something like that and not follow through."

"Everything will unfold in due time." Corrine stopped when she saw where Sofia was headed. "I believe she'll want to have a private conversation with you."

Sofia was taking steady, purposeful strides headed right out of the Catacombs. Her shoulders were heaving. I wondered if she was sobbing. Annoyed at the witch, I sped up to catch up with Sofia just before she reached the tunnel that would lead us out of the human slaves' quarters.

"Sofia…"

I held her arm, but she shrugged my hand away. The idea of her being angry at me dragged my spirits down. I kept pace with her until we finally reached the end of the tunnel and she walked directly to the exit of the Black Heights. The moment we reached the woods and breathed in the fresh night air, Sofia spun around to face me. The pained look in her eyes was a heavy weight on my chest. I gulped.

"You're ruler of The Shade, Derek. Powerful vampire. Feared by everyone. I've seen them tremble before you." She pointed toward the direction of the caves. "How could you allow *this*? Are they not your subjects too?"

Something caught in my throat and I found myself momentarily mute. *Why must I defend myself to her? She's a nobody here. I can bend her to my will just as I can everyone else on the island.* I caught the thoughts before they could run rampant. *Don't be a fool, Derek. Vivienne sacrificed herself for Sofia and Corrine hinted that the girl is of more importance than you originally thought. She is worth far more than all the humans combined.*

I gave her a lingering gaze, taking note of the agitation marring her countenance. *She is worth far more than all the citizens of The Shade combined.* The thought sent my mind spinning. Having someone mean *that* much to me brought forth an emotion entirely foreign to me.

"Well?" She was still waiting for an answer from me.

"What do you expect me to do, Sofia?"

"I don't know… something! Anything!"

"I'm not all-powerful, Sofia. I can't stop the vampires from satisfying their cravings and feeding on humans. I can barely stop myself." I stepped forward, wanting her to understand.

She lifted both hands in the air as if to ward me off. "In the chronicles of The Shade back at the lighthouse, it was written that the first time most of you shed human blood was at the battle of First Blood. How were you able to survive before then?"

"Animal blood." I cringed.

"You survived with that before the hunters forced you to take this murderous path, why can't you do it again?"

"You don't understand, Sofia. Animal blood nourishes, but never satisfies. Not many can embrace that kind of living."

"Living?" She was livid. "How can you call this kind of lifestyle living? You continue to kill even when there's an alternative to all this bloodshed."

I couldn't come up with a defense.

"Is there not a single vampire here living on animal blood alone?"

"Vivienne. She never fed on a human… at least not that I knew of." I longed for the company of my twin. She would've known just the right words to ease my conscience. Then again, perhaps that was what Sofia was for, to drag me away from my excuses and escapes.

"If she was able to do it, why can't the rest of you?"

"It's not that easy. You have to understand, Sofia. The vampires will turn on us if we put the fate of humans over them. We can't just…"

Sofia shook her head. "For a widow to look at her children and find only fear and sorrow because she finds them beautiful… something's wrong with that and you know it." She wet her lips and ran a hand through her long red locks. Her eyes momentarily fell on me. "I can't even look at you right now."

She began to walk away, into the dark woods.

"Where are you going?" I called after her.

"Anywhere away from you. *Don't* follow me."

Stubborn human. I inwardly groaned, part of me wanting to knock some sense into her, part of me wanting to get away from her, exhausted by the helplessness I felt. Even I found my defenses hollow.

I watched her form fade into the distance, secure that her affiliation with me would keep her from danger. I'd never once thought of the welfare of the humans occupying The

Shade. They were always a means to an end—the end being keeping our kind safe and satisfied. Standing there, debating with myself whether to run after Sofia, I knew that the humans' fate would haunt me as long as she was around.

I was unable to move from that spot long after she left. Dread enveloped me when I realized: *A culling is inevitable. What will she think of me when she finds out?*

CHAPTER 45: SOFIA

I followed the pathway through the woods, not certain where I was going or what I planned to do. My body was trembling. The pounding in my veins refused to subside. I didn't even know whom I was angry at. Was it Derek and the excuses he had for every atrocity committed at The Shade? Or was it me and all the doubts I had over what I was supposed to be doing on this mad island?

When I eventually reached the Vale, I was exhausted from my trek. All I could think about was Derek. *What's wrong with me? How could I care so much about someone like him?*

My gaze was set straight ahead as I meandered through the cobblestone streets of the Vale's marketplace. So preoccupied was I, I didn't notice a familiar face until I bumped into her. Upon seeing the mass of blonde curls, the pretty round face and those big eyes, I froze. *Claudia.* A wide and wicked smile formed on her lips upon seeing me.

"Well, if it isn't the little twig herself." She brushed her fingers over my hair. "The prince's pet walking about The Shade as if she owned the island."

I stepped away from her, unnerved by her touch. Glaring at her, I gathered all self-control to keep myself from venting all my anger for what she'd put my dear Ben through—yet another atrocity Derek had turned a blind eye to.

"I don't want any trouble."

"Neither do I." She raised her brow and tilted her head. "Send my regards to the prince. Do let him know that he can share my bed anytime he pleases." Claudia smiled, her eyes twinkling with malice. "I owe him that much after he arranged for my quick release from the Cells."

I swallowed hard. Her words pierced a dagger through my heart. I tried to appear unaffected, but the thought of any other girl sharing his bed made my stomach turn.

"You don't think you're the only one sharing Derek Novak's bed, do you?" Each taunt scarred me. "Poor little thing. Did you think him in love with you? That his heart beats for only you? I don't know what kind of pleasures you provide him that he would be so enamored with someone like you, but you're just a temporary pleasure… one he will grow tired of soon enough."

I forced a smile and gave her a curt nod. "I'll be on my way." I tried to remember that I shouldn't take anything Claudia said seriously, but the words nagged at me even as I passed by her.

I'd only taken a few steps when I noticed a chain she was holding with one hand. She pulled on it, the clang of metal filling the air, and a young man with red hair stumbled behind her. The chain was attached to a collar around his neck.

He looked at me with familiar eyes as he stumbled forward. He was just about my age—tall, lean and attractive with work-hardened hands and eyes that had seen too many horrors for a life as short as his.

Before I could second-guess myself, the words came out of my lips. "Claudia, wait."

Both Claudia and the young man halted.

"Who is he?" I asked.

Claudia raised a brow. "A slave. *My* slave. Is he your best friend too? Would you have him taken from me the way you took Ben? Where is he anyway? I do miss him. You know, I find it rather odd that I don't crave him. If he's still on the island, just his presence should drive me insane in an attempt to quench my appetite for him."

She still doesn't know that Ben and I escaped. I stood my ground. The thought of what she was going to put that young man through had sealed my decision.

"What's your name?"

His eyes flitted from Claudia to me. I searched for a sign of fear but found none of it in his eyes. Just defiance.

"Gavin."

The name was too familiar. I gasped. *Lily's son.*

"I owned his father. It only makes sense that I own him too, does it not?" Claudia began running her fingers over Gavin's arms, her eyes sultry and full of heat as she eyed him. Fists balled, I took a step forward to assert myself.

"I demand that you let him go."

Claudia's brown eyes grew wide open. "You *demand?* Who do you think you are, you little bitch?"

"I claim him for the prince. You do know by now how important it is to his highness that I am pleased, don't you?" Gaining confidence even while making the biggest bluff of my life, I stepped forward and pushed Claudia away from the boy.

She stumbled backwards more out of surprise than my strength. The moment she recovered, fury blazed in her eyes. Her raging demeanor made my blood turn cold. Her fingernails grew into claws and she used them to scratch nasty gashes over Gavin's upper torso. He screamed and her eyes flickered with delight at the sight of his blood before she turned on me. Her hands found my neck and pushed me backwards until my back hit the wall of one of the nearby buildings.

"You overstep your ground, slave. It doesn't matter who owns you. That's what you still are. A slave." She pressed one claw against my neck, threatening to draw blood.

I sneered at her, feigning confidence. "Go ahead, Claudia. Do it. Let's see what Derek does to you once he finds out."

Her hand caught my jaw before a manic smile formed on her face. "The same thing he did to me the last time I defied him, I guess. I can take whatever he throws my way, little girl. I can take the lashes. I can take the prison cell. I can take it when he uses me the way he uses you. I've been through hell and back, so think twice, redhead. Do you really want to threaten me again?"

I saw then how someone like her had been able to break my best friend. Her brokenness made her give in to pure evil and there wasn't a single sign of guilt or even hesitation in her eyes. *The wounded can inflict the most painful wounds without hesitation.* She wouldn't hesitate to kill me, so I kept my words few.

"Let Gavin go. You are not to touch him or his family again."

The back of her hand slammed against my cheek and I

tumbled to the ground. She stood over me and was about to deliver a blow across my face with her claws when someone pushed her back against the wall she'd had me pinned against only moments ago.

Derek pressed against her, keeping her in place. "Did I not make it clear that she is not to be touched?"

Gavin was lying on the ground, recovering from the pain. I put my arms around him and helped him sit up. A crowd of vampires was now beginning to circle us. More than one of them eyed his bloody torso hungrily. I positioned myself protectively in front of Gavin.

"She demands to take my slave from me. She has no right to. I was merely protecting my property."

"He's Lily's son. I can't bear the thought of him suffering the same fate as Ben." I intervened.

Derek's shoulders were heaving, the muscles in his back tensing up. Silence filled the air as he weighed the decision before him. He let go of Claudia, stepping away from the vampire. "Do as she says, Claudia."

"What?" Claudia spat. "You forget who you've sworn to protect, prince."

"I never swore to protect *you*, Claudia."

"What has she done that you are so enamored by her, that you would have even vampires submit to her whims?"

"My word is law on this island. She is the woman I love.

So shall her words also be law upon The Shade… *unless* I say otherwise. Do you understand?"

I froze. *The woman I love.* The words echoed inside my head—so loud and so clear I barely understood the rest of what he said.

"The woman you *love*? Were you thinking of her when you visited me in my cell and…"

"Be silent, Claudia. My patience wears thin."

My heart broke when Derek cut her off. It was confirmation to me that Claudia could be speaking truth about Derek having been in bed with her. My jealousy rekindled at the thought of the last time I'd seen them together and the way Derek had held her as he'd asked her to give him Ben for my sake. I hated the way he was making me feel. Conflicted. I wanted to believe that he loved me, but how could he?

Claudia glared at Derek, then at me. "You're going to get your comeuppance one day, redhead. You'll see."

"Enough! Just leave, Claudia." Derek finally turned to face me and I found myself trembling when he perused me. "Are you all right, Sofia?"

I nodded.

"You don't have to be afraid of her any longer. I'm right here."

The only person I'm afraid of on this island is you, Derek. I had let him penetrate my heart and soul. He consumed me. This terrified me, because despite my instincts that he was a good man worth fighting for, the circumstances surrounding us said otherwise.

Fear enveloped me, because as he embraced me, whispering words of comfort into my ear, I couldn't help but wonder, *What if I've allowed myself to fall in love with a complete monster?*

Chapter 46: Lucas

I puffed on a cigarette as I stood beside a flickering lamp post in Amsterdam. My hunt for my father was proving to be a greater undertaking than I had initially predicted. I was hoping this would be the last stop.

I was there to meet with an old acquaintance, Natalie Borgia. The gorgeous Italian vampire didn't belong to any of the covens. She was one of the few rogue vampires, the only one who knew all the locations of the covens and was allowed entrance into all of them. She was the ultimate diplomat, a woman I found irresistible and unattainable.

"Lucas Novak." Natalie approached, her dark brown hair lifted into an updo, her sultry curves covered by a chic red coat.

"Hey, beautiful." I smiled.

She rolled her eyes and stared at me with a poker face. "You look like crap." She took the cigarette from my mouth and threw it on the ground, crushing it with her heel.

"That's not a very diplomatic thing to say, Natalie."

"Oh, please, Lucas. We both know diplomacy is lost on you."

We began walking over a bridge toward a small street café so we could talk. The moment we were comfortably seated, she crossed her legs and nodded for me to speak.

"I'm a busy person, so make it quick. And please don't hit on me. We both know it's not going anywhere."

I frowned. "Don't flatter yourself, Natalie. I just want to find my father. You're the best person to tell me where he is."

"I don't know where he is at this moment in time, but I did get in touch with him after you contacted me. He can't see you right now."

My blood began to boil. "Excuse me?"

"Word's out on you, Lucas. You're not the most subtle person and you've been burning through all the contacts you have outside of your coven. To your disadvantage, you're not a well-loved person either. You certainly pale in comparison to your brother and sister."

"I don't care what anybody thinks about me. Where's my father? Why doesn't he want to meet with me?" My knuckles gripped the edge of the metal table between us.

"Your father is afraid your presence would only compromise what he is trying to accomplish with the other covens. He thinks that it's best you return to The Shade and resolve whatever issues you have with your brother on your own."

"He doesn't understand. I can't go back there. Derek will kill me." I slammed my hand on the table, making a waitress who was about to take our order back up and leave. "Why is he doing this? Why are they all turning against me?"

"I'm just relaying the message I was given, Lucas." She was treating me so flippantly, I wondered where all her diplomatic skills had disappeared to. "I'll make sure your father hears your response."

I was fighting the urge to attack her. She was at least a century older than me. I was sure to lose.

"What am I supposed to do now?"

"That's entirely your choice." Natalie shrugged. "But I do have another message for you. From Borys Maslen."

"Borys Maslen?"

"As I already implied, your rogue status has become known throughout the covens."

My head was spinning. The thought that my father could

turn on me was something I'd never considered possible. And now our family's worst adversary was trying to get in touch with me.

"What does he want with me?"

"He's offering you sanctuary at the Oasis."

The world has gone mad. "In exchange for what?"

"Loyalty to the Maslens."

At this, I scoffed. "Loyalty? To them?"

"So what do you want me to tell them, Lucas? Does this mean you're refusing?"

I gave it some thought. I shook my head. "I think my choice was made for me the moment my family turned their backs on me. Let Borys Maslen know that I'll be on the first flight to Cairo. Finally, make sure to let my father know that I've joined the Maslens."

Natalie nodded. Her expression remained stoic. No judgment. No condemnation. She was a channel, our central hub of communication. "I'll make sure your message is received. Anything else?"

"Yes. Tell my father that the one person to blame for our falling out is Derek. He's obsessed with a human slave named Sofia Claremont. Tell my father to beware of her."

"Of course." Natalie rose from her seat. "If that's all, goodbye, Lucas. I hope everything works out for you." Without bothering to hear my response, she walked away.

My eyes followed her until she disappeared. I smiled. I knew the damage my father was going to inflict on Sofia just based on the message I'd relayed through Natalie. The knowledge that I had contributed to making her life and Derek's a little bit more miserable was enough consolation.

Thoughts of Sofia made my blood pound and my senses tingle. "You'll be mine someday, Sofia. Oh, you'll be mine."

CHAPTER 47: DEREK

News spread quickly throughout the island that Sofia had defied a vampire—a member of the Elite at that—and got away with it. Outrage followed soon after.

"What if the rest of the humans follow her example and decide they can start defying their masters?" Felix, one of my most distrusted among the Elite, brought up during a council meeting at the dome.

"We can't afford to have another human uprising." Xavier voiced his concern—one I also shared.

Felix scoffed, his hands raised in the air. "A human uprising! Perhaps it's best. With the abductions halted, an uprising would give us all the blood we need for years to come."

Eli, the only one at the stand amidst all the talk being thrown from the seats of the council, stared at Felix as if he were insane. Despite the tension in the room, I couldn't help but notice. He always looked at Felix as if he had no patience for the man. "There's a reason we avoided touching the Naturals, prince. They are the backbone of this island. All the labor required to keep The Shade in its self-sufficient state is done by the humans born out of generations of humans loyal to the work they were given on this island."

"We cannot continue to abduct humans from the outside, if that's what you're trying to imply, Eli." In this, I was not to be dissuaded. "They endanger The Shade by risking discovery from the hunters."

"We've been abducting humans for years, Derek," Cameron chimed in. "We've never been discovered. The scouts are trained to be stealthy enough not to risk discovery."

"The hunters grow more powerful as we speak. We cannot press our luck. Eli can attest to that based on the little information he managed to squeeze out of one of them we've taken captive."

"Yet another human slave you seem to favor," Claudia hissed. "I take punishment for aiding one of our own—our prince, your own brother. These slaves defy everything we stand for and yet they run free."

"They are my slaves and I will do with them as I see fit. That's the end of this discussion." I stood up to better make my point. "There will be no abductions, and while we still have a reserve of blood from the last culling in the chilling chambers, no humans will be taken from the Catacombs."

"And when the blood runs out?" Xavier asked.

My gut clenched at what I knew was necessary to be done. "Then we conduct another culling."

"I want fresh blood," Felix demanded, seconded by *ayes* and *yeahs* echoing throughout the dome.

"Your wants don't concern me, Felix. It's what this island needs that is of greater priority."

"We fear the human slave you favor—Sofia, is it?—has made you weak, prince." He rose from his seat and walked toward the stand.

I feared the same thing. The guilt, the pressure and the shame that I felt whenever Sofia asked me to change the kingdom weighed heavily upon me. She did not understand the pressures of ruling a kingdom, of serving one's subjects and making tough decisions on their behalf. And yet she moved me like no other. Even though she'd been spending the past few days ignoring my existence and had barely spoken a word to me for reasons I couldn't fathom, I was satisfied just knowing that she was there.

I stared at Felix for a moment before speeding toward him, my claws sinking into his chest. Fear sparked in his eyes when he realized that he'd gone too far and that I could break his neck in two with my bare hands.

"Broach the subject again, Felix, and I will demonstrate just how *weak* I am by ripping your heart out with my bare hands. Her name is never to escape your lips again. Do you understand?"

He nodded. "Yes. Of course. My apologies."

With no further attempt to address the rest of the council, I walked out of the dome with Cameron and Liana trailing behind me.

"You're treading dangerous waters, prince," Cameron warned as he stepped to one side of me while Liana stepped to the other.

"There hasn't been this much unrest with the vampires in centuries," Liana added. "Word is out that some of the Elite have already sent scouts to retrieve your father and get him back here to take you under control."

"Get to the point."

"You can't keep making enemies out of the Elite, Derek." Cameron's voice was tinged with concern. "Even those who have been loyal to you from the very beginning—the Vaughns and Lazaroffs—are finding it difficult to defend you."

"What would you have me do, Cameron? We both know that the tides are about to turn. War is brewing. You agreed with me on this, did you not?"

"Yes, I did, but the importance you place upon this girl of yours... enough that you would make enemies out of Claudia and even your own brother on her behalf..." Cameron paused. "Is she worth it, prince?"

I gave one of my dearest comrades a lingering look before heaving a sigh. I had to be honest—if not with them, at least with myself. Was Sofia really worth losing what had taken centuries for our kind to build?

CHAPTER 48: SOFIA

Vivienne stared at her appearance in the mirror. She sighed as she set her long dark hair in its proper place. The violet halter dress she was wearing highlighted not only her pale skin but also her eyes—more violet than blue against the candlelight. She looked stunning, but there wasn't a hint of pleasure in her face. Instead, she appeared afraid.

A knock on her door made her turn around. Xavier appeared in the doorway, his dark hair closely cropped and his eyes betraying how much he adored her.

"They've arrived," he announced. "Your father asked me to come and escort you to the dome." The way he spoke revealed that neither of them was fond of the guests.

"Has my father forgotten what I went through under that monster's hands?" Vivienne ran both hands over her slender form, smoothing out the slight creases in her dress.

Xavier's gaze darkened, pain looming over his handsome face. "Vivienne…"

She nodded bitterly. "It has to be done. I guess peaceful relations must be made between the Maslens and Novaks. I just can't help but think that if Derek were awake, he'd never allow Borys Maslen anywhere near this island."

"To be fair to your father, all precautions were taken so that Borys and his company won't remember how to get back here should a peaceful agreement not be made between the clans." Xavier sighed. "Still, we both know that your father and older brother combined make for a pale reflection of the kind of leader your twin is."

"Be careful that they don't hear you say that. Father and Lucas already have enough resentment toward Derek as it is."

They stared for a couple of seconds, neither saying a word, seemingly lost in their own thoughts until Xavier broke the silence. "Vivienne, we must go."

Vivienne stepped forward hurriedly. "Of course."

Just as she reached the door, expecting Xavier to follow, he halted.

"What is it?" Vivienne's blue-violet gaze was marred with more fear.

"Borys told me that Ingrid Maslen sent this for you to wear."

He was hesitant and slightly trembling as he retrieved a red velvet pouch from his pocket. He handed it to Vivienne.

Vivienne raised a brow. "Ingrid Maslen? His new woman? She's here with him?"

Xavier shook his head. "No, he would never risk losing someone as valuable as her." He looked at the pouch. "He said that Ingrid insisted that you have this. He says that it rightfully belongs to you."

Vivienne swallowed before taking the pouch from Xavier. She undid the knots that kept the pouch sealed, her fingers shaking as she did. She retrieved a stunning necklace with a large ruby red heart-shaped pendant. Fury loomed in her eyes as tears began streaming down her face. Clutching the necklace, she screamed with such anguish that Xavier stepped back.

"Vivienne, what…"

The piece of jewelry hit her vanity mirror. Glass shattered on the floor. Vivienne marched past Xavier. "How dare he!"

Of the many memories Vivienne had shared with me, that encounter with Xavier—a vampire I'd only recently met during preparations for Vivienne's memorial—often revisited me. I couldn't ignore it, because the mere mention of the names Borys and Ingrid Maslen sent chills down my spine. *Who are the Maslens? What was it about that necklace that got Vivienne so angry? Does Derek know about them? Should I ask Xavier about this day?* The memory bothered me, but the one person who should be answering them was nowhere in sight.

Vivienne… Why on earth did you dump all these memories into my head? I can't make head or tail out of them.

"Earth to Sofia Claremont." Paige waved her hand in front of my face. "Are you still with us, Sofia?"

I blinked several times, recalling that I was with my friends after a visit to the Vale for some new clothes. They were a little more friendly toward me after Ashley's release.

"Huh? What?"

"You keep spacing out on us." Ashley chuckled. "Are you all right?"

"I just…" I didn't know how to explain what Vivienne had done to me. "I'm fine."

"Are you still not talking to Derek?" Rosa asked.

I nodded. Ever since that encounter with Claudia, I'd moved back into one of the guest rooms.

"Why? He sided with you *again* against Claudia." Paige was staring at me like I'd gone mad. "You should be rewarding him, not punishing him."

I slowed down my steps as we walked past the woods that led to the Residences before voicing the questions I feared most.

"Is it true that Derek has been sleeping with other women?"

We all stopped walking and they exchanged concerned glances. Their reactions answered my question. Pain gripped my heart. Suddenly, breathing became quite a task.

"Sofia..." Rosa, the most sensitive and gentle among us, brushed her hand over my arm.

"I don't even know why I'm so disturbed. It's not like we're together, and besides, I left him."

"Sofia, he's a vampire who's been on Earth for centuries. It's amazing that he's developed such loyalty and affection for you, but whatever's going on between the two of you, it can't possibly last," Paige, ever the voice of reason, explained. "He's a vampire. You're human. Such relationships—if you could even call it that—don't last long."

That dose of reality from a dear friend was enough to shake everything I stood for. I didn't know what the proper reaction was, but to me, it made what I had with Derek more precious—as if the time I had with him was borrowed and I had to make the most of it.

I started walking again, not knowing how to respond. They followed my pace, the atmosphere tense.

Ashley, to my relief, finally broke the silence. "For all it's worth, Sofia, he's different when you're here. He doesn't seem to be as dark compared to when you were away." She rubbed a palm over the back of her neck. "Look, I'm not one to pretend to understand how the mind of Derek Novak works, but maybe... just maybe... he had Vivienne send him those girls so he could get his mind off of you."

She was the last person I expected to defend Derek. The fact that she did took me aback.

"I guess what I'm saying is that the best person for you to ask would be him."

We finally reached the lift that would lead us to the walkway branching toward Derek's penthouse. We were silent as the lift rose up the full length of the giant redwoods supporting Derek's home. It didn't take long before we stepped into the hall that led to the living room. I drew a breath when we found Derek waiting there, standing in the middle of the room, fists clenched and muscles tensed.

"Where were you?" he asked.

"We went to the Catacombs to make sure Gavin has begun to heal of the gashes Claudia inflicted upon him, then we stopped by the Vale." I motioned to the shopping bags we were holding.

He didn't even bother looking at the bags. His eyes were on me and suddenly, I felt vulnerable under his gaze—as if his glare alone could break me. "Leave us," he ordered.

Ashley pried the shopping bags from my hands as all three of them left for their rooms, leaving me with a brooding vampire, drinking in the sight of me like I was a feast he wanted to partake of.

Derek stepped forward—slowly and tentatively. He stopped a few inches in front of me, close enough for me to be aware of how tense he was and how his breaths were coming in slow heaves and sighs. I could sense how powerful he was, how small I was compared to him and for some reason, I couldn't make myself look up into his face. Instead I kept my gaze on his torso, wondering what was going through his mind.

I froze when he began circling me, his hands clasped behind his back. His eyes were still on me. I wanted to shrink away from him.

"You're trembling."

I hadn't even noticed.

"Why? Since when do you fear me, Sofia?"

Was it because the past few days had given me a clear picture of what he was capable of? Was it because the selfish bubble had finally burst and I now saw him for what he was? I didn't know, but I feared him and I hated it. I wanted to see him as I had before—capable of good—but all I saw when I looked at him was a powerful vampire, a prince of The Shade, whose whims could change at a moment's notice.

"I'm sorry," was all I could think of to say.

He stopped circling me and stopped by my side, his breath cold against my temple as he spoke, his face close to mine. "You're sorry? What are you sorry for, Sofia?"

Again, I didn't know how to answer, so I sealed my lips shut, unwilling to dig myself any deeper.

"I've been defending you and your crusade to save the humans of The Shade since you got here and how do you repay me?" One of his large hands crept around my waist. His other hand cupped my jaw, his thumb running the length of my lower lip.

I wanted to flinch away from him, but I stood frozen under his touch.

He nudged me so that I was facing him. He lifted my chin, forcing me to look him in the eye. "Why do you shut me out, Sofia?"

Before I could hold it back, a tear ran down my cheek. I knew he couldn't understand what I was going through. I couldn't admit to myself that I feared losing him. I feared that going on with my "crusade to save the humans of The Shade", as he so aptly called it, meant that I might lose him. I feared how his touch made me ache with so much longing. I feared how much the idea of him being with anyone but me was tearing me apart inside. I feared treasuring him only to have him ripped away from me—something everyone said was inevitable.

I didn't fear Derek Novak. I feared what loving him could mean for me.

CHAPTER 49: DEREK

The enigma that was Sofia Claremont stood before me, trembling and tearing up at the sight of me. I would've given the world to catch a glimpse of what was going through her mind. Was she so disappointed in me that she still couldn't bear to look at me even after I'd taken her side against Claudia? Was she unaware of all the heat I was under because of that choice?

Her green eyes—moistened with tears—pierced straight through me and I couldn't help but wonder why she had such an effect on me. Why was I willing to turn my entire world upside down on her behalf? And why didn't any of it seem to be enough for her?

What I would give to have you look at me the way you used to... My hand on her waist tightened and she tensed even more. "Why do you resist my touch?"

It was another question that she refused to answer. It felt as if she was slipping away from my fingers, and the question once again haunted me. *Are you worth it, Sofia?*

My confusion gave way to frustration, then to anger over her silence, over her cold treatment of me. My grip on her jaw tightened. The terror that flashed in her eyes fueled my determination. I pulled her body flush against mine and claimed her lips with mine. Her tears were hot against my face. They stung.

She didn't resist, but she didn't respond either. She just hung limply in my arms, letting me have my way. When I felt her waist under my palms, my hands creeping beneath her blouse, I knew I was treading dangerous ground. I couldn't trust myself around her.

She gasped when my mouth parted from hers. I set her feet on the floor and stepped away from her, afraid of what I was capable of doing to her. Her knees buckled, but I made no motion to help her steady herself. The idea of touching her unnerved me.

This time, I was shaking too, fully aware of how powerless she was against me and yet whether she was aware of it or not, she held power over me the likes of which no one else had ever had before.

The mere sight of her swollen lips reminded me of the warmth of her blood and the coldness of mine. We had no business being together, yet I couldn't think of a life apart from her.

Her voice was broken when she finally managed to speak. "What am I to you, Derek?"

My life. The thought was a blow that knocked the wind out of me. I stared at Sofia, taking in her beauty from the small splash of freckles on her cheeks to her slender hourglass form to the length of her legs and then to her soft feet. She was my life and I was about to tell her that, but my silence outgrew her patience and she stepped toward me.

"Am I just your human pet? Your slave? Your toy? Will you one day tire of me? What will become of me when that day comes? Will you discard me as you would any other human on this island?"

I was caught breathless at how stunning she looked, her red locks as fire over her pale face, her eyes—listless only moments ago—now burning with rage. Her beauty distracted me from the absurdity. She meant the world to me, and as far as I was concerned, her fears, though understandable, were unfounded. I smiled when her lips finally settled into a small pout.

"You have a habit of asking one question after another

before hearing the answers to any of them. Do you realize that?"

She glared at me. "Don't make light of this, Derek. You hold my life and that of all other humans on this island in your hands. Can you blame me if I'm so fearful of you?"

I put on a straight face and cupped her face with both hands. "What do I have to do to ease your fears, Sofia? You mean everything to me. I've never loved a woman in my life. Not since you came along and…"

She pulled my hands away from her as if my touch somehow burned. "Don't say things like that." She stepped away from me. Her lips quivered as she spoke. "Not unless you mean it."

Her withdrawal confused me and it took a couple of seconds for what she was saying to register in my mind. Once I understood, clarity came over me. I moved toward her and tilted her chin up. She moved her face to the side, refusing to look at me. I used my thumb to direct her face toward me, willing her to look at me. When she did, I planted a kiss—as tender as I could manage—on her forehead, her temple, her cheekbone, then on her lips.

"I love you, Sofia," I whispered. "And I honestly believe that I could never love another woman for the rest of my life. For the first time in the past five hundred years, I am sincerely thankful for my immortality, because without it, I never would've found you."

The words rushed out without hesitation, but it never dawned on me that she might not feel the same way until I confessed my heart to her. I felt foolish under her gaze, her silence killing me.

"For crying out loud, Sofia. Say something."

All I got from her was a soft, sweet smile as her hands found mine. Wordlessly, she led me to my bedroom. She bared herself to me and lay down in the center of my bed. Her surrender was my challenge. She was a fragile porcelain doll in my hands, one I loved, one I couldn't afford to shatter. I took great lengths to be as gentle with her as possible, afraid to hurt her. Her gasp of pain made me ache with guilt when her maidenhead gave way beneath me. Still, somewhere between the pleasure and the pain, I knew everything was going to be all right when her warm lips brushed the lobe of my ear, her arms clinging over my neck.

She whispered, "I love you too, Derek."

Chapter 50: Sofia

When I woke up, eyes still closed, half-asleep, half-awake, the first sensation that greeted me was the slightest ache between my legs. *What have I done?*

I kept my eyes shut as I thought over what I'd just allowed myself to do. My head rested on his arm. *Rock solid. Not exactly the most comfortable pillow.* I could feel the weight of his arm over my waist, his fingers brushing the ends of my long hair. I felt the heave and sigh of his chest, my hands curved in front of me, the only thing keeping our bare bodies apart. The recollection of his toned torso, his strength, his brilliant blue eyes and the way he held me, the control he had sent shivers throughout my body.

I recalled what Ben had told me back at the beach after our escape from The Shade. *Sandcastles always fall, Sofia… you might as well bid it farewell sooner rather than later.*

I opened my eyes and noticed how serene Derek looked asleep. I couldn't remember if I had ever woken up before him. It felt like the first time I'd ever seen him in deep slumber, looking more content than I'd ever seen him. There was a faint smile on his face and my heart leapt.

What I have with you… Is it a sandcastle? Will I one day have to watch it broken by time and nature's waves?

I lifted his arm away from my waist, careful not to wake him. I sat up on the bed, over the edge of it, groaning at the slight ache in my body. I got up and picked up my black lace lingerie from the floor, slipping them back on. As I pulled a silk night shift over my body, I kept my eyes on Derek, trying to recall what had been going through my mind as I'd bared myself before him the night before.

He was immortal and I wasn't. I would grow old one day and he would remain the same. I dreaded the day he might grow tired of me. What we had was a sandcastle, beautiful but temporary. *So why did you give yourself to him in this way, Sofia?*

I made my way to my bedroom as noiselessly as I could and retrieved my sketchbook and pencil from my belongings. I returned to his bedroom relieved to find that he was still asleep. I saw the trace of blood on his bed sheet, a reminder of what I had surrendered to him.

I pulled the red velvet ottoman near the edge of his bed and sat down across him, and began sketching him, never wanting to forget that moment. I knew why I'd given myself to him and I didn't regret it. *Just because sandcastles are temporary, it never stopped me from making them as beautiful as possible.* As I sketched his appearance, I couldn't shy away from the truth that was staring me right in the face. I was in love with Derek Novak and the idea that he returned my affections thrilled me.

Focusing on the sketch, I didn't realize that he'd woken up until I looked up to find his stunning eyes on me.

"You're so beautiful." His gaze was hooded, his voice husky.

I blushed in response, winking at him before continuing to put the finishing flourishes on my sketch.

"Come here." He tapped the empty space on the bed beside him. "What are you doing all the way over there?"

"Creating a masterpiece." I grinned, crossing my legs as I lifted my sketch in the air to get a better look at it.

"Show me." He was speaking in his typical authoritarian tone.

I pouted at him. "No."

"Will you just come over here, Sofia?" As an afterthought,

he grinned and spoke the magic word. "Please?"

I placed my pencil on the nearby bedside table and dragged my feet toward the bed. I sat on the edge of the bed, sketchbook still clutched in one hand. When I got close enough, he pulled me on the bed beside him, making me gasp.

Before I could object, he grabbed the sketchbook from my hand and lay flat on his back. Mischief traced his face as he watched me for a reaction. I curled up on the bed beside him and gave him my blessing.

"Go ahead. Look."

When Derek shifted his gaze toward the most recent sketch, my stomach fluttered at the reaction on his face.

"Sofia, this is... incredible. I had no idea you could draw."

I chuckled, recalling what he'd told me when I first saw him play a tune on his grand piano. *There are lot of things you don't know about me.* I rolled to my stomach and rested my arm and chin over his chest and shoulder, watching his reactions as he thumbed through my sketches.

I knew every sketch by heart. They contained fond memories of him. *A sketched copy of the Polaroid picture Corrine sent over. The confused look on his face as he tried to figure out how to navigate through a smartphone. His fingers over a grand piano. Our hands clasping each other's, fingers intertwined. The way he looked standing on the balcony during our first night at The Shade, breathtaken by the incredible view.*

After he finished browsing through my sketches, he eyed me questioningly as if to ask what it all meant.

"I never stopped thinking of you."

Guilt marred his countenance. My gut clenched. He set the sketchbook aside and brushed a hand over my hair. His fingers trembled. I ran a hand over his bare torso. All those times Ben had tried to get me in bed with him, I'd held out. I hadn't known it then, but now I understood. I'd been holding out for Derek. He was the man I wanted to share this with, yet the apprehension looming over his countenance shook me.

"What's wrong, Derek?"

"You were constantly on my mind too, Sofia. Trust me when I say that. But while you were away, I just... I lost myself. I can't even..."

Vivienne, Corrine, the girls... they all said that he was different apart from me, but it still meant a lot more when I heard from him. "I'm here now. I'm here for as long as you want me here."

"You promise never to leave me again?"

I didn't even hesitate. "I promise."

"How could you trust me this way, Sofia? Trust me enough that you would give all that you are to me?"

Before insecurity could take a hold of me, his lips were on mine, his fingers tangling in my hair. I responded to his kiss wondering if I would ever fully understand him, not caring at that moment if I ever would. He was a mystery I was willing to take time unraveling.

When our lips parted, I slapped his shoulder with my palm. Of course, there was more pain in my palm than on his shoulder. Still, he scowled at me and grabbed the assaulted area.

"What the hell was that for?"

"You can't ask questions like those and then just kiss me without waiting for me to give an answer, Derek."

"Oh yeah?" Amusement flashed through his eyes. The boyish charm he rarely showed surfaced during our stolen moments of intimacy. "What else can't I do? Enlighten me, will you?"

"I'm serious." I frowned.

He tried to put on a straight face, but burst out laughing anyway, his hand running the length of my waist down to my hips. "Well, can you blame me if I can't keep my hands off of you? After you seduced me last night?"

I blushed even as I feigned offense. "I did *not* seduce you."

"It's nothing to be embarrassed about, Sofia. You were seduction personified from the moment I laid eyes on you."

"You can't say things like that."

"Why can't I?" He quirked a brow at me.

"I never know how to react to it."

He chuckled. "But it's true. I've wanted you for the longest time. I don't even think you realize how attractive you are, Sofia. Do you have any idea the kind of hell you put me through every night you spent here in my bed? The kind of self-control I needed not to make you mine?"

"Is that what I am? Yours?"

"That's what you've always been since you stepped onto this island. I keep telling you that you belong to me, but it never seems to sink in to that stubborn mind of yours."

I should've been offended by the way he was once again referring to me as if I were an object he could own, but I'd already lost count of the number of times I'd clarified to him that I wasn't his. Besides, at that moment, it actually felt like I was. Still, my stubborn self just had to clarify. "I don't belong *to* you, Derek."

"Oh?" he challenged me.

"I belong *with* you."

He grinned. "Fair enough, just as long as I know you're with me." His arms wrapped around me and pulled me against him. I gasped slightly when his hand rested on a sore spot on my back.

His eyes registered surprise, his brows meeting as he made me lie on my stomach so he could check my back. I heard a gasp escape his lips as he lifted up my nightshift to get a better look.

"Sofia, I'm sorry. I tried to be gentle…"

"I'm fine." *It's not like this island hasn't dealt me my share of pain. Whatever pain you caused me is nothing.* I could feel the blood rise to my cheeks as I recalled the pleasures we'd shared together. I didn't want to ruin the light mood we were both in.

"Do I have to drink your blood again?" I rolled my eyes. "At this rate, I'm more the vampire in this relationship than you are."

All I got from him was a grunt in response to my jibes. He stood up and cut a gash on his palm. He gently helped me up on the bed, making me sit over the edge of it.

"Don't beat yourself up over this, Derek. I barely feel any pain."

He offered his hand to me and I drank from him once again.

"I've failed to protect you so many times. Now, I can't even protect you from myself."

The ache in my body subsided the moment his blood ran through me. I rose from the bed, careful to cover myself with the blankets, wrapping the same sheets around him as I drew close to him.

"Self-pity is unbecoming of you, Derek. You've protected

me plenty of times. I certainly wouldn't be here if it weren't for you. Besides, when was the last time you slept with a human without feeding on her?"

He tensed at the thought.

"I felt your fangs on my neck and you were about to break skin, but you didn't. You can control yourself like I always knew you could… like I know you can now."

I led him to the shower and had another tumble in bed with him before we both headed off to breakfast, our appetites for each other's company temporarily sated, giving in to actual hunger. I came out of it relatively unscathed and he seemed more confident in his own self-control.

"Jam and butter on toast… you never get tired of it," he noted, as I took a bite of my favorite breakfast.

"The same way you never seem to get tired of *that*." I eyed his glass of blood. "You should try my breakfast. It tastes really good."

Before he could stop me, I shoved a piece of my sandwich inside his mouth. Derek sat frozen in his seat, his bright blue eyes staring in shock at me, the toast beginning to get soggy inside his gaping mouth. He looked like he was about to spontaneously combust.

"You chew and then you swallow, Derek. Have you forgotten how to eat?"

I squinted teasingly at him before finally doubling over

with laughter. I found myself wondering what I could get away with doing to him. He reached across the table for my plate and spat out the toast all over my half-finished sandwich.

"Derek, ewww! What did you do that for?"

"It was either that or I make you taste *my* breakfast." He lifted his glass of blood midair and raised a brow at me.

I wrinkled my nose and scowled. "No thanks."

A smug smile formed on his face as he crossed his arms over his chest. "I thought so."

"Now you have to make me a new plate of breakfast." I pushed my plate toward him.

"What's wrong with that one?"

"Your spit's all over it."

"Eating it would just be like kissing me."

"That's gross."

"Serves you right." He grinned. "And for the record, I don't find you complaining that it's disgusting whenever I kiss you."

"Oh, yeah?" I raised a brow in challenge. "Well, I just might find the idea of kissing you gross *until* you make me breakfast." I winked at him.

He rolled his eyes and took my plate from the table. I smiled at him in triumph.

"The things I do for you," he muttered under his breath.

He quickly went about making me breakfast, knowing exactly how I wanted it considering how many times he had watched me prepare the same meal. He then offered the newly made sandwich to me, but not before kissing me full on the mouth as he laid the plate on top of the table.

The things he does that leave me breathless... I was barely able to gather my wits about me before anxiety registered in his eyes.

"What's wrong?"

"Someone just came in." He walked out of the kitchen and into the living room, where sure enough, the front door had been left open. He took my hand and sped toward his bedroom.

A man with the same bright blue eyes as Derek's stood by the bed, his graying hair and facial features clearly indicating that he was related to Derek, so I wasn't all that surprised when Derek addressed him with, "Father?"

Chapter 51: Derek

My first instinct upon seeing Gregor Novak standing in the middle of my bedroom was to protect Sofia and I wasn't even sure why. He was my father. *Why would I need to protect her from him?*

Still, my gut clenched when his eyes brushed past me and settled on her.

"Is this her? The beauty everyone's been harping about? The one who made you turn against your own brother? The one your sister gave up her life to bring back to you?" He eyed Sofia as if she was the most despicable thing he'd ever laid eyes on. "She isn't much to look at. Attractive, yes, but she isn't exactly above and beyond all the other lovelies you've had in your bed, so what is it that makes you willing to turn the world upside down just so you can have her?"

I pushed her behind me to shield her from my own father. Her hands clasped mine as I faced off with him.

"What are you doing back here?"

"Vivienne's been caught by the hunters. Lucas has gone off to join the Maslens, and I hear alarming news that you're putting my kingdom to ruin for the sake of indulging the whims of a human wench."

I could easily take your kingdom away from you and you know it. "What do you mean Lucas joined the Maslens?"

"Borys Maslen and his baby vampire, Ingrid, have managed to convince him to join their coven, something he willingly embraced after you had him hunted down for *her.*"

"He had it coming. I warned him not to lay a hand on her."

"Borys and Ingrid Maslen," Sofia muttered from behind me, sparking both my interest and my father's, our eyes turning toward her.

"You've heard of them?" I asked.

"One of Vivienne's memories has been recurring recently. It's the day Borys Maslen visited the island. Borys gave her a necklace with a ruby pendant. It drove her mad. I don't fully understand why. Their names... especially Borys'... they are oddly familiar."

"My daughter gave *you* her memories?" Gregor spat.

"Not all, just…"

I cut Sofia's explanation off. "You allowed Borys Maslen onto the island? After what he did to Vivienne?"

"Don't look at me that way, Derek. You escaped from all the chaos and we had to deal with it. Don't you dare look at me like you're better than me because I was man enough to face the issues that you ran away from. This island survived because of me, Lucas and Vivienne. You wake up after four hundred years and now you're running this kingdom into the ground."

"I'm trying to save The Shade, because you let it grow weak with all its indulgences. *That's* why you have to run around attempting to secure alliances with various vampire covens who want nothing other than to take us down."

"Indulgences? Like the human abductions? Those weren't indulgences, Derek. They were necessities. We did what we needed to do in order to survive."

"Hunters were the only human threat we had. When you started abducting teenagers to populate your harems, you made the entire world a threat to the island. How can you not see that? We never had to end the life of someone who wasn't a hunter until you ruled."

"Don't be a hypocrite, son. The young beauty you're so adamant to protect is here because of these abductions. Is it not her sweet young blood staining your bed? You always did have a penchant for virgins. Perhaps now that you've had her, she'll be less of a threat to us all."

Sofia's breath hitched behind me. It killed me to think what kind of effect my father's words could have on her.

"Don't ever talk about her that way again, Father. Better yet, don't talk about her at all unless you want to see me use the power you know I have against you."

"How dare you." My father's fists clenched and he looked as though he was about to attack me, but he directed his rage toward Sofia instead. "Beware of the day he loses interest in you, little girl. I doubt you'll have him to protect you then."

I stepped forward, my tightened fists a clear warning that he was overstepping his boundaries. "I *love* her. You of all people should know me well enough to realize what that statement means. She's the girl I love and if you ever lay a hand on her, make no mistake about it, I *will* turn against you."

The moment the confession spilled out of my lips, his eyes widened with shock. He looked at Sofia as if she'd just become an enormous threat to his life and I had no doubt in my mind that it had something to do with what Corrine had told me about after our visit to the Catacombs: *Vivienne's prophecy about you can never be fulfilled unless the young woman Cora spoke about does her part.*

I didn't fully comprehend then the situation I found myself in, but based on my father's reaction, Sofia was far more important than I gave her credit for. And it wasn't just because she was my heart and my life. She was so much more and I would soon find out how and why.

At that moment, however, I knew that no other person had ever mattered to me as much as Sofia Claremont.

Epilogue: Lucas

The Oasis, the underground Egyptian tombs that were now home to the Maslen coven, was every bit the fascinating legend it was rumored to be. The triangular gate, the seven levels, the circular glass lift, the lavish royal quarters… It was a worthy abode of the second most powerful vampire coven existing.

I wasn't too happy about being in the arid deserts of Egypt, but I wasn't about to complain. The Oasis was the only place I could think of running to—especially after the Maslens had offered me sanctuary after my own coven, my own flesh and blood, had turned against me.

Two guards led me to a large opulent chamber, at the

center of which was a black throne made of human skulls. Borys Maslen still looked the same way he had hundreds of years ago—dark, muddy brown hair, dark brown, almost black eyes, a stocky, well-built physique, wide and muscular. I recalled his obsession with my sister and couldn't help but imagine how frail Vivienne looked compared to him.

He was sitting on the skull throne with a smug smile on his face as he watched me being escorted closer to him. "The great Lucas Novak turning on his own kind to join the Maslens... I never thought I'd see the day."

"I came to claim the sanctuary you offered me," I answered dryly.

"I'm sure you understand that sanctuary comes with a price?" he asked. "You are, after all, a Novak. One I can't fully trust."

"Of course."

"Answer me a couple of questions first." Borys rose from his seat and descended down the steps that led to me. "Is it true? Your brother is finally awake?"

"It's true. This is a matter of concern to you?"

"Should it be? After all the sleeping he's done, I doubt your brother is still much of a threat." He began circling me like a vulture.

I scoffed. "Don't be a fool, Borys. We've played this game for hundreds of years. You know what my brother is capable of. Besides, his power and influence aren't the only reasons you ought to tremble. He's found the girl prophesied to establish his reign by bringing all vampires true sanctuary. He's in love with her. I'm sure of it."

"True sanctuary? And yet it's me you're running to for sanctuary?"

"Let's just say that, like you, I don't want to see my brother succeed."

"Very well then. Who is this girl you speak of? This girl you say Derek is so enamored with?"

"Her name is Sofia Claremont."

At the mention of Sofia's name, Borys Maslen's face contorted with fury. "How dare he! How dare your brother lay a hand upon her! She was mine! The Claremont girl *is* mine!"

He tackled me to the ground and began pounding my face. It was beyond me how he even knew who Sofia was, much less understand why she was so important to him. I knew how she had this inexplicable way about her that drew me to her, but what was it about her that had caused my entire world to start spinning around her?

I tasted blood on my lips as Borys continued to attack me. All I could think of was how much I wished that blood belonged to Sofia. *What I would give to taste her again.* I was already sure that Borys' attacks weren't going to stop until he'd pounded the brains out of me until a sharp female voice called out his name.

"Borys! What are you doing?"

Borys immediately stopped hitting me and turned toward her. "He has Sofia. Derek Novak has her! She's mine, Ingrid. Sofia Claremont is *mine*."

"Of course she is. Sofia is yours, Borys. We'll get her back." Ingrid spoke soothingly, like a mother calming a young boy.

Ingrid Maslen. The newest vampire in their coven. I trembled at the mention of the name and all the rumors that came with it. I staggered to my feet. Rumors of Ingrid Maslen's beauty and how she came to be a part of the Maslen clan resurfaced in my mind and I couldn't wait to catch a glimpse of her.

Her face was hidden by Borys' large, imposing form as she embraced him, whispering calming words into his ear. Something Borys said caught my attention and sent chills running down my spine.

He pulled away from her and said, "You gave her to me, Ingrid. You remember that."

"Of course... I did."

I strained to catch a glimpse of Ingrid and gasped. She was the spitting image of Sofia, albeit an older version. Her eyes met mine and she brushed past Borys to face me.

"You can either tell us what we need to know, Novak, or I will use the means that *I* know to get the information out of you. Either way, we're going to take Sofia away from your brother and bring her here where she belongs."

"Who are you?"

"Suffice it to say, I was once Camilla Claremont…"

Want to read the next part of Derek and Sofia's story?
A Shade of Vampire 3: A Castle of Sand is available now!

Visit www.bellaforrest.net for more information.

Note from the Author

Dear Shaddict,

If you want to stay informed about my latest book releases, visit this website to subscribe to my new releases email list: www.forrestbooks.com

You can also check out my other novels by visiting my website: www.bellaforrest.net

And don't forget to come say hello on Facebook.
I'd love to meet you personally:
                www.facebook.com/AShadeOfVampire
You can also find me on Twitter: @ashadeofvampire
And Instagram: @ashadeofvampire

Thank you for reading!

Love,
Bella

Made in the USA
Lexington, KY
27 June 2016